英語自學策略!!

U0080729

英文 Email 懶人包

複製、貼上、替換，瞬間搞定!

不傷腦筋、不 NG，與時俱進，最實務性的商用 Email，一貼搞定！

1 重要必備商務情境全收錄，話題分類明確，目錄查找好方便！

精準規劃 9 大主題、130 種辦公室或生活中最常會用到的完整商務情境，舉凡各領域的拓展業務、商品交易、公告、服務、道歉、致謝、慰問……必要的商務情境一次準備到位，隨時查找目錄快速又方便。

Part 1. 拓展業務 ✉

01 公司簡介（含大致業務
02【回應】公司簡介
03 業務開發
04【回應】業務開發
介紹新產品

Part 7. 邀請函 ✉

01 邀請出席新品展示會
02【回應】邀請出席新品展
03 邀請參觀貿易展覽會
04【回應】邀請參觀貿

2 有來有往，雙向溝通往來無礙，信手捻來完美 Email！

每一情境皆附兩則有來有往範本，能寫也能回。不必再 Google、不必東拼西湊，直接快速複製一篇主旨明確、格式完整、進退合宜、文法正確、用字漂亮、 易讀好懂的完美 Email，專業加分不出錯！

照著抄～

（範例 1）**Title : We a**

Dear Mr. Johns.
We are so ple
service in H

（範例 2）**Title :**

Dear M
You

3

擴充／替換句型，讓 Email 隨時更多彈性變化！

全書提供超過 500 句的關鍵替換／擴充句，能巧妙因應更多不同的需求、情境，靈活地替換／擴充句型，即使複製 Email，內容也能更生動，有更多變化。

> **E-mail 這樣寫也行！**
>
> ① 能否查看庫存貨物的狀況？
> Would you do the inventory check for us?
>
> ② 我查過了庫存中您要的那種商品。
> I checked our supply of the commodity you asked for
>
> ③ 目前，我們的貨物庫存有限。
> At present, we have only a limited stock of goods.

4

關鍵詞彙、慣用語特別醒目提示，隨需求靈活更換

範例中關鍵字、片語或重點句型用特別色塊呈現，不僅達到提醒需隨時依實際需要做更換之外，亦能幫助加速抓到信件重點；更可同時在潛移默化中認識／學會更多字彙，真正做到工具＋學習雙效合一。

nat I have **received** complete
o take this opportunity to thank
ner with us.
e find the **receiving slip**.
forward to serving you again ir

5

只要輕輕一掃 QR Code，Email 一貼搞定

全書「Email 懶人包」電子檔貼心地收錄在雲端裡，隨掃即用：複製、貼上、替換、寄出，Email 快速完成，就是這麼簡單！

PART 2
商品交易

因各家手機系統不同，若無法直接掃描，仍可以（https://tinyurl.com/uxmb2rs）電腦連結雲端下載，一貼搞定！

★ Email 懶人包全書下載網址：https://tinyurl.com/fmpu9mze

時代日新月異，時間分秒必爭。英文郵件往來，費時傷腦筋，讓人望紙興嘆。因此，選擇一本符合自身需求、言之有物的工具書，方能掌握效率，同時提升工作能力。有鑑於此，作者與專業編輯群經過開會、研發和討論，擬定出幾十種常見英文電子郵件往來主題，讓讀者能多方選擇，找出適合自己需求的模組。

全書每一章節嚴選出現代忙碌的工商業社會裡，常見且重要之商業往來互動情境，只要從標題／主旨裡，就能輕易的找出所需要的信件範例，不僅可以一來一往的雙向互動，同時提供兩篇不同範本供您選擇，現學現用，能寫能回，快速提高工作效率與專業能力，讓撰寫電子書信不再傷腦筋，不再是苦差事。另外，每篇文章特別挑出關鍵詞彙、慣用語，還有全書超過 500 句以上的替換句、擴充句，讓你在面臨不同情境時，能充分多元化的運用，舉一反三，書信更豐富有變化，還能在潛移默化中提升英文力及兼顧實用性。

時間，應該用在對的事情上；學習，應該節省寶貴時間。當學習變得有趣和有效，書籍之益處不遑多論。《英語自學策略：英文 Email 懶人包，複製、貼上、替換，瞬間搞定！》定能助你在撰寫郵件時不怕詞窮，還能文思泉湧，也更專業、更輕鬆。

Sheila

目錄
Contents

Part 3. 婉拒請求 ✉

PART 1
拓展業務

因各家手機系統不同，若無法直接掃描，仍可以（https://tinyurl.com/3ncbzxw3）電腦連結雲端下載，一貼搞定！

Part 1.
拓展業務

01 公司簡介（含大致業務方向）

照著抄 ～ Email 簡單搞定！　　　　　　　　　　　— ⤢ ✕

（範例 1）

Title : What We Do

Dear Mr. Roberts,

We are a **software company**, specializing in web and app development.

We have long-term experience in delivering a variety of services ranging from branding to ecommerce.

In terms of providing a better user experience, the latest technologies are utilized, known as Single Page Application (SPA), as opposed to the conventional approach of multiple pages.

In contrast, SPA takes less time to render pages without having to reloading and redirecting.

Let us know your requirements, and we will take it from here.

Yours sincerely,
Ted Stone

SEND　　　　　　　　　　　　　　　　　　　　A ⬍ ⬚ ☺

主旨：公司服務內容

親愛的羅伯茲先生：

我們是一家**軟體公司**，專門從事網路和應用程式開發。

我們提供從品牌到電子商務的各種服務，經驗非常悠久。

在提供更佳的用戶體驗方面，我們使用最新的技術，稱為單頁應用程式（SPA），而不是傳統的多頁方式。

相比之下，SPA 無需重新載入和重新定向的情況下，呈現頁面所花的時更短。

讓我們知道您的要求，由我們來負責您的需求。

您誠摯的，

泰德・史東

照著抄 ～ Email 簡單搞定！

Title : Company Introduction

Dear Mr. Jones,

The purpose of this letter is to introduce the company **Happy Furniture**, which has been opened since 2001. We offer high quality furniture and service with no complaints from our clients.

We offer you the products that are the highest standards. Enclosed with this letter is documentation about our products. Please feel free to contact us if you are interested in our products.

Yours truly,
Anna Miller

SEND

主旨：公司簡介

親愛的瓊斯先生：

這封信的目的是介紹**快樂家具公司**，本公司從 2001 開始營業。提供客戶零抱怨的高品質和服務。

我們為您提供最高標準產品。隨函附上我方產品的檔案。

如果您對本公司產品感興趣，請隨時與我們聯繫。

誠摯地，

安娜‧米勒

Email 這樣寫也行！

① 我藉此機會向您介紹軟體公司。

I am taking this chance to introduce you the software company.

② 為了跟上網路世界的快速變化，我們有一組專門的開發人員來成功實現這一切。

To keep pace with rapid changes in the web world, we have a group of dedicated developers to make it all happen.

③ 我們全世界有十家店，台灣有五間店。

We own 10 offices worldwide and 5 within Taiwan.

④ 我們公司專門生產沙發和餐桌為主的家具。

Our company specializes in manufacturing furniture mainly sofas and tables.

⑤ 希望我們未來能有機會合作。

Hope that we will have the opportunity to cooperate in the future.

⑥ 同樣等待您的來電。

Await your call for the same.

⑦ 期待我們未來的合作。

I'm looking forward to our future cooperation.

⑧ 我們隨時恭候您的來電。

We are always waiting for your call.

02【回應】公司簡介

Re : What We Do

Dear Mr. Stone,

I was referred to you by Mr. Will and learned that you are the best at what you do.

Please allow me to introduce my company. We are a *clothing company* that is seeking a reliable contractor to develop a new large scale website.

I was intrigued by the idea of SPA and would it very much to integrate the new site with it.

It would be greatly appreciated if you could get back to me at your earliest convenience.

Yours sincerely,
Ken Roberts

SEND　　　　　　　　　　　　　　　A ‖ ⇔ ☺

回覆：公司服務內容

親愛的史東先生：

我是由威爾先生介紹而得知，了解到您們是領域中最優秀的。

請讓我先介紹本公司。我們是一間**服裝公司**，正在尋求可靠的承包商開發新的大型網站。

我對 SPA 的想法很感興趣，非常想把新的網站與其相結合。

若方便請儘早回復，我將不勝感激。

真誠地，
肯・羅伯茲

照著抄 ～ Email 簡單搞定！

 範例 2

Re : Company Introduction

Dear Mrs. Miller,

I'm glad to receive your introduction letter. We're interested in your products.

I would be grateful if you would send me some information. Could you please send us a ***catalog*** and your ***current price list*** of all your products?

We look forward to hearing from you soon.

Yours truly,
Larry Jones

SEND

中譯

回覆：公司簡介

親愛的米勒女士：

我很高興接到您的來信。我們對貴公司的產品深感興趣。

如能寄給我一些資訊，我將不勝感激。可否請您寄給我們貴公司所有商品的**最新價格目錄**？

我們期待儘快收到您的回信。

誠摯地，
賴瑞‧瓊斯

Email 這樣寫也行！

① 我想先介紹一下本公司。

I'd like to introduce my company first.

② 我們對五種產品感興趣。

We are interested in five different items.

③ 如果您寄一本全商品的冊子給我方，那就太棒了。

It would be great if you would send us a brochure of all your products.

④ 我對此專案有嚴格的截止期限，想更詳細地討論。

I have a tight deadline on the project and would like to discuss it in more detail.

⑤ 我相信速度效能是非常重要的。

As I believe the performance of speed is essential.

⑥ 請盡速與我們聯繫。

Please contact us as soon as possible.

⑦ 我們想要和貴公司開會。

We'd like to fix a meeting with your company.

⑧ 若能近日接獲回信我們將會非常感激。

Your prompt reply will be highly appreciated.

03 業務開發

範例 1

Title : We have a new product you may be interested.

Dear Mr. Alston,

You will be interested to hear that we have recently developed a product, which is selling very well in most of our clients' markets.

As we thought there might be a **sales potential** in your market, too, we shall be glad to supply you with our samples as well as the price list.

Your prompt reply will be highly appreciated.

Yours sincerely,
Henry Brown

SEND   A  🔗 😊

主旨：您可能會對我們的新產品感興趣

親愛的阿爾斯頓先生：

相信您樂於知道我們公司最近研發了一項新產品，並且在我們大多數客戶的市場中都很暢銷。

由於我們公司認為這項新產品在貴市場也**具有潛力**，因此特向貴公司提供相關樣品和報價。

如能即時回覆，不勝感謝。

您真誠地，
亨利‧布朗

照著抄 ～ Email 簡單搞定！

 Title : We have a new product you may be interested.

Dear Mr. Affleck,

I learned from your message by chance on the internet that your company is in need of all kinds of ***car parts***.

Our company is such a manufacturer. If you are interested in our products, please let us know. We do hope there is an opportunity for us to cooperate with each other in the near future.

An early reply will be obliged.

Yours sincerely,
Roger Hamilton

SEND

主旨：您可能會對我們的新產品感興趣

親愛的阿弗萊克先生：

偶然從網路上看到貴公司正需要各類**汽車零配件**的消息。

我們公司正好是汽車零配件製造商。如果您對我們的產品感興趣的話，請告訴我們。我們衷心希望彼此能很快有進行合作的機會。

期待您的早日回覆，謝謝。

您誠摯地，

羅傑‧漢密爾頓

Email 這樣寫也行！

① 我們生產的產品範圍廣泛。

We manufacture a wide range of products.

② 我確信您一定會對我們的產品感興趣的。

I am sure our products will attract you.

③ 希望我們能有機會合作。

Hope that we will have the opportunity to cooperate.

④ 我們隨時恭候您的來電。

You can call us whenever you want.

⑤ 我們可以為貴公司提供各種產品。

We can provide you with all kinds of products.

⑥ 我們最近生產了三種新產品。

We produced three different new items recently.

⑦ 我們願意嘗試各種可能，以開拓新的業務。

We are willing to explore every possibility for new business.

⑧ 我們很樂意提供樣品給您們。

We are willing to provide you with our samples.

04【回應】業務開發

範例 1

Re : We have a new product you may be interested.

Dear Brown,

This is an intriguing proposal. As good as it sounds, some ***critical information*** are missing such as its name, features and a specification.

If possible, please kindly elaborate more on the developed product. By doing so, it would help us make a decision as whether to place an order on it or not.

Yours sincerely,
Paul Alston

SEND　　　　　　　　　　　　　　　　　A 📎🔗☺

 中譯

回覆：您可能會對我們的新產品感興趣

布朗先生您好：

這是個有趣的提案。聽起來很棒，但一些**關鍵資訊**遺失了，譬如名稱、特徵和規格。

如果有可能，請詳細說明開發的產品。如此一來，將有助於我們是否要訂購的決議。

祝好
保羅‧阿爾斯頓

Re : We have a new product you may be interested.

Dear Hamilton,
Thank you for getting back to us. Due to the recent heavy rains in the city, many cars were soaked in floodwater. Among those, many were damaged and towed into my shop. My lot is now ***filled with flood-damaged cars***. Car parts are urgently needed. Please refer to the attachment for more information and have them shipped immediately.

Sincerely,
Vic Affleck

SEND

回覆：您可能會對我們的新產品感興趣

漢密爾頓先生您好：
謝謝您的回覆。由於最近都市豪雨，許多汽車浸泡在大水中。其中，許多汽車已經損壞，拖吊到我的工作場。我的地方現在**停滿被洪水浸壞的車子**。急需汽車零件。請參閱附件獲得多資訊，並立即運送這些商品。

真誠地，
維克 · 阿弗萊克

Email 這樣寫也行！

① 很榮幸收到您的回覆。

It is my pleasure to receive your reply!

② 如果有任何問題，請隨時與我聯繫。

If you have any questions, please do not hesitate to contact me.

③ 這個提案很有用。

The proposal is very useful.

④ 如果無法打開附件，請讓我知道。

Shall you have any problem opening the attachment, please let me know.

⑤ 如果可以，請寄給我們此商品更多的資訊。

If possible, please kindly send us more information about the product.

⑥ 希望不久的將來能與您合作。

Hope we can cooperate with you in the near future.

⑦ 讓我知道您將如何執行。

Let me know how you want to proceed.

⑧ 若能及時回覆將不勝感激。

A prompt reply will greatly oblige.

05 介紹新產品

範例 1

Title : We are sure you would be interested in our new (product name).

Dear Mr. Brown,

We are pleased to inform you that we have recently brought out a new product – the **Wireless mouse**.

Since the quality is superior to other old products, there will be an increasing demand for it in the near future.

By another air parcel, we have sent you one sample along with the manual for your kind appraisal and test. We look forward to receiving your comments or trial order shortly.

Yours sincerely,
Mary Evans

SEND   A 📎 🔗 ☺

中譯

主旨：我們確定您會對我們的新產品（產品名）有興趣

親愛的布朗先生：

很高興通知貴公司我們最近推出了一種新型的**無線滑鼠**。由於品質較其他舊產品優異，在不久的將來，它的需求量肯定會大增。

特地以航空郵件寄上樣品及說明書一份供參考與試用。盼能獲反饋和試訂。

您誠摯地，

瑪麗・埃文斯

範例 2 Title : We are sure you would be interested in our new (product name).

Dear Mr. Walker,

We are so glad to inform you that we have just marketed our new products.

You will find our new products more ***competitive*** than similar products in other companies in both its quality and price. They should get a very good reception in your market. Please let us know if you would like to take the matter further. Look forward to hearing from you.

Yours sincerely,
Paul Keating

SEND   A 📎 🔗 ☺

中譯

主旨：我們確定您會對我們的新產品（產品名）有興趣

親愛的沃克先生：

很高興通知貴公司我們最近推出了新產品。

您會發現與其他的同類產品相比，我們的新產品在品質和價格上都更**具競爭力**，定能吸引顧客選購。

如果願意做更進一步的了解，請讓我們知道。

敬候佳音。

您誠摯地，

保羅 · 基汀

① 我們的新產品已經在這週五上市，相信您樂於知道。

You will be interested to hear that we marketed our new product on Friday.

② 我們的主要優勢之一是產品的超棒品質。

One of our main strengths is its superb quality.

③ 它包含了最新的設計，並已經供貨上架。

It covers the latest designs, which are now available in stock.

④ 時尚產品在市場上有很大的商機。

There is a good market opportunity for snazzy products.

⑤ 相信您會對我們最新的產品感興趣。

I believe you will be interested in our latest products.

⑥ 這一特點將吸引許多用戶。

This unique feature will appeal to many users.

⑦ 我們盼望與您聯繫。

We are pleased to get in touch with you.

⑧ 如果對我們的商品有興趣，請盡速與我們聯繫。

Please contact us as soon as possible if you are interested in our products.

06 【回應】介紹新產品

照著抄 ～ Email 簡單搞定！　　　　　　　　　— ⤢ ✕

範例1

Re : We are sure you would be interested in our new (product name).

Dear Mrs. Evans,

We have been expecting the new model of the wireless mouse. Base on the *feedback* from our customers, one major issue was constantly reported.

When used in an uneven or glassy surface, its cursor was somehow not as responsive as it should be. There was a delay for a fraction of a second.

Hopefully, the issue has been addressed on the coming model.

I am looking forward to hearing from you.

Yours sincerely,
Neil Brown

SEND　　　　　　　　　　　　　　　　　　A ! ⌐ ☺

回覆：我們確定您會對我們的新產品（產品名）有興趣

埃文斯女士您好：

我們一直在期待無線滑鼠的新款上市。基於客戶**反饋**，有個主要問題一直被回報。當在不平或玻璃表面使用滑鼠時，在某種程度上，它的游標反應不夠靈敏。延遲了一秒鐘左右。

希望在即將上市新款中，這個問題已經解決。

期待您的回覆。

尼爾・布朗

Re : We are sure you would be interested in our new (product name).

Dear Mr. Keating,

Fantastic, it's finally out. We are confident in your previous products you had offered. They were with high-quality. We are definitely interested in your new products and would like to have the ***first-hand information***.

In regards to the price, we look into the quality of the products more as we believe it's the key to be distinct and recognized in the competitive market.

Please contact us as soon as possible.

Sincerely,
Tom Walker

SEND

回覆：我們確定您會對我們的新產品（產品名）有興趣

基汀先生您好：

太棒了，商品終於問市了。我們對您們以前提供的產品很有信心。它們品質卓越。我們對您的新產品很有興趣，希望得到**第一手資料**。

相較在價格方面，我們對於產品的品質更關注，因為我們相信品質在競爭市場中，才是眾不同的重要關鍵。

請盡快與我們聯繫。

誠摯地
湯姆·沃克

Email 這樣寫也行！

① 基於客戶反饋，大部分的人對此商品不滿意。

Base on the feedback from our customers, most of them are not satisfied with the product .

② 希望在即將上市新款中，這個問題已經解決。

The problem has been solved on the coming model.

③ 我們喜歡貴公司的產品，想得到更多的資料。

We like your new products, and would like to get more information.

④ 您之前提供的商品品質很高。

The previous products you had offered are high-quality.

⑤ 如果月底拜訪您，不知是否方便。

It is convenient for you if I visit you by the end of this month.

⑥ 謝謝您的慎思。

Thank you for your consideration.

⑦ 我們期待和貴公司合作。

We are looking forward to doing business with you.

⑧ 期待您盡速回應。

We look forward to receiving your early reply.

07 附加服務介紹

 照著抄 ～ Email 簡單搞定！

範例 1　**Title : We are now providing ... service.**

Dear Mr. Johns,

We are so pleased to inform you that we offer maintenance service in Hong Kong from now on.

Purchasers can enjoy *a two-year free warranty service* and *a life-long maintenance* in our branches nationwide.

If any questions, please dial our Customer Service Hotline on 666-666.

Yours sincerely,

Brian William

SEND　　　　　　　　　　　　　　　A 〇 ⊖ ☺

 中譯

主旨：我們現在有提供……服務

親愛的約翰斯先生：

很高興通知貴用戶，自即日起，本公司將在香港地區提供維修服務。

購買者可在我們全國各大分部享受產品 **2 年免費保固**及**終生維修**的服務。

如有疑問，請撥打我們的客服熱線：666-666。

您誠摯地，

布萊恩‧威廉

照著抄 ～ Email 簡單搞定！

 範例 2

Title : We are now providing ... service.

Dear Mr. Block,

You will be very interested to hear that from now on, our company will allow our mobile phone users to download music from our official website for free for one year.

You will find our music better than that you download from elsewhere. That is because the music we provide is of good quality and most importantly, it is *legitimate*.

If you want to know more, please call us on 888-888.

Yours sincerely,
John Peters

SEND

 中譯

主旨：我們現在有提供……服務

親愛的布洛克先生：

相信您樂於知道從現在起，我們公司將允許我們的手機用戶可從官方網站免費下載音樂一年。

您將會發現我們的音樂優於您從別處所下載的音樂，這是因為我們所提供的音樂品質好，而且最重要的是，它是**正版音樂**。

如果您想瞭解更多，請撥打我們的電話：888-888。

您誠摯地，

約翰‧彼得斯

Email 這樣寫也行！

① 我們願為顧客提供免費配套服務。

We are willing to offer a free backup service to customers.

② 我們為顧客提供個人服務。

We offer a personal service to our customers.

③ 公司承諾為用戶提供專業服務。

We commit to provide professional service to our customers.

④ 這台筆記型電腦的保固期為一年。

The notebook PC comes with one year guarantee.

⑤ 請允許我介紹我們公司所能夠提供的各項服務專案。

Please allow me to make a presentation of the services we can offer.

⑥ 敝公司擁有一套很好的售後服務體系。

Our company has an excellent sales service system.

⑦ 保固服務只適用於該種類的產品。

This warranty service applies to the product of this kind only.

⑧ 您會發現我們的服務比以前好很多。

You will find our service is much better than before.

08 【回應】附加服務介紹

範例 1

Re : We are now providing ... service.

Dear Mr. William,

I tried your hotline several times without success. For some reason, it didn't get through. I am writing regarding the warranty service issue.

Recently, I was reached by a potential buyer online and was inquired whether the warranty service is ***transferrable***. If not mistaken, it's good for another year.

Enclosed is my purchased info as attached below and please have a look into it.

Sincerely,
Adam Johns

SEND   A ‖ ⌐ ☺

回覆：我們現在有提供……服務

威廉先生您好：

我嘗試撥打您的專線未果，由於某些因素未能接通。我正在寫關於保固服務的問題。

最近，網上有個潛在買主聯繫我，詢問保固服務是否可**轉讓**。如果無誤，那還能有效使用一年。

隨信附上我的購買資訊，請查收。

真誠地，
亞當‧約翰斯

Re : We are now providing ... service.

Dear Mr. Peters,

It's finally here, open to download music. However, I wish there was one step could be taken further. As tempting as it sounds, it's just not quite matched for the streaming service. In comparison, streaming music allows user to just click and listen instantly without having to wait for the whole download to complete. In addition, it's a lot quicker to switch from one song to another.

That's *one humble opinion* wish to be heard.

Yours sincerely,

Sam Block

SEND　　　　　　　　　　　　　　　　　　　　A ⬙ ⤬ ☺

回覆：我們現在有提供⋯⋯服務

彼得斯先生敬安：

終於完成了，下載音樂吧。不過，我希望能更上層樓。雖然聽起來很酷，但與串流服務並不太搭。

相比之下，串流音樂允許用戶只需點擊就能馬上聽，不必等到整首下載完成。另外，從一首歌切換到另一首歌速度快很多喔。

希望能聽**個人拙見**。

您誠摯地，

山姆・布洛克

Email 這樣寫也行！

① 我很高興收到了您的電子郵件。
I'm glad to have received your email.

② 我試圖用電話聯繫您，但無法接通。
I tried to reach you by phone but can't get through.

③ 我們提供最有質感的音樂。
We provide the best quality music.

④ 相信問題將很快解決。
I trust that the problem will soon be resolved.

⑤ 謝謝您撥空考慮我的意見。
Thank you for taking the time to consider my opinion.

⑥ 我希望那些資訊將有所助益。
We hope that information will help.

⑦ 如果您需要更多資訊，請與我聯繫。
If you need any further information, please contact me.

⑧ 我相信很快會收到您的回覆。
I trust that you will reply us immediately.

09 主動報價

範例 1

Title : Quotation of (product) from (company name).

Dear Sir or Madam,
Since we know that you are interested in ***Taiwanese furniture***, I am pleased to introduce our company and goods to you.
Westport Dining Table: $ 4,000
Brown chairs: $ 5,200
Wooden Wall Shelf: $ 900
Enclosed is our company's profile and quotations.
We hope you will be satisfied with our service and ***quotes***.
I appreciate your early reply.

Faithfully,
Don Cruise
Sales Manager
Home Mall

SEND

 中譯

主旨：詢問（公司名）的（產品名）報價

先生、女士您好：
因為我們知道您對**台灣的家具**有興趣，很高興能向您介紹本公司和商品。
西港餐桌：$ 4,000
棕色椅：$5,200
木製壁架：$ 900
隨信附上本公司的簡介和報價。希望您對我們的服務和**報價**能滿意。

忠實地，
堂 · 克魯斯
銷售經理家庭購物中心

照著抄 ～ Email 簡單搞定！

Title : Quotation of (product) from (company name).

Dear Sir or Madam,
We are writing this letter to tell you that we deal in the **business of bikes**. Our company is known as Frank Company.
Truly, we are very interested in doing business with you. We appreciate this opportunity to provide you with a **sales quote**.
1. Trekking Bike: $ 12,000
2. Touring Bicycle: $8,000
3. European City Bicycles: $ 20,000
For further information, kindly contact us.

Best Regards,
Dora Williams
Lucky Bike

SEND

主旨：詢問（公司名）的（產品名）報價

親愛的先生、女士：
我們寫這封信是想向您介紹本公司做**腳踏車方面**的生意。我們是法蘭克公司。
誠然，我們非常有興趣想和您做生意。很高興有機會為您提供**報價**。
1. 通勤自行車：$ 12,000
2. 旅行自行車：$ 8,000
3. 歐洲城市自行車：$ 20,000
煩請聯絡我們，以獲得更多資訊。

誠摯問候，
朵拉 ‧ 威廉斯
幸運自行車公司

Email 這樣寫也行！

① 我們提供您一份問題清單，以便我們能提供您準確的報價。
We provide a list of questions so that we may reply you with an accurate quote.

② 我們期待幫助您找到最佳的商品和價格。
We look forward to helping you find the best products and prices.

③ 敬請回答所有問題。
Kindly respond to all questions.

④ 敬請不要猶豫與我們聯繫。
Please don't hesitate to contact us.

⑤ 我們將提供估價單給您。
We will provide an estimated quotation to you.

⑥ 請填寫表格以便讓我們了解您的情況。
Please fill out the form so that we can understand your situation.

⑦ 希望我們的報價能滿足您的要求。
Hope our quotations can meet your specifications.

⑧ 如果需要幫助，請隨時撥打免付費專線 0800-383-838。
If you need assistance, please feel free to call 0800-383-838.

10【回應】對方報價

照著抄～ Email 簡單搞定！

— ⤢ ✕

範例1

Re : Quotation of (product) from (company name).

Dear Mr. Cruise,

I am pleased to receive your letter. Taiwanese made furniture has a good reputation in the marketplace. I should look no further than the one who has everything I desire for.

Listed might be the ones suit my needs. However, there are no photos and dimensions attached. If available, being able to **browse online** with the above information is even better.

I shall be pleased to receive an early reply.

Best Regards,
Molly Pitt

SEND

中譯

回覆：訊問（公司名）的（產品名）報價

克魯斯先生您好：

很高興接獲來信。台灣製家具在市場上聲名遠播。我不應該成為只是因為想要而買下一切的人。

列出的那些家具可能適合我的需求。然而，附件沒有照片和尺寸。如果可以的話，最好能**線上瀏覽**上面的（物品）資訊。

很高興收到您及早回信。

誠摯問候，

茉莉 · 彼特

Re : Quotation of (product) from (company name).

Dear Mrs. Williams,

I am the owner of a bike shop. Based on the last quarter numbers, one of the bestselling bikes was the ***trekking bike***.

For the next generation, a major improvement is said to be done on enhancing its comfort as well as stability. Before closing a deal with you, a ***specification*** for the bike must be available for further assessments.

Best Regards,
Emma Jones

SEND

A ⏻ ⊖ ☺

回覆：詢問（公司名）的（產品名）報價

親愛的威廉斯女士：

我是自行車店老闆。基於最後一季的數字，最暢銷的自行車之一是**徒步自行車**。

對於下一代來說，在提高舒適性和穩定性方面，有重大改進。在與您達成交易之前，提供自行車**規格**是必要的，以供進一步評估。

誠摯問候，
艾瑪 · 瓊斯

Email 這樣寫也行！

① 很榮幸收到您的來信。

It is my pleasure to receive your letter!

② 煩請盡快回答我的問題。

Please respond in your earliest free time..

③ 台灣製家具以品質和服務聞名。

Taiwanese made furniture is famous for its quality and service

④ 我對貴公司的一些家具感興趣。

I am interested in some furniture in your company.

⑤ 您能提供貴公司的網站給我嗎？

Can you provide me with your company's website?

⑥ 在完成交易前，我需要更多腳踏車相關資訊。

Before closing a deal with you, I need more information about the bike.

⑦ 請提供估價單給我。

Please provide an estimated quotation to me.

⑧ 請盡早回信。

Kindly reply at your earliest convenience.

11 議價（提出降價要求）

範例 1

Title : We wish to have a price reduction.

To Whom It May Concern,
I regret to send a request for price reduction. Please bear my price reduction letter in mind.
In fact, we have been running into some difficulties in selling our merchandise. The sales **fell** 20% in July and August.
We hope you can understand our difficulties.
Please call our representatives at 0800-888-888.
I look forward to hearing from you soon.

Best regards,
Brenda Foster

SEND

 中譯

主旨：我們希望可以議價

敬啟者：
我很遺憾地提出降價要求。煩請記住這封降價要求信。
事實上，我們在銷售商品時面臨了一些問題。7 月和 8 月的銷售量比起之前同期**下跌**了 20%。
我們希望您能理解我們的苦衷。
請與本公司聯繫 0800-888-888。
敬請回音。

謹致，
布蘭達 ・ 弗斯特

照著抄 ～ Email 簡單搞定！

Title : We wish to have a price reduction.

Dear Mrs. Jones,

I am writing to request *a rent reduction*.

There are two reasons for this request. Firstly, I have lived here for five years without any trouble. The second reason is the money I put into *repairs*. I had spent ten thousand dollars repairing the refrigerator and air-conditioner.

As a result, I request that you reduce the rent to seven thousand dollars per month.

Thank you.

Sincerely yours,
Dora Lopez

SEND

主旨：我們希望可以議價

瓊斯先生您好：

我寫這封信是為了要求**調降房租**。

提出此要求的原因有兩個。首先，我已經在這裡住了 5 年，沒製造過任何麻煩。

第二個原因是**維修費**，我花了 1 萬元修了冰箱和冷氣。

因此，我要求將每月租金降到 7 千元。

謝謝你。

誠摯地，
朵拉 ‧ 羅佩茲

Email 這樣寫也行！

① 若您需要更多資訊，我們很高興回答您的問題。

Should you need further information, we would be pleased to answer the questions.

② 謝謝合作。

Thank you for your collaboration.

③ 我們想提醒您注意附加檔的價目表。

We would like to bring your attention to the price as attached.

④ 感謝您慎重地考慮。

Thank you for considering.

⑤ 我們有財務困難。

We have financial difficulties.

⑥ 請撥打免付費電話 0800-000-000。

Please call our toll-free number 0800-000-000.

⑦ 請多加考慮。

Please take it into consideration.

⑧ 我們期待您的協助。

We look forward to assisting you.

12【回應】議價（答應降價，降價幅度／不答應降價）

範例 1

Re : We wish to have a price reduction.

Dear Mrs. Foster,

Unfortunately, our price is **non-negotiable**. It's the strict company policy one must enforce. As much as I would like to help you on that, there is really not much I can do.

However, there is an alternative. Though it's not a price reduction, it's a **discount** on bulk orders. If it works for you, let me know ahead, and I will forward the paperwork to you. Please contact me at 0800-123-456.

Sincerely yours,
Roger Smith

SEND

中譯

回覆：我們希望可以議價

弗斯特女士您好：

很遺憾，我們的價格是**不容商榷的**。這是公司嚴格執行的政策。儘管我很想幫助您，但真的無能為力。

然而，您還有另一種選擇。雖然這不是降價，是大宗訂單的**折扣**。如果這方案對您有用，請提前告知，我會把資料交給您。

請撥打 0800-123-456 與我聯繫。

誠摯地
羅傑 · 史密斯

Re : We wish to have a price reduction.

Dear Mrs. Lopez,

First of all, thank you for liking my place and I believe you had wonderful stay. Knowing that you have the appliances fixed, I'd like to express my appreciation by **reimbursing** you for the expanses of the repairs.

As far as the rent is concerned, the reduction to seven thousands per month does not seem to be a reasonable request. However, I am still willing to meet you half way, which is to reduce the rent by one thousand dollars per month. Once again, thanks for being a wonderful tenant. Look forward to hearing from you.

Sincerely yours,
Meg Jones

SEND

回覆：我們希望可以議價

親愛的羅佩茲女士：

首先，謝謝妳喜歡我的房子，相信住得很愉快。知道您修了電器，我想讓您的修理費**報帳**，以茲感謝。

就租金而言，每月減至七千元似乎不是合理要求。不過，我還是願意各退一步，每月租金減少一千元。再次感謝您成為一名優質房客。

期待您的回音。

誠摯地
梅格 · 瓊斯

Email 這樣寫也行！

① 事實上，降價是不可行的。
In fact, a price reduction is not available.

② 如果您有興趣，我會將資料傳給您。
If you are interested in it, I will forward the information to you.

③ 我很高興您喜愛我的房子。
I am glad that you like my house.

④ 您一個月可以省一千元。
You can save one thousand dollars each month.

⑤ 就我看法，您是一個好房客。
In my opinion, you are a good tenant .

⑥ 如果需要更多資訊，請與我聯絡。
Please let us know if you need more information.

⑦ 請撥打免付費電話 0800-123-456。
Please call our toll-free number 0800-123-456.

⑧ 您的即早回覆我們將不勝感激。
Your early reply will be greatly appreciated.

13 諮詢產品使用情況

範例 1

Title : How do you like our product/service?

Dear Mr. Farrell,

You purchased a **Mac** in our store in Boston last year. Thank you for choosing our brand.

Now we want to know whether your Mac is still in a good state. Please fill out the following **questionnaire** about its service condition and email us so that we can improve the technology.

Looking forward to hearing from you.

Yours sincerely,
Susan Smith

SEND   A ⬚ ⊝ ☺

主旨：請問您如何看待我們的產品／服務？

親愛的法瑞爾先生：

去年您曾在我們的波士頓分店買過一台**蘋果電腦**。感謝您選擇蘋果的產品。

現在，我們想瞭解一下您的電腦是否仍然狀態良好。請您填寫下列有關電腦使用情況的**問卷**，並郵寄給我們，以期改進技術。

期待您的回覆！

您誠摯地，

蘇珊‧史密斯

照著抄 ～ Email 簡單搞定！ — ⤢ ✕

範例 2

Title : How do you like our product/service?

Dear Mr. Affleck,

It has been one year since you bought our machine. Thank you for your purchase.

We would like to know about its **working status**. Do you have any problems or any suggestions about it?

Please fill out the following questionnaire and tell us all about it.

Any **opinion** from you will be of great value to us. We really appreciate it.

Yours sincerely,

John Brown

SEND   A 📎 🔗 😊

 中譯

主旨：請問您如何看待我們的產品／服務？

親愛的阿弗萊克先生：

您購買我們的機器已經有一年了。謝謝您的購買。

我們想知道這台機器目前的**工作情況**。同時，關於這台機器您有什麼問題或是建議嗎？

請填寫下列問卷，以告訴我們有關它的一切情況。

來自您的任何**意見**都十分寶貴。我們對此深表謝意。

您誠摯地，

約翰‧布朗

① 希望我們的產品一直都使用狀況良好。

I hope our product works in good condition all the time.

② 填寫這份問卷，只需花您 5 分鐘的時間。

It will only take you five minutes to fill out the questionnaire.

③ 您曾在專賣店購買過我們的商品。

You bought the product from our franchised store.

④ 我們仍需再努力改進技術。

It is still necessary to try and improve our technology.

⑤ 我們想詢問一下它的工作狀況。

We would like to inquire about its working status.

⑥ 謝謝您的耐心和理解！

Thanks for your patience and understanding.

⑦ 感謝您使用我們的產品，也希望它們能夠幫上您的忙！

Thanks for using our products and hope they will help you.

⑧ 請填好表格，並在 8 月前寄給我。

Please fill out the form and send it to me by August.

14【回應】諮詢產品使用情況

照著抄 ～ Email 簡單搞定！

範例 1

Re : How do you like our product/service?

Dear Mrs. Smith,
It's flattered to receive an email from Apple checking the condition on my Mac. However, I am a bit concerned about the validity of this email since it's unprecedented to be reached this way.
As well, filling out the questionnaire requires downloading an unverified attachment and submitting my personal information.
As a precaution, I would **put it on hold**. Alternatively, filling it out online is preferred because it's straightforward for one to verify the web address and be more willing to complete the request.
Thank you for the courtesy of your early attention.

Yours sincerely,
Tom Farrell

SEND

回覆：請問您如何看待我們的產品／服務？

史密斯女士您好：
很高興收到 Apple 查看我 Mac 使用情況的郵件。不過，我有點擔心這封電子郵件的有效性，因為從沒用這種方式收到過。
此外，填寫問卷需要下載未經證實的附件，還要提交我個人資訊。
為以防萬一，我會把這封信**擱置**。或者，最好在網上填寫，因為網路驗證比較簡單，讓人更有意願完成要求。
感謝您及早回覆。

您誠摯地，
湯姆‧法瑞爾

Re : How do you like our product/service?

Dear Mr. Brown,
I have been calling **customer service** several times to file a complaint. As of now, I am not content with the responses I received from the representative. The responses all seemed to lean toward improper use. The fact I followed the step-by-step instruction manual to operate it.
There are a couple of issues I have been running into. Firstly, it gets overheated quickly in 10 minutes or less. Secondly, a squeaking sound is apparent when it's set in a high mode. Having said that, I hope these two issues **can be addressed** before filling out the questionnaire.
I look forward to receiving your response.

Sincerely,
David Affleck

SEND

回覆：請問您如何看待我們的產品／服務？

布朗先生您好：
我多次打電話給**客服部**客訴。到目前為止，我不滿意從客服得到的答覆。這些回答似乎都傾向於使用不當。事實上，我依照指導手冊來循序漸進地操作。
結果碰到幾個問題。首先，在 10 分鐘以內，甚至更短的時間內迅速過熱。第二，在高速模式下很清楚聽到發出的尖銳聲。誠如所言，在填寫調查表之前，我希望這兩個問題**能獲得解決**。
期待收到回覆。

您誠摯地，
大衛‧阿弗萊克

Email 這樣寫也行！

① 我很開心收到這封電子郵件。

I am happy to receive the email.

② 我擔心這封電子郵件的有效性。

I am worried about the validity of this email.

③ 我比較想在線上填寫。

I prefer filling it online.

④ 我對客服部的回答不甚滿意。

I'm not satisfied with the answers I received from the customer service.

⑤ 期待您的答覆。

I look forward to hearing your reply.

⑥ 還有一些問題要解決。

There remain some issues to be solved.

⑦ 以防萬一，我晚點再做這件事。

As a precaution, I'll do it later.

⑧ 盼您及早回覆。

A prompt reply would help us greatly.

15 請求擔任獨家代理

照著抄 ～ Email 簡單搞定！ — ⤢ ✕

範例 1

Title : We would like to be your sole agents in Taiwan.

Dear Sir or Madam,
Our company is APP Shoes. We represent a reliable Taiwanese *importer of shoe apparel*.
We are interested in your outstanding shoes, and shall be pleased to act as your *sole agent* here and market your products successfully in Taiwan.
Attached is our company profile for your kind perusal.
Please feel free to contact us.

Yours faithfully,
APP Shoes
Molly Huang
General Manager

SEND   A 🔗 ☺

主旨：我們想要取得您的台灣獨家代理

敬啟者：
本公司是 APP 鞋業。我們是台灣**進口鞋類**的可靠代表。我們對貴公司精製的鞋子很感興趣，很希望能取得貴公司**獨家代理**，並在台灣成功地推銷貴公司的鞋子。
附件是本公司簡介資料，請您仔細審閱。
請隨時與我們聯繫。

忠實地，
APP 鞋業
黃茉莉
總經理

照著抄～ Email 簡單搞定！ — ⤢ ✕

Title : We would like to be your sole agents in Taiwan.

Dear Sir or Madam,

We'd like to inform you that we have successfully acted as the sole importers for many manufactures.

We are really interested in your products, so it would be my pleasure if you could appoint us as your sole agent.

Please see the attached document as our company **profile** for your reference.

We look forward to your prompt reply.

Sincerely,

Jason Yip

SEND　　　　　　　　　　　　　　　　　A ⎘ 🔗 ☺

主旨：我們想要取得您的台灣獨家代理

敬啟者：

我們想告訴您，我們已經成功獲得許多進口商的獨家代理權。

我們真的對您的產品很感興趣，如果您能讓我們取得貴公司的獨家代理權，這將是我的榮幸。

附件是敝公司的**簡介**，僅供您參考。

期待您盡速回覆！

誠摯地，

傑森‧葉

Email 這樣寫也行！

① 如果您同意我的提案，請提供我們貴公司的商業條款。

If you agree to our proposal, please send us the terms of business you propose.

② 我們對成為貴公司的獨家代理商非常感興趣。

We are interested in an exclusive arrangement with your company.

③ 我們很榮幸成為貴公司的獨家代理商。

We have the pleasure to be your sole agent.

④ 請閱讀本電子郵件內的附件簡介。

Please find the attached document with this email.

⑤ 如果我們能被選為貴公司的獨家代理商，我們將會提供最棒的服務。

We will provide the best service if we are appointed as the sole agent for your company.

⑥ 您的及早回應是我們的喜悅。

We shall be pleased to receive an early reply.

⑦ 事實上，我們已經做好成為公司獨家代理商的準備。

In fact, we are ready to act as sole agent for your company.

⑧ 我們期待和貴公司合作。

We look forward to doing business with you.

16【回應】請求擔任獨家代理

照著抄～ Email 簡單搞定！ — ⤢ ×

範例 1

Re : We would like to be your sole agents in Taiwan.

Dear Mrs. Huang,

Thank you for contacting us. We are very pleased to know that our products are seen overseas.

To work with a local sourcing agent is definitely a plus in growing our business.

Regulations on importing shoe products to Taiwan are beyond the scope of our expertise.

We'd like to know more about how the ***process*** goes such as making documentations, product inspections and shipping.

I'm looking forward to hearing your feedback.

Sincerely,
Emma Cruise

SEND

 中譯

回覆：我們想要取得您的台灣獨家代理

黃女士您好：

感謝您聯繫我們。很高興得知我們產品在國外也能看得到。

與當地採購代理合作，對我們的業務發展絕對是有利的。在台灣進口鞋類產品的規定，超出了我們專業的知識範圍。

我們想了解更多的**過程**該如何進行，如製作檔案，產品檢查和運送。

期待聽到您回應。

誠摯地，
艾瑪．克魯斯

範例 2

Re : We would like to be your sole agents in Taiwan.

Dear Mr. Yip,

Thank you for considering us. We have been contacted by several sourcing agents lately.

To find the best fit among all the proposals, an ***assessment*** is a must and will take place shortly. In the meantime, in addition to the profile you have attached, it would be helpful to also see some of your works or clients you have worked with as ***reference***.

Thank you again for your time and consideration.

Yours faithfully,
Doris Holmes

SEND   Ａ 🔗 ⊝

中譯

回覆：我們想要取得您的台灣獨家代理

葉先生您好：

謝謝您考慮我們。最近我們已經和一些採購代理商聯絡過。

為了找出所有提案中最合適的一位，進行**評估**是必要的，並且不久我們就會進行。

同時，除了您所附的簡介之外，還想看到您的一些作品或曾合作過的客戶，以茲**參考**。

再次感謝您的時間和考量。

您忠實地，
朵莉絲‧福爾摩斯

Email 這樣寫也行！

① 我們想知道更多貴公司的資訊。
We'd like to know more information about your company.

② 謝謝您寫信給我們。
Thank you for writing to us.

③ 我們最近有和幾間當地代理商談過。
We have been talked by some local agents recently.

④ 請列舉一些您的成果或是曾合作過的客戶。
Please list some of your works or clients you have worked.

⑤ 我們期待收到更多關於您們的相關資料。
We look forward to receiving your more information.

⑥ 貴公司已經被本公司選為獨家代理廠商。
You have been appointed as the sole agent for our company.

⑦ 感謝您慎重地考慮。
Thank you for your kind consideration.

⑧ 從合約中提到的日期起，您將成為我們公司的獨家代理。
You will act as sole agent for our company from the mentioned date in the agreement.

17 請求介紹客戶

照著抄 ～ Email 簡單搞定！

範例 1

Title : Would you be kind and introduce us some clients?

Dear Mr. Scott,

We would like to explore the potential market in your country and increase the export of ***electronic products***.

Therefore, we shall appreciate it very much if you will kindly introduce us to some of the most capable importers who are interested in them.

Your early reply will be greatly appreciated.

Yours sincerely,
Dawn Smith

SEND

主旨：請問您是否能為我們介紹一些客戶？

親愛的史考特先生：

我們準備在貴國開拓潛在市場，以增加**電子產品**的出口貿易。

因此，若您們能介紹幾個對上述產品感興趣，且實力雄厚的進口商，我們將十分感謝。

期待您的回覆！

您誠摯地，

唐恩‧史密斯

照著抄 ～ Email 簡單搞定！

Title : Would you be kind and introduce us some clients?

Dear Mr. Brown,

We are well established in manufacturing various **bicycles** to which we have devoted many years of research. As we desire earnestly to **increase** the sales of our products in your market, we shall appreciate it very much if you can introduce us to some clients.

We are confident that our products will not disappoint our future partners.

We look forward to hearing from you.

Yours sincerely,

Henry Peters

SEND

中譯

主旨：請問您是否能為我們介紹一些客戶？

親愛的布朗先生：

我們公司在生產各種**自行車**有著多年的深入研究，經驗豐富。我們很想**擴展**貴國市場，如果您能介紹一些客戶給我們的話，我們將不勝感激。

相信我們的產品不會讓未來的合夥人失望的。

期待您的回覆。

您誠摯地，

亨利·彼得斯

Email 這樣寫也行！

① 我們期望進一步拓寬國際石油市場。

We hope to expand in the international petroleum market.

② 這些年來，我們的生意發展得很快。

Our business has developed rapidly these years.

③ 我們在尋找專案投資商。

We are looking for some companies to invest in our project.

④ 我們的目的是想找到一個可以建立合資企業的合作夥伴。

Our purpose is to find a partner in setting up a joint venture.

⑤ 您們那裡有沒有合適的客戶可以介紹給我們？

Are there any right customers to introduce in your city?

⑥ 我們計畫要在今年擴大我們的貿易。

We are planning to expand our trade this year.

⑦ 我們決定要擴大市場範圍。

We have decided to expand the market reach.

⑧ 如果您們能替我們介紹一些客戶的話那就太棒了。

It would be great if you can introduce us to some customers.

18 【回應】請求介紹客戶

範例 1

Re : Would you be kind and introduce us some clients?

Dear Mr. Smith,

We were glad to receive your letter. Unfortunately, we are not familiar with the market of electronic products. To expand the network of meeting importers, one efficient way is to ***attend conferences***.

Base on my personal experience, I was able to discover my potential clients/partners and establish a long term business relationship with them. Be more engaged at social gatherings and take advantage of the opportunity to build connections.

Yours sincerely,
John Scott

SEND　　　　　　　　　　　　　　　　　A ⌀ 🔗 ☺

 中譯

回覆：請問您是否能為我們介紹一些客戶？

史密斯先生您好：

很高興收到您的來信。不幸的是，我們對電子產品的市場並不熟悉。為了擴展進口商的圈子，有效的方式是**參加會議**。

根據個人經驗，我有辦法找出潛在客戶／合作夥伴，與他們建立長期業務關係。參與更多地社交聚會，利用機會建立聯繫關係。

您誠摯地，
約翰·史考特

範例 2

Re : Would you be kind and introduce us some clients?

Dear Mr. Peters,

As much as I'd like to help, this is above my pay grade.
Having a strict policy in place at work, it's forbidden to refer firm's clients to others.

Alternatively, you might want to shift your focus to the ***online shoppers***. To create a global market and reach the unlimited potential bicycle buyers. All you have to do is to put them online, and start to sell all over the world.

Should you need further assistance, please don't hesitate to contact me again.

Sincerely,
Jack Brown

SEND　　　　　　　　　　　　　　　　　A ⋃ ⊖ ☺

回覆：請問您是否能為我們介紹一些客戶？

彼得斯先生您好：
正如我想說明的那樣，這超出了我的薪水等級範圍。在工作中有嚴格的政策，禁止將公司的客戶介紹給其他方。
或者，您可能想把注意力轉移到**線上購物者**身上。打造全球市場，獲得無限潛力的自行車買家。您所要做的就是將它們放在網上，開始進行全世界銷售。
如果需要進一步的說明，請馬上與我再次聯繫。

您誠摯地，
約翰‧布朗

Email 這樣寫也行！

① 非常感謝考慮本公司。

Thank you so much for considering us.

② 有效擴展進口商圈子的方式是參加會議。

One efficient way to expand the network of meeting importers is to attend conferences.

③ 我們對此領域不熟。

We are unfamiliar with the field.

④ 因為已經超越我的薪水階級範圍，我無法幫您。

Because this is above my pay grade, I can't do anything for you.

⑤ 抱歉，我沒辦法介紹客戶給您。

I'm sorry I can't introduce you to some customers.

⑥ 我們期待和貴司合作。

We look forward to doing business with you.

⑦ 若有任何問題，請隨時與我聯繫。

If you have any questions, please feel free to contact me.

⑧ 您可以藉由將商品放上網路，而行銷全世界。

You can sell your products all over the world by putting them online.

19 尋求合作

範例 1

Title : We are looking for chances of cooperation.

Dear Mr. Brody,

We are writing to you to seek your cooperation.

We are very well connected with many major dealers here of electronic products, and feel sure that we can sell large quantities of them if you can make us a **special offer**.

Your early reply will be greatly appreciated.

Yours sincerely,
James Wright

SEND A 🔗 😊

主旨：我們正在尋找合作機會

親愛的布羅迪：

我們特寫此信尋求合作機會。

敝公司與當地眾多電子產品大經銷商都有著很好的聯繫，若貴公司可以提供我們**優惠價**，我們肯定能賣出大量產品。

期待您的回覆！

您誠摯地，

詹姆斯‧懷特

照著抄 ～ Email 簡單搞定！

Title : We are looking for chances of cooperation.

Dear Mr. Green,

Our company is specialized in manufacturing ***household appliances***. We are to expand our market this year and desire to find a suitable partner.

In the past several years, we have been extending the scope of our products. I am sure that some items would be of great interest to you even though you have not seen them.

Please let us know if you want to cooperate with us.

Yours sincerely,
Jessica Yang

SEND

中譯

主旨：我們正在尋找合作機會

親愛的格林先生：

我們是一家專門生產**家用電器**的公司。今年我們計畫拓展市場，希望找到一位合適的合作夥伴。

在過去的幾年裡，我們一直在擴大產品範圍。雖然您未曾見到我們的產品，但是我們相信您一定會對我們的某些產品很感興趣。

如有意合作，請聯繫我們。

您誠摯地，

潔西卡 · 楊

Email 這樣寫也行！

① 我們正在尋求合作機會。

We are seeking cooperation opportunities.

② 如果您對這個計畫感興趣的話，請與我們聯繫。

If you are interested in this plan, please contact us.

③ 如果您想知道有關我們產品的所有資訊，請致電給我們。

If you want to know all the information regarding our products, please call us.

④ 我們在尋找為我們提供此類貨物的合作夥伴。

We are looking for a partner who can supply us with such goods.

⑤ 如果您對此感興趣的話，請告知具體資訊。

Please let us know with specific information if you are interested in it.

⑥ 想要找到一個合適的合作夥伴對我們來說並不容易。

It is not easy for us to find a suitable partner.

⑦ 為了擴大市場，我們正在國外尋求合作夥伴。

We are looking for partners abroad to expand our market.

⑧ 如果您有興趣合作，請撥打免付費電話 0800-111-111。

If you are interested in cooperation, please call toll-free number 0800-111-111.

20 【回應】尋求合作

照著抄 ～ Email 簡單搞定！ — ↗ ✕

範例1

Re : We are looking for chances of cooperation.

Dear Mr. Wright,

Thank you for your consideration. Since we are a startup company, our objective at this point is not to sell large quantities yet.

Instead, we are aiming to **expand our user base**. To get consumers really like with every single electronic product we make. Ideally, one would leave a positive impression after trying it out.

Thanks again for reaching out to us.

Sincerely,
Willy Brody

SEND   A ! ⊝ ☺

中譯

回覆：我們正在尋找合作機會

懷特先生您好：

謝謝您的考慮。因為我們是一家草創公司，目前的目標並非大量銷售。

相反地，我們的目標是**擴大基本用戶**。讓消費者真正喜歡我們生產的每種電子產品。在理想情況下，使用過的人會後留下正面印象。

再次感謝您支持我們。

誠摯地，
威力‧布羅迪

Re : We are looking for chances of cooperation.

Dear Mrs. Yang,

Your company has a good business reputation in the market and is well known for household appliances. We would be more than happy to join a ***partnership***.

As mentioned, there are some recent products I am not familiar yet and I can't wait to get my hands on them.

In short, we appreciate for the opportunity to work with you and look forward to the partnership.

Sincerely yours,
Gary Green

SEND   A 🖉 🔗 ☺

回覆：我們正在尋找合作機會

楊女士您好：

貴公司在市場商業信譽優良，以家用電器聞名。我們很樂意加入和貴司成為**夥伴關係**。

如上所述，有些新產品我還不熟，迫不及待想趕快上手。

簡而言之，感謝有機會與您合作，期待彼此的合作關係。

您誠摯地，

蓋瑞‧格林

Email 這樣寫也行！

① 建立合夥關係是我們的榮幸。

It's our pleasure to join a partnership.

② 我們很開心和貴公司有合夥關係。

We are happy to have the opportunity to partner with you.

③ 我們希望顧客真的喜愛我們的電子產品。

We hope our customers really like our electronic products.

④ 謝謝您的推薦。

Thank you for your recommendation.

⑤ 期待與您合作。

We are looking forward to cooperating with you.

⑥ 如果有任何疑問，請隨時打電話給我。

If you have any questions, feel free to call me.

⑦ 謝謝您的諒解。

Thank you for your understanding.

⑧ 我們期待與貴公司在未來有良好的合作關係。

We are looking forward to having good partnership with your organization in the future.

PART2

商品交易

因各家手機系統不同，若無法直接掃描，仍可以（https://tinyurl.com/uxmb2rs）電腦連結雲端下載，一貼搞定！

Part 2.
商品交易

01 詢問公司資訊

照著抄 ～ Email 簡單搞定！　　　　　　　　　　─ ⤢ ✕

範例 1

Title : Information inquiry of your company.

Dear Sir or Madam,

We are manufacturers of ***leather shoes*** in Taiwan. I am
writing to request information about your company. We
Actually, I am very interested in learning more about your
company. I would appreciate any corporate brochures or
marketing materials with which you could provide me.

I am looking forward to hearing from you soon.

Thank you very much for you kindness.

Yours sincerely,

John Brown

SEND　　　　　　　　　　　　　　　　　　　　A ⫾ 🔗 ☺

主旨：貴公司的資訊諮詢

敬啟者：

我們是台灣的**皮鞋**製造商。這封信是為了諮詢貴公司的相關資訊。事實上，我很有興趣更進一步瞭解貴公司。如果您能將一些可公布的公司業務簡介或市場銷售資料提供給我，將不勝感激。

期待您儘快回覆。

非常感謝您的熱心幫助。

您真誠地，

約翰・布朗

照著抄 ～ Email 簡單搞定！ — ⤢ ✕

範例 2

Title : Information inquiry of your company.

Dear Mr. White,

I would like to request more information about your company.

I am planning to invest your company on the **hearing aids** because of their better performances compared with other similar products.

I would appreciate any brochures or marketing materials with which you could provide me.

Thank you in advance. I am looking forward to your reply.

Yours sincerely,

Lincoln Miller

SEND   A 🖉 🔗 ☺

中譯

主旨：貴公司的資訊諮詢

親愛的懷特先生：

我想請教有關貴公司產品的更多資訊。

與其他同類產品比較之後，發現您們的**助聽器**性能更佳，因此我打算投資您們公司的助聽器生產。

如果您能將公司業務簡介或市場銷售資料提供給我，將不勝感激。

先謝謝您了，期待您的來信！

您誠摯的，

林肯・米勒

Email 這樣寫也行！

① 我想要一份貴公司的簡介。

I would like to request a copy of your company brochure.

② 我很有興趣更進一步地瞭解貴公司。

I am very interested in knowing more about your company.

③ 可以在網站上找到有關貴公司的詳細資訊嗎？

Is further information about your company available on your website?

④ 我想要諮詢貴公司的相關資訊。

I am writing to request some information about your company.

⑤ 您可不可以給我一份貴公司的年度報告？

Is it possible to have a copy of your annual report?

⑥ 如果您能給我一些貴公司的資訊將不勝感激。

I would appreciate if you could give me some of the detailed information about your company.

⑦ 您能提供給我貴公司的詳細資訊嗎？

Could you provide me with detailed information about your company?

⑧ 先謝謝您的關注。

Thank you in advance for your kind attention.

02 【回應】詢問公司資訊

 Re : Information inquiry of your company.

Dear Mr. Brown,

Thank you for your letter of cooperating brochures and marketing materials.

We are pleased to enclose our ***latest brochure***. We would also like to inform you that it is possible to visit us at www.browncompany.com.tw

Enclosed you will find the information you request.

We look forward to hearing from you.

Yours sincerely,

Lisa Simpson

SEND　　　　　　　　　　　　　　　　　A ₿ 🔗 ☺

回覆：貴公司的資訊諮詢

布朗先生您好：

感謝您要求公司宣傳手冊和行銷物料的來信。

很榮幸隨函附上**最新的手冊**，同時期望您可以瀏覽本公司的網站：

www.browncompany.com.tw

隨信附上您所需求的資訊。

期待您的回音。

您真誠地，

麗莎‧辛普森

Re : Information inquiry of your company.

Dear Mr. Miller,

Thank you for your letter of **_inquiring_** about the hearing aids.

Enclosed you will find the brochures about our products.

We would like to thank you for your letter of asking for information about the hearing aids.

We look forward to hearing from you.

Yours sincerely,

Jordan White

SEND

回覆：貴公司的資訊諮詢

親愛的米勒先生：

感謝您來信**詢問**關於助聽器相關產品。

隨信附上本公司產品手冊。

非常感謝您來信諮詢助聽器的相關資料。

我們期待您的來信。

您誠摯的，

喬丹‧懷特

Email 這樣寫也行！

① 感謝您對本公司產品有興趣。

Thank you for your interest in our product.

② 可以在網站上找到本公司的詳細資訊。

Further information about our company is available on our website.

③ 很高興附上我們最新商品指南。

We are pleased to enclose our latest brochure.

④ 我已隨信附上公司手冊和行銷物料。

I have enclosed our brochures and marketing materials.

⑤ 我們期待並歡迎您成為我們的客戶。

We look forward to welcoming you as our client.

⑥ 感謝您查詢本公司資訊。。

Thank you for your enquiry about our information.

⑦ 期望您認為我寄送的公司資料有所助益。

Hope you will find the information of our company I have sent is useful.

⑧ 我們歡迎您成為本公司的客戶。

We are welcoming you as our client.

03 詢問產品資訊

範例 1

Title : Product information inquiry from ... company.

Dear Sir or Madam,

I am writing to request ***further information*** about your latest products. May I ask you to provide me with their detailed information on prices, delivery costs and the like?

I wonder if there are any discounts available for bulk order. In addition, do you accept an overseas order?

I appreciate your early response.

Yours sincerely,

Bill Smith

SEND

中譯

主旨：諮詢貴公司的產品資訊

敬啟者：

我想諮詢貴公司最新產品的**更多資訊**。貴方能否提供價格、運輸價格等詳細的產品資訊？

我想知道如果大量購買的話能否有折扣呢？另外，請問您接受海外訂單嗎？

即早回覆不勝感激。

您真誠地，

比爾・史密斯

照著抄 ～ Email 簡單搞定！

範例 2

**Title : Product information inquiry from ...
company.**

Dear Mr. Brown,

We learned from the advertisement that your company is producing electronic products of high quality.

We are going to get more of them for we find they are in a great demand in the local shops. Is it possible for you to send us a ***detailed catalog or any material*** about your products in terms of price, specification and payment mode?

We look forward to hearing from you.

Yours sincerely,

John Cook

SEND

中譯

主旨：諮詢貴公司的產品資訊

親愛的布朗先生：

我們從廣告中獲悉，貴公司致力於生產高品質的電子產品。

由於您們的電子產品在當地商店中頗為暢銷，因此我們打算買進更多的此類產品。

不知您是否可以寄給我們一份產品**目錄**或任何價格、規格和付款方式方面的**產品資料**呢？

期待您的回覆！

您誠摯地，

約翰‧庫克

① 寫這封信是想諮詢貴公司的產品資訊。

I am writing to request information about your products.

② 您能告知我們有關產品的詳細資訊嗎？

Can you inform us of your products in detail?

③ 您們的產品在當地很暢銷。

Your products are well received in the local place.

④ 如能寄來一份商品目錄，我們將不勝感激。

We would appreciate if you would send us your catalog.

⑤ 您們正在生產高品質的電子產品。

You are producing high quality electronic products.

⑥ 這將會是一個極具挑戰性和發展前景的產業。

This is a very challenging but potential industry.

⑦ 我們需要利用優勢，快速佔領市場。

We should make use of its advantages to occupy the market quickly.

⑧ 我們的產品用途廣泛。

The appliances of our products are diverse.

04【回應】詢問產品資訊

照著抄 ～ Email 簡單搞定！　　　　　　　　— ↗ ✕

範例 1　Re : Product information inquiry from ... company.

Dear Mr. Smith,

Thank you for your email enquiry about our latest products detailed information on prices, delivery costs.

We generally give a **5% discount** for a bulk order. In addition, we **accept an overseas order**.

If you require more information, please do not hesitate to contact me.

Yours sincerely,
Johnny Thomas

SEND　　　　　　　　　　　　　　　　　A 🖉 🔗 😊

回覆：諮詢貴公司的產品資訊

史密斯先生您好：

謝謝您來信諮詢本公司最新產品的相關資訊。附件是本公司產品的價格、運輸費的詳細資訊。

針對大量訂單我們會給予**九五折優惠**。另外，我們**接受海外訂單**。

如果需要更多資訊，請隨時與我聯繫。

您真誠地，

強尼‧湯馬仕

範例 2

Re : Product information inquiry from ... company.

Dear Mr. Cook,

Thank you for your inquiry of electronic products for the latest edition of our catalog.

We enclose our latest brochure about our products in terms of price, specification and ***payment mode***.

If you have any questions, please don't hesitate to contact us.

We look forward to welcoming you as our customer.

Yours sincerely,

Allen Brown

SEND   A ⬆ 🔗 ☺

 中譯

回覆：諮詢貴公司的產品資訊

庫克先生您好：

感謝您諮詢電子產品的最新目錄。

隨函附上最新目錄，包含產品、價格、規格和**付款方式**。

如果您有任何疑問，請隨時與我們聯繫。

期待並歡迎您成為我們的客戶。

您誠摯地，

艾倫・布朗

Email 這樣寫也行！

① 感謝您透過電子郵件諮詢本公司產品。

Thank you for your email enquiry about our products.

② 您能提供貴公司的詳細資訊給我嗎？

Can you provide me with detailed information about your company?

③ 感謝您對本公司的電子產品感興趣。

Thank you for your interest in our electronic products.

④ 如果能進一步協助您，請不吝告知。

If we can be of any further assistance, please let me know.

⑤ 根據您的要求，附上本公司簡介。

As you requested, I enclose a brochure about our company.

⑥ 先謝謝您關注（本公司產品）。

Thank you in advance for your kind attention.

⑦ 我們很高興附上本公司最新目錄。

We are pleased to enclose our latest catalog.

⑧ 我們期待您的回音。

We are looking forward to hear from you soon.

05 詢問交貨日期

範例 1

Title : Inquiry of date of order delivery for ... product.

Dear Mr. Hines,

Would you please inform us how long it usually takes you to make delivery of our order of July 2nd (Order No. 35287) for **car components**. I wonder if it is possible for you to ship the goods before early mid-July?

Moreover, please mail the **invoice** of this order to our company.

We look forward to hearing from you soon.

Yours sincerely,
Robert Wilson

SEND

主旨：詢問產品訂單的運送時間

親愛的海因斯先生：

敬請告知敝公司於 7 月 2 日訂購的訂單編號：35287 **汽車零配件**什麼時候能出貨？我想知道您能不能於 7 月中旬之前出貨呢？

此外，能否將**發票**寄送到本公司？

煩請儘快與敝公司聯繫。

您誠摯地，
羅伯特‧威爾森

照著抄 ～ Email 簡單搞定！

Title : Inquiry of date of order delivery for ... product.

Dear Sir or Madam,

As mentioned in the last letter, we would like to purchase ***two hundred air conditioners*** from you.

As it is the best season for sales of air conditioners at present, could you please let us know your earliest delivery date? As you know, the time of delivery is a matter of great importance to us.

We look forward to hearing from you soon.

Yours sincerely,
Bill White

SEND

主旨：詢問產品訂單的運送時間

敬啟者：

如上封信提到的，我們想購買貴公司**兩百台空調冷氣**。

由於現在是空調冷氣的暢銷季節，可否請貴公司告知最早的交貨日期呢？您知道交貨時間對我們來說是很重要的。

期待您儘早回信。

您真誠地，

比爾‧懷特

① 能否儘快告知交貨日期？

Can you please communicate delivery date as soon as possible?

② 我們可以同意其他條件，除了發貨日期。

We can live with the other terms, except the delivery date.

③ 交貨日期如有變更，我們將予以告知。

We will advise you of any changes in the delivery dates.

④ 您們什麼時候可以交付貨物給我們？

When will you deliver the products to us?

⑤ 貴方不能在發貨日期上對我方失約。

You must not let us down on delivery dates.

⑥ 關於出貨日期這方面，應該沒有問題了吧！

As far as delivery dates are concerned, there shouldn't be any problems.

⑦ 您們能否於 9 月初之前把貨物運送過來？

Will it possible for you to ship the goods before early September?

⑧ 最早的交貨日期是 10 月。

Our earliest time of delivery is October.

06【回應】詢問交貨日期

照著抄 ～ Email 簡單搞定！ ー ⤢ ✕

Re : Inquiry of date of order delivery for ... product.

Dear Mr. Wilson ,
This is in regard to your Order No. 35287 which you placed with our company on the 2nd of July.
We sincerely *apologize* to you for the delay in delivery of car components you ordered with us. Your shipment shall be dispatched for delivery on July 15.
Moreover, we will mail the invoice of this order to your company.
Once again we apologize to you. We really appreciate your support.

Yours sincerely,
Tommy Hines

SEND   A ✐ 🔗 ☺

回覆：詢問產品訂單的運送時間

親愛的威爾森先生：
這封信是關於您於 7 月 2 日向我們公司訂購商品，編號：35287。
對於您訂購的汽車零件的延遲交貨，我們深表**歉意**。您的商品將於 7 月 15 日發貨。
此外，我們會將此訂單的發票郵寄到貴公司。
再次向您致歉。非常感謝您的支持。

您誠摯地，
湯米‧海因斯

Re : Inquiry of date of order delivery for ... product.

Dear Mr. White,
We have received your letter of the 5th January asking of early in the delivery of two hundred air conditioners.
We understand the time of delivery is a matter of great importance to you, so we would do our best to support you.
Our earliest delivery date would be 15th January, 2022.
We fully ***appreciate*** the indulgence you have shown to us in the date of delivery.
We look forward to your early reply.

Yours Faithfully,
Lisa Wilson

SEND

回覆：詢問產品訂單的運送時間

懷特先生您好：
我們已收到您 1 月 5 日，要求提早運送兩百台空調冷氣的來信。
我們了解交貨時間對您來說至關重要，因此我們將竭盡所能給予支持。本公司最早會於 2022 年 1 月 15 日交貨。
貴司對本公司交貨日期的延期寬容，十分**感謝**。
期待您儘早回信。

您真誠地，
麗莎‧威爾森

Email 這樣寫也行！

① 我們這週晚點會告知出貨日期。

We would communicate delivery date later this week.

② 請稍等一封確認訂單發貨日期的信件。

Please wait for an email confirming the delivery date for your order.

③ 這所有原因造成延誤。

All this has led to this delay.

④ 我們已檢查出延遲發貨的原因。

We have checked to find out the reason why your shipment was delayed.

⑤ 本公司最早的交貨日期在三月。

Our earliest time of delivery is March.

⑥ 在您下一次訂購本公司商品時，我們會提供九五折給您。

We offer 5% discount to you on your next purchase order with us.

⑦ 根據合約內容，交貨時間是訂在 2021 年 4 月。

Under the terms of the contract, delivery is scheduled for April 2021.

⑧ 下訂單時，將會自動安排交貨日期。

Your delivery date is automatically scheduled when you place a delivery order.

07 詢問庫存狀況

範例 1

Title : Inventory inquiry from ... company.

Dear Mr. Brown,
In consideration of your electric fan which sells well here because of its high quality and favorable price, we have decided to purchase more of them.
Please **check** your inventory to see if you have **one hundred more** for another delivery.
Thank you very much for your kind attention and we look forward to hearing from you soon.

Yours sincerely,
Paul Smith

SEND   A ✎ 🔗 😊

主旨：詢問公司庫存

親愛的布朗先生：
鑒於貴公司的電風扇品質不錯而且價格優惠，銷量不錯，我們決定再多買進一些。
請**確認**該產品是否還有庫存，我們需要再購買 100 台。
非常感謝您的關注，期待您儘快回覆！

您誠摯地，
波爾‧史密斯

照著抄 ～ Email 簡單搞定！

範例 2

Title : Inventory inquiry from ... company.

Dear Sir or Madam,

We are very interested in your products which were ***advertised on Facebook***. Therefore, we are writing to request about your stock availability.

If we place a considerable order, could you provide enough products for us? In addition, could you give us any discount? An early reply will be obliged.

Yours sincerely,
Steven Stone

SEND

 中譯

主旨：詢問公司庫存

敬啟者：

我方對貴公司在**臉書廣告中**的產品非常感興趣，因此寫信詢問貴公司的庫存情況。如果我方大量訂購，貴公司有足夠的產品提供給我方嗎？另外，貴公司可否給予我方一些折扣呢？

如能儘早回覆，不勝感激。

您真誠地，

史蒂芬・史東

Email 這樣寫也行！

① 能否查看庫存貨物的狀況？

Would you do the inventory check for us?

② 我查過了庫存中您要的那種商品。

I checked our supply of the commodity you asked for.

③ 目前，我們的貨物庫存有限。

At present, we have only a limited stock of goods.

④ 現有庫存無法滿足需求。

The current inventory of the product can not meet the demand.

⑤ 如果可能的話，我們想再購買 50 台，希望盡速運送。

If possible, we need fifty more for immediate delivery.

⑥ 您們庫存有什麼型號的商品？

What type of model do you have in stock?

⑦ 我很遺憾，我沒有按時收到庫存單。

I regret not receiving the inventory on time.

⑧ 我剛剛獲知我們現有的庫存量。

I just got an answer about the stock we have on hand.

08 【回應】詢問庫存狀況

照著抄 ～ Email 簡單搞定！ － ⤢ ✕

 範例 1

Re : Inventory inquiry from ... company.

Dear Mr. Smith,

It was a pleasure to receive your inventory inquiry about the product of our company.

We are pleased to **satisfy your inquiry** with the attached information.

We have checked our inventory. We have one hundred more for another delivery.

If you need more details, we are always ready to help.

We look forward to hearing from you soon.

Yours sincerely,

Frank Brown

SEND   A ⬭ ⊝ ☺

 中譯

回覆：詢問公司庫存

史密斯先生您好：

很榮幸收到您對本公司商品的庫存詢問。

很高興所附訊息能讓您的**諮詢滿意**。

我們已經檢查過庫存。本公司還有一百台產品可以再次交貨給您。

如果貴公司需要更詳細資訊，我們將隨時為您提供協助。

期待您儘快回覆！

您誠摯地，

法蘭克‧布朗

Re : Inventory inquiry from ... company.

Dear Mr. Stone,

First of all, we would like to express our thanks for your interest in our products which were advertised on Facebook.

I regret to inform you that these items are currently *out of stock*.

Should there be any questions, please don't hesitate to contact us.

Thank you for your support.

Yours sincerely,
Helen Jordan

SEND

回覆：詢問公司庫存

史東先生您好：

首先，我們感謝貴公司對我們在臉書廣告中的產品非常感興趣。很遺憾地通知您，這些物品目前已經**缺貨**。

如有任何疑問，請隨即與我們聯繫。

謝謝您的支持。

您真誠地，

海倫‧喬登

Email 這樣寫也行！

① 感謝貴公司諮詢本公司的商品庫存。

Thank you for your inventory inquiry regarding our product.

② 如果您需要進一步說明，請隨時與我們聯繫。

If you require further clarifications, please do not hesitate to contact us.

③ 如有需要，歡迎您隨時來電。

If necessary, we always welcome a call for you.

④ 現有商品庫存可以滿足貴公司需求。

The inventory of our product can meet the demand.

⑤ 我們已經檢查過您詢問的庫存商品。

We have checked our supply of the commodity you asked for.

⑥ 感謝您來信諮詢本公司的商品庫存。

We would like to thank you for your letter inquiring about our inventory.

⑦ 如果您對本公司產品有其他疑問，請直接撥打 XXX-XXXX 與我聯繫。

If you have any further questions about our products, you may call me directly on XXX-XXXX.

⑧ 希望您覺得我方提供的資訊對您有用。

Hope you will find the information I have provided useful.

09 詢問交易條件（含製作日期）

 照著抄 ～ Email 簡單搞定！

(範例1) **Title : Questions about the deal we made.**

Dear Mr. Black,

Thanks for your call last week. To confirm our conversation, we'd like to inquire about your trading terms and conditions for ***providing related equipments and services***.

We also want to know how long it will take if you work on this project.

Please offer us a ***quotation*** specifying terms and conditions of business and a ***work schedule***.

We look forward to hearing from you.

Yours sincerely,

Peter Green

SEND   A 🖉 ⊖ ☺

 中譯

主旨：關於我們交易的問題

親愛的布萊克先生：

謝謝您上周的來電。我想確認一下電話中提到的，關於提供**相關設備及服務**的事宜。

此外，我們還想知道，如果將工程交給您們，需要多長時間完成。

最後，麻煩您提供一份詳載交易條件的**報價單**以及一份**工作日程表**。

期待您的回覆！

您誠摯地，

彼得・格林

照著抄 ～ Email 簡單搞定！

Title : Questions about the deal we made.

Dear Sir or Madam,

We are writing to ask if it would be possible for us to have credit facilities in the terms of **_payment by 30-day bill of exchange_**. If possible, please let us know as soon as possible.

In addition, we still want to know **_your earliest delivery date_** and **_discounts for regular purchases_**.

We expect that you would give us a definite reply at your earliest convenience.

Yours sincerely,
Blare Field

SEND

主旨：關於我們交易的問題

敬啟者：

請問貴公司能否接受我們以 **30 天匯票支付的條件**進行信用交易？如有可能，請儘快回覆我們。

另外，我們還想請貴公司說明**最早的交貨日期及定期購買的折扣**。

期盼貴方能儘早給我方一個明確的答覆。

您真誠地，

布雷爾·菲爾德

Email 這樣寫也行！

① 這次，讓我們來探討一下其他條款和條件。

We'll go on to the other terms and conditions this time.

② 請惠寄價格表，如能告知最好的交易條件，非常感激。

I shall be glad if you will send me your price list, and state your best term.

③ 當這些條款和條件均為雙方所接受時，交易即達成。

The business is settled when the terms and conditions are agreed upon.

④ 感謝貴公司惠告交易條件，並贈以樣品和其他輔助資料。

We shall thank you to let us know your trade terms, and forward samples and other helpful literature.

⑤ 這次貿易合作的條件是什麼？

What are the terms and conditions on this trade cooperation?

⑥ 所有條件和情況都應在報價單中進行清楚的敘述。

All the terms and conditions shall be clearly stated in the estimate.

⑦ 請告知我方，貴方是否同意這些交易條件。

Please inform us if you agree upon these terms.

⑧ 我們需要討論一下基本的交易條件。

We need to talk about the basic terms of the transaction.

10【回應】詢問交易條件（含製作日期）

範例 1

Re : Questions about the deal we made.

Dear Mr. Green,

Thank you for your inquiry regarding our trading terms and conditions for providing related equipment and services.

According to your inquiry, we have enclosed a quotation specifying terms and conditions of business and a work schedule.

Moreover, it will take us **two weeks** if we work on this project.

We look forward to doing business with you.

Yours sincerely,
Allan Black

SEND

 中譯

回覆：關於我們交易的問題

格林先生您好：

感謝您對本公司提供相關設備及服務的事宜之諮詢。

根據您的諮詢，我們隨信附上一份詳載交易條件的報價單以及一份工作日程表。

此外，如果工程讓我們負責，時程約**兩週**可以完成。

期待與您有業務往來！

您誠摯地，
艾倫・布萊克

Re : Questions about the deal we made.

Dear Mr. Field,

We truly appreciate your letter asking for billing information.

We would like to inform you that we accept credit facilities in the terms of payment by 30-day bill of exchange.

In addition, we offer huge discounts on ***special occasions***.

Earliest delivery date and discounts for regular purchases were enclosed with the letter.

We hope that the details mentioned are useful for you.

Yours sincerely,

Sally Roberts

SEND   A ✎ 🔗 ☺

回覆：關於我們交易的問題

菲爾德先生您好：

十分謝謝您來信要求提供帳單資訊。 謹在此通知您，我們接受 30 天匯票支付的條件進行信用交易。

此外，在**特別情況**下，我們會提供大量折扣。

隨信附上說明最早的交貨日期及定期購買的折扣。

希望提及之相關細節對您有助益。

您真誠地，

莎莉・羅伯特

Email 這樣寫也行！

① 提供之服務將按照預計時間表完成。

The services will be completed in accordance with the schedule in the estimate.

② 我們公司合約以商業條款為基礎。

Business terms and conditions set the contract foundation between our companies.

③ 我方為您提供了特價商品的價目表。

We have attached a price list of all the items with special discounts for you.

④ 我方還附上了價目表和時程表，以茲參考。

I also attached the price list and a work schedule for you to refer.

⑤ 期待與貴公司有業務往來。

Looking forward to doing business with you.

⑥ 本公司希望所提供的資訊能對貴公司提供協助。

We hope the information given was helpful.

⑦ 希望您對以上資訊感到滿意。

Hope you are satisfied with the above information.

⑧ 更多資訊，請參閱附件。

For further information, please refer to the attachment.

11 詢問運送方式及運費

照著抄～ Email 簡單搞定！ — ↗ ✕

範例 1 **Title : Inquiry of shipment and the fee.**

Dear Sir or Madam,

I regret that I might ignore an important thing in the last letter. I wonder that whether your price includes the ***freight and insurance*** or not. If not, what are your charges?

In addition, would you like to transport our goods by train or by boat? Please let me know about the details of the ***type of conveyance and freight***.

I look forward to your early and definite reply. Thank you very much.

Yours faithfully,
John Brown

SEND   A 🖉 🔗 ☺

主旨：詢問運輸費用

敬啟者：

很抱歉我在上封信中可能忽略了一件重要的事。我想知道您的價格是否包含了**運費和保險**，如果沒有，那麼您們的收費方式是怎樣呢？

另外，貴方是要用火車運輸還是船運呢？請告知我關於**運輸方式和運費**的相關事宜。

期待您儘早明確回覆。非常感謝。

您忠誠地，
約翰‧布朗

照著抄 ～ Email 簡單搞定！

Title : Inquiry of shipment and the fee.

Dear Mr. Robinson,

I am writing to ask about the goods transportation.

May I know the shipping method of our goods? How do you mean to convey our ***500 cases of apples***? Further, could you let me know about the transport costs?

I would appreciate your kindness for your ***particulars and total charges***.

I hope for your response at your earliest convenience.

Yours sincerely,
Barney Marshall

SEND

主旨：詢問運輸費用

親愛的羅賓森先生：

謹以此信詢問運輸相關事宜。

請問我方貨物的運輸方式是什麼？貴方打算如何運送我們的 **500 箱蘋果**呢？另外，我可以知道運輸費用是多少嗎？

如果貴方能告知我**費用明細和總共費用**，將不勝感激。

期待您方便時儘早回覆。

您誠摯地，
巴尼‧馬歇爾

Email 這樣寫也行！

① 您會採取哪種運輸方式？

Which transport mode would you like?

② 我可以將一件行李托運嗎？

Can I send one of these by unaccompanied baggage?

③ 將貨物按指定的運輸方式發送。

It refers to dispatch the goods in the specific transportation mode.

④ 他們是否按體積計算運費？

Do they charge carriage by bulk?

⑤ 請告訴我們幾種可能的運輸方式的價格。

Please show us the shipping costs for several possible methods.

⑥ 如果可以，請問我該支付多少運費？

If possible, how much freightage should I pay?

⑦ 運送方式和包裝將由貴方決定。

The delivery method and packaging shall be decided by you.

⑧ 超重行李每公斤多少運費？

What about the rate per kilo for overweight goods?

12【回應】詢問運送方式及運費

範例 1

Re : Inquiry of shipment and the fee.

Dear Mr. Brown,

Thank you for contacting us regarding the inquiry of shipment and the fee. We are pleased to inform you that our price **includes** the freight and insurance.

In addition, we would like to transport your goods **by boat**.

Please find enclosed the requested details.

Please let me know about the details of the type of conveyance and freight.

We look forward to your prompt reply.

Sincerely,

Mark White

SEND　　　　　　　　　　　　　　　　A 🔗 ☺

中譯

回覆：詢問運輸費用

布朗先生您好：

感謝您聯繫本公司諮詢運費相關事宜。很高興地通知您，本公司價格**包括**運費和保險。

另外，貴公司的貨物將用**船運**運輸。

隨函附上詳細資訊。

運輸方式和運費的相關事宜，請不吝賜教。

期待您儘早明確回覆。

真誠地，

馬克‧懷特

範例 2

Re : Inquiry of shipment and the fee.

Dear Mr. Marshall ,

Thank you for contacting us regarding the transportation of goods.

We will convey your 500 cases of apples by boat. Further, I have ***enclosed a brochure*** that contains more detailed information about the shipping method, the particulars and t otal charges.

Looking forward to doing business with you.

Yours sincerely,

Danny Robinson

SEND   A

回覆：詢問運輸費用

親愛的馬歇爾先生：

感謝您就貨物的運輸事宜與我們聯繫。

我們將透過船運寄送您 500 箱蘋果。此外，**隨函附上**包含運輸方式、明確資訊和總費用細節的介紹**手冊**。

期待與您有業務往來。

您誠摯地，

丹尼‧羅賓森

Email 這樣寫也行！

① 貴方若能盡早答覆，以便我方加速裝船速度。

An early reply from you will help us to speed up shipment.

② 隨函附上我們的運費資訊。

Enclosed please find our delivery rates.

③ 請見附件中幾種運輸方式的費用。

Please find the attachment for the shipping costs for several possible methods.

④ 本城市所購買物品將免運費。

The purchased items will be delivered free of charge anywhere in the city.

⑤ 貨物如果需轉運，您方必須多付運費。

In case of transshipment, you have to pay extra transportation charges.

⑥ 如果您想了解更多資訊，我們很樂意以電話聯繫。

In case you would like to have more information, we are happy to arrange a call.

⑦ 抱歉我們無法按貴方要求將貨物裝船。

We regret we can't ship as you desired.

⑧ 如果您需要進一步的說明，請隨時與我們聯絡。

If you require further clarifications, please contact us at anytime.

13 詢問未到貨商品

範例 1

Title : We haven't received our order of...

Dear Mr. Smyth,

We ordered ***eight computers*** on June 27th. However, we have not received them yet. Would you tell us when you will be delivering these computers which should have arrived a week ago?

Since we ***desperately need*** them for our new employees, would you please be kind enough to check this matter and inform us your prompt solution by return?

Yours sincerely,
Thomas Brown

SEND

 中譯

主旨：我們尚未收到訂購……

親愛的史密斯先生：

我們於 6 月 27 號在貴公司訂購了 **8 台電腦**。但至今還未收到商品。貴公司能否告知，這些原本一週前就應該到貨的電腦將何時發貨？

由於我們**急需**這些電腦供新員工使用，可否儘快查明此事，並告知即時的解決方案？

您誠摯地，

湯瑪斯・布朗

照著抄 ～ Email 簡單搞定！

Title : We haven't received our order of...

Dear Sir or Madam,

We wish to remind you that at this moment we still have not received our order NO. 657238 which should have arrived before **the end of May**.

As we need these goods badly, would you please inform us when we can expect them? According to our records, there have been **similar delays on previous transactions**. We wish you could give us a reasonable explanation.

Your prompt reply is urgently awaited.

Yours sincerely,
CPT Co.

SEND

主旨：我們尚未收到訂購……

敬啟者：

在此提醒貴公司，我們訂單號碼 657238 本應該在 **5 月底**就收到的貨物迄今仍未收到。

由於我公司急需這批貨物，請告知我們貨物何時抵達？依照記錄，**類似延誤交貨的情形已發生數次**。我方希望貴公司能給予合理的解釋。

期待您儘快回覆。

您真誠地，
CPT 公司

① 非常遺憾，我們至今還未收到訂購的產品。

We greatly regret to say that the goods we ordered have not reached us yet.

② 您們告知我們說一週內到貨。

We are informed that we will get the goods within one week.

③ 剛才知悉我公司 9 月 10 日的新產品還未到貨。

I was just informed that our new September 10th product had not arrive yet.

④ 跟蹤訂單以確保物品準時到貨。

Follow up purchase order to ensure the punctual arrival of goods.

⑤ 商品早在 5 天前就應該到貨。

The goods were supposed to arrive five days ago.

⑥ 他們計畫的到貨時間是 8 月 15 日。

The date of delivery they arranged is August 15th.

⑦ 估計本星期二就會到貨。

We expect to have a supply this Tuesday.

⑧ 如果不能很快拿到貨，我們只有取消訂購了。

We will have to cancel if we do not get that order soon.

14【回應】詢問未到貨商品

照著抄 ～ Email 簡單搞定！

範例 1

Re : We haven't received our order of...

Dear Mr. Brown,

This is in regard to your order which you placed with our computers on the 27th of June. I'm sorry that we are experiencing a delay in these computers.

We have checked to find out the reason. Your package was delayed due to *a routing error*.

We hereby inform you that your goods will be delivered tomorrow.

I have included *a discount code worth $500* with this email.

Thank you for your understanding.

Yours sincerely,
Daniel Smyth

SEND

 中譯

回覆：我們尚未收到訂購……

親愛的布朗先生：

本封信是關於您在 6 月 27 日向本公司訂購電腦事宜。抱歉，我們電腦運送時間上有延遲情形。

本公司已查明原因。您的貨物延遲是因為**發貨路線錯誤**。

我們特此通知您，貨物明天將於明天發貨。

本封電子郵件中已附上 **500 元折扣代碼**。

感謝您的理解。

您誠摯地，
丹尼爾‧史密斯

Re : We haven't received our order of...

Dear Sir or Madam,
It is with regret that we received your letter regarding an order
NO. 657238 that you still not received before the end of May.
Thanks for informing us about your undelivered order.
This delay was due to a problem with **communication**. We
would like to apologize for any inconvenience this has
caused you. We have made sure that your order will be with
you in the next two days.
Please accept our deepest apologies.

Yours sincerely,
Neil Harris

SEND

回覆：我們尚未收到訂購……

敬啟者：
關於編號 657238 訂單原定五月底到貨， 但迄今貴公司尚未收到，對此事感到抱
歉。
感謝您通知我方尚未收到。
此延遲情形是因為**溝通問題**引起。對於任何不便，我們深表歉意。本公司確保您
的貨物將於兩天內收到。
請接受我們最深的歉意。

您真誠地，
尼爾‧哈里斯

Email 這樣寫也行！

① 請接受我代表 CPT Co. 向您致歉。

Please accept my apologies on behalf of CPT Co.

② 這封信是關於您在 2021 年 3 月 20 日郵件的回覆。

This letter is in regard to the one you sent on 20th March 2021.

③ 商品應該星期五之前會到貨。

The goods will be arrived by this Friday.

④ 延遲發貨是因為行程表合併所引起。

This delay is due to a consolidated schedule.

⑤ 我方保證此事不會再發生。

I promise that this incident will not occur again.

⑥ 請允許我對延遲發貨表達深深歉意。

Please allow me to offer my apologies with reference to the delay.

⑦ 在此通知您，貴公司的貨物明天將交貨。

We hereby inform you that your goods will be delivered tomorrow.

⑧ 我們向您保證，此類問題將不會再出現。

We guarantee you that this will never be rehashed ever.

15 商品訂購通知

範例 1

Title : Online ordering available/Initial order confirm notification.

Dear members,

To begin with, I wish everyone a Happy New Year in advance! I am honored to inform you that you can order any commodities as usual during the holiday. You just need to choose what you want on the website of our mall, and write down your ***detailed address***, and then we will provide the service of ***cash on delivery***.

Please enjoy your shopping!

Yours sincerely,
Molly Roberts
OU Ya Mall

SEND

 中譯

主旨：網路訂單可用的／最初的通知

親愛的會員：

首先，預祝大家新年快樂！

很榮幸通知各位在假日期間仍能正常訂購商品。只要在購物網站上選擇您要的商品，寫明您的**詳細地址**，我們就會提供**貨到付款**服務。

祝您購物愉快！

您真誠地，
莫莉‧羅伯茲
歐亞購物廣場

照著抄 ～ Email 簡單搞定！

範例 2

Title : Online ordering available/Initial order confirm notification.

Dear Sirs,

We have received your quotation dated November 17th. As a trial order, we are pleased to enclose our order NO. 007 of **100 pieces of auto parts** to you.

Since we **urgently need** the above items, we kindly ask you to put the trial order into your production program as soon as possible.

If the quality proves satisfactory, we will send you regular orders in the near future.

Yours sincerely,
Fred Pitt
QQ AUTO

SEND

中譯

主旨：網路訂單可用的／最初的通知

敬啟者：

我方已收到貴公司 11 月 17 日之報價單。在此附上試產訂單號碼 007 訂購貴方 **100 個汽車零件**。

由於本公司**急需**上述產品，請儘快安排生產日程。

如此次試作產品質令人滿意，本公司今後將向貴公司下長期訂單。

您真誠地，
弗瑞德‧彼德
QQ 汽車公司

① 我方希望能按照訂貨單從您處訂購貴方的產品。

We wish to order your products as per our purchase.

② 我們堅持貨到付款，不打任何折扣。

We insist on paying by cash on delivery without allowing any discount.

③ 貴方所訂購貨物之其餘部分，待我方進貨即可供應。

The balance of your order will be supplied when we receive fresh stock.

④ 我們暫時只接受貨到付款。不便之處，敬請原諒。

We accept cash on delivery only up to this moment. Sorry for any inconvenience caused.

⑤ 請以傳真確認您方訂單。

Please confirm your order by fax.

⑥ 如果您要訂購產品，請與我們聯繫！

If you want to order the products, please contact us.

⑦ 感謝您方向我們訂購網球拍。

We thank you for ordering this tennis racket.

⑧ 歡迎廣大客戶訂購、洽談！

Customers are welcome to order, negotiate!

16 【回應】商品訂購通知

照著抄 ～ Email 簡單搞定！

範例
1

Re : Online ordering available/Initial order confirm notification.

Dear Mrs. Roberts,

Thank you for your kind notice. There are several products I would like to place during the holiday. I am pleased to know you **provide the service of** cash on delivery.

Thank you for your service!

Happy New Year.

Yours faithfully,

Anne Cuthbert

SEND   A ⬙ ⬩ ☺

回覆：網路訂單可用的／最初的通知

羅伯茲女士您好：

謝謝您的通知。我想在放假時訂購幾種商品。很高興得知您**提供**貨到付款服務。

感謝您的服務（假日期間依然可以照常購物）！

祝您新年快樂！

您真誠地，

安·卡森博特

Re : Online ordering available/Initial order confirm notification.

Dear Mr. Pitt,

We thank you for your order of November 20th for **the 100 pieces of auto parts**.

Moreover, we will put the trial order into our production program **as soon as possible**.

Hope that you will find them highly satisfactory.

We thank you for this order.

Yours sincerely,

Harry Smith

SEND

回覆：網路訂單可用的／最初的通知

彼德先生您好：

感謝您在 11 月 20 日訂購的 **100 項汽車零件**。

此外，我們將**盡快**安排試產日程。

希望產品品質會令貴公司滿意。

感謝您的訂單。

您真誠地，

哈利·史密斯

 **Email 這樣寫也行！**

① 我們將在約定時間內提供所訂購的產品。

We are supplying the ordered products within the stipulated time.

② 我們提供貨到付款服務。

We provide the service of cash on delivery.

③ 我們向您保證提供最好服務。

We assure you of our best services.

④ 我方對於 100 項汽車零件的品質和包裝格外謹慎。

We have taken special care for the quality and packing of the 100 pieces of auto parts.

⑤ 希望我們的產品能讓您滿意。

Hope our product will meet your satisfaction.

⑥ 感謝您提供的資料。

Thank you for the information.

⑦ 您的訂單預計於 2021 年 6 月 25 日交貨。

Your order has been placed and delivery is expected on 25 June 2021.

⑧ 希望本公司商品品質能讓您喜愛並再次回購。

Hope the quality will induce you to favor us with further orders.

17 商品出貨通知

範例 1

Title : Shipment notification of order...

Dear Mr. White,

This is a notification of shipment.

We have shipped your order NO. 1794128 as of June 24th, 2021. I also sent you the relevant shipping documents **by fax**. Please check.

You should receive the goods you ordered by June 29th, 2021 if there is no accident.

Please let us know if they arrive. Thank you very much.

Yours truly,

Vic Cage

Eastern Wind Co.

SEND

A 🖇 🔗 ☺

主旨：訂單出貨通知

親愛的懷特先生：

此為出貨通知。

訂單號碼 1794128 的貨物已於 2021 年 6 月 24 日出貨。相關出貨資料也**已經傳真**給您，請注意查收。

如無意外，您的貨物應在 2021 年 6 月 29 日就能收到。

如果貨物到達，請通知我們。謝謝！

您忠誠地，

維克・凱基

東風公司

照著抄 ～ Email 簡單搞定！ — ⬈ ✕

Title : Shipment notification of order...

Dear Sir or Madam,

Thank you for placing an order for our product. We are pleased to inform you that your transaction ***has been completed*** and your order ***has been shipped***.

I am sure you will receive your shipment within three to four work days.

We hope that you will be satisfied with our product.

Thanks again for you order.

Yours sincerely,
Bill Jackson
11-7 Company

SEND　　　　　　　　　　　　　　　　A 𝟙 ⌗ ☺

主旨：訂單出貨通知

敬啟者：

感謝您訂購我們的產品。很高興通知您，您的交易**已經完成**，訂單也**已經出貨**了。

我們保證貨品將於 3 到 4 個工作日內送達。

希望您能對我們的產品滿意。

再次感謝您的訂貨。

您真誠地，

比爾‧傑克森

11-7 公司

① 我們已將您訂單號 KS 1688 的貨物於 2021 年 8 月 21 日出貨。

We have shipped your order NO. KS 1688 as of August 21st, 2021.

② 以下商品已於昨日出貨到貴公司的所在地。

The following goods were shipped to your address yesterday.

③ 貴公司所訂購的 T 恤已於 4 月 27 日重新出貨。

Your corrected order of T-shirts was shipped on April 27th.

④ 這些貨物一定會小心地遞送給您。

This freight must be carefully delivered to you.

⑤ 該船運送的 200 包棉花提單已收悉。

I have received Bill of Lading for 200 bales cotton by that vessel.

⑥ 我已經把相關的出貨資料傳真給您。

I have faxed you the relevant shipping documents.

⑦ 一旦貨物到達，請通知我們。

Please let us know once they are arrived.

⑧ 貨物已於 10 月 30 日送出。我會把出貨明細表傳真給您。

They are shipped on October 30th. We'll send you the shipment details by fax.

18【回應】商品出貨通知

照著抄 ～ Email 簡單搞定！

Re : Shipment notification of order...

Dear Mr. Cage,

Thank you for the notification of shipment that you sent us.

We **have receive**d your relevant shipping documents **this Monday**.

In addition, we**'ve received the goods** we ordered on June 28th, 2021.

Thank you very much.

We look forward to doing business with you again in the future.

Yours truly,
Sean White

SEND

回覆：訂單出貨通知

親愛的凱基先生：

謝謝您寄給本公司的出貨通知。我們**已於星期一收到**出貨資料。

另外，**貨物**已於 2021 年 6 月 28 日**收到**。

非常感謝。

期待未來能繼續和貴公司合作。

您忠誠地，
史恩‧懷特

Re : Shipment notification of order...

Dear Mr. Jackson,

The purpose of this letter is to inform you that we have received your shipment notification of order. We are looking forward to receiving our shipment by Friday.

If we are satisfied with your product, we would ***place further orders*** since your prices were the most reasonable that we've found.

Thanks for your cooperation.

Yours sincerely,

Beth Hathaway

SEND

回覆：訂單出貨通知

傑克森先生敬安：

本封信的目的是通知您，本公司已收到您的訂單運送通知。

我們期待在星期五之前收到貨物。

如果我們對貴公司產品**感到滿意**，再加上商品價格最為合理，我們將會**再次訂購**。

謝謝您的合作。

您真誠地，

貝絲‧海瑟威

Email 這樣寫也行！

① 我們很高興通知咖啡機已經收貨。

We are delighted to announce the arrival of a new shipment of coffee makers.

② 本司已於 3 月 12 日收到訂購的風衣。

We received order of coats on March 12th.

③ 我希望最近能再下更多訂單。

We hope to place further orders with you in the the near future.

④ 我方尚未收到出貨明細表傳真。

We haven't received the shipment details by fax.

⑤ 我們期待再次向貴公司購買商品。

We look forward to purchasing from you again.

⑥ 您們將商品寄到錯誤的地址。

You have shipped our goods to the wrong address.

⑦ 謝謝您寶貴的業務。

Thank you for your valued business.

⑧ 我們在 2021 年 4 月 1 號收到 訂單號 KS1688 。

We received our order NO. KS 1688 as of April 1st, 2021.

19 商品缺貨通知

範例 1

Title : [Notification] The product you ordered was temporarily out of stock.

Dear subscriber,

Due to **booming sales**, we are so sorry to inform you that The Audacity of Hope you ordered is out of stock.

However, we will **replenish stock at once**. If you still wish to order it **three days later**, please let us know if you would like to have it delivered by airmail or by surface mail.

We are looking forward to hearing from you soon.

Yours faithfully,

Judy Wisdom

World Book Co.

SEND   A ⬚ ⊖ ☺

 中譯

主旨：〔通知〕您訂購的商品暫時缺貨

親愛的訂戶：

由於**銷售激增**，很抱歉通知您訂購的《無畏的希望》目前已經沒有存貨了。

不過我們會**馬上補貨**。如果**三天後**您還希望訂購的話，請告知我們是用航空郵寄還是普通平信郵寄。

期待您的回信。

您真誠地，

茱蒂‧威斯登

世界圖書公司

範例 2 itle : [Notification] The product you ordered was temporarily out of stock.

Dear customer,
To our regret, we must inform you that what you ordered are out of stock now. I am afraid it will take us **three or four days to replenish** them.
We are sure to inform you right away, as soon as they are available.
We are very sorry for any inconvenience caused and thank you very much for your understanding.

Yours truly,
Rose Jobs
Ameritech

SEND   A ✏ ⊖ ☺

主旨：〔通知〕您訂購的商品暫時缺貨

親愛的客戶：
很遺憾，我們不得不通知您，您訂購的商品目前缺貨。我們大約需要 **3 到 4 天的時間補貨**。
我們保證一旦到貨就立刻通知您。
很抱歉給您帶來不便，同時非常感謝您的理解。

謹致問候
羅絲‧賈伯斯
美瑞泰克公司

Email 這樣寫也行！

① 您訂購的產品目前缺貨。

The product that you ordered is out of stock now.

② 很抱歉這種紅裙子已經沒有現貨了。

I am sorry that the red skirts are out of stock.

③ 很抱歉，該商品目前已無存貨。

I am sorry, but that product is out of stock at the moment.

④ 很抱歉，鑽石牌縫紉機已經沒有存貨。

We are sorry that the Diamond Sewing machine is out of stock.

⑤ 事實上我們已缺貨幾個星期了。

As a matter of fact, we have run out of stock for a few weeks.

⑥ 您來信要買的辭典現在缺貨。

The dictionary you asked for is in short supply.

⑦ 您近日詢問的書暫時無貨，謹此奉告。

In answer to your recent inquiry, the book you mentioned is not in stock.

⑧ 很抱歉您要的這本書現在缺貨。

I am sorry that the book you need is not available now.

20【回應】商品缺貨通知

範例 1

Re : [Notification] The product you ordered was temporarily out of stock.

Dear Mrs. Wisdom,

This is to acknowledge receipt of your email. Indeed, I would like to order it three days later. When you have the book in stock, **please notify me**.

Please have it delivered **by airmail**.

I look forward to hearing from you soon.

Yours faithfully,
Steve Taylor

SEND   A 🛈 ⌐ ☺

 中譯

回覆：〔通知〕您訂購的商品暫時缺貨

親愛的威斯登女士：

本封是收到您的電子郵件的確認信。事實上，我三天後還想訂購商品。當貴公司有存貨時，**煩請通知我**。

我想用**航空郵寄**商品。

希望盡速收到您的回音。

真誠地，

史帝夫·泰勒

Re : [Notification] The product you ordered was temporarily out of stock.

Dear Mrs. Jobs,

Thank you for the letter that you sent me, addressing the concerns for my order are *out of stock* now.

Please inform me right away, as soon as they are available.

Thank you for your immediate response.

Yours truly,

Fiona Adams

SEND

回覆：〔通知〕您訂購的商品暫時缺貨

賈伯斯女士您好：

感謝您的來信，通知我訂購的商品目前**缺貨**。

一旦到貨請立刻通知我。

感謝您立即回覆。

謹致問候

費歐娜‧亞當斯

Email 這樣寫也行！

① 請問把商品寄給我們需要花多久的時間？

How long will it take you to send the product to us?

② 我想要諮詢貴公司的相關資訊。

I am writing to request some information about your company.

③ 我來信詢問的洋裝目前缺貨嗎？

Is the dress I asked for in short supply?

④ 我 5 月 1 號訂購 100 個茶杯而且同時付款。

I have placed an order of 100 cups on May 1st and made payments for the same.

⑤ 請盡速將剩餘的費用寄還給本公司。

Please return the remaining money to us as soon as possible.

⑥ 當產品到貨時請通知我。

Please notify when you have the item in stock.

⑦ 我訂購的品項目前缺貨。

The item that I ordered is out of stock now.

⑧ 謝謝您迅速回應！

Thank you for replying quickly!

21 付款確認通知

範例 1

Title : We have completed the payment process.

Dear Ms. Lewinsky,

On June 28th, 2021, we **transferred to you for amount** of 5698.00 US dollars as payment for your invoice NO. DB 1798523. **Please kindly check.**

I have also faxed a copy of **the remittance slip** for your reference.

When you receive the remittance, your prompt reply would be highly appreciated.

Yours sincerely,
Carl Clair

SEND

主旨：已完成付款

親愛的萊溫斯基女士：

我方已於 2021 年 6 月 28 日將帳單編號 DB1798523，金額 5698 美元**匯到您的戶頭。請查收。**

我也已經將**匯款通知單副本**傳真給您，以供參考。

如已查收，請速回覆。

您真誠地，
卡爾．克雷爾

照著抄 ～ Email 簡單搞定！ — ↗ ✕

範例 2

Title : We have completed the payment process.

Dear Sirs,

Enclosed, please find herewith our **bank check** for US$ 4,000 drawn by **Taipei Bank, Da-an Branch**, as full settlement of your invoice NO. 13680, our order NO. 34672. Please kindly **confirm your receipt of the above**. Thank you for you cooperation and assistance on this matter.

Yours faithfully,
Vic Thomas
Kai Hsin Company

SEND

A 📎 🔗 ☺

 中譯

主旨：已完成付款

敬啟者：

隨信附上本公司**銀行支票**一張，金額為 4000 美元。由**臺北銀行大安分行**支付。此為支付貴公司發票編號 13680，訂單編號 34672 之貨款。

請查收並來信告知。

感謝您對此事之協助與合作。

您忠實地，

維克‧湯瑪士

凱信公司

① 您可以匯款到我們的銀行帳戶。

You could electronically transfer the payment into our bank account.

② 我已將匯款通知單副本傳真給您以供參考。

I have faxed you a copy of the remittance slip for reference.

③ 我們希望能很快收到來函與匯款。

We expect to hear from you at once with a remittance.

④ 自動轉帳比用支票支付需要多 3 個工作天處理。

Payment by direct deposit into bank account will usually take three additional working days than by check mailing.

⑤ 所有的訂單在確認付款後，將會透過快遞服務送出。

All orders will be sent out via courier service upon confirmation of payment.

⑥ 錢已由銀行直接轉帳匯入您的戶頭。

Money has been credited to your account by bank giro.

⑦ 銀行已把支票上的款項匯入您的戶頭。

The bank has credited your account with the amount of the check.

⑧ 隨信附上帳單一份，如能儘快將款項匯出，不勝感激。

We enclose you a statement of account, for which your remittance at your earliest convenience will oblige.

22 【回應】付款確認通知

照著抄 ～ Email 簡單搞定！

Re : We have completed the payment process.

Dear Mr. Clair,

It is confirmed that I have ***received*** complete payment.

We would like to take this opportunity to thank you for being a valued customer with us.

Attached please find the ***receiving slip***.

We are looking forward to serving you again in the future.

Yours sincerely,
Fiona Lewinsky

SEND   A ⫯ ⇔ ☺

回覆：已完成付款

克雷爾先生您好：

本封信是**確認**我已經收到款項。

我們想藉此機會感謝您成為本公司的重要客戶。

隨信附上**收據**。

期待將來再次為您服務。

您真誠地，

費歐娜‧萊溫斯基

Re : We have completed the payment process.

Dear Mr. Thomas,
The purpose of this letter is to **inform** you that we have received your payment for US$4000. Thank you for remitting this payment to us.
If you have any other concerns, please don't hesitate to contact us.
We look forward to doing business with you.

Yours faithfully,
Paul Walls

SEND

回覆：已完成付款

湯馬仕先生您好：

本封信的目的是**通知**您，本公司已收到您的 4000 美元款項。感謝您的匯款。

如果您還有其他疑問，請隨時與我們聯繫。

期待與您有業務往來。

您忠實地，

保羅・沃爾思

Email 這樣寫也行！

① 我們誠摯感謝您付 4,000 美元款項。

We earnestly acknowledge your payment of US\$ 4,000.

② 非常高興地通知，我已經收到款項。

I am very pleased to report you that I have just received the payment.

③ 您的下一筆款項將於 2021 年 7 月 10 日到期。

Your next payment will be due by July 10, 2021.

④ 我們寫信確認已經收到您的款項。

We are writing to confirm that we have received your payment.

⑤ 隨本電子郵件付上收據。。

Please find the receiving slip attached to this email.

⑥ 我們期待繼續與貴公司合作。

We look forward to continuing cooperating with you.

⑦ 非常感謝與您有生意往來。

We appreciate doing business with you.

⑧ 款項已被授權並核准。

The payment has been authorized and approved.

23 催繳貨款通知

範例 1 **Title : Your payment has been delayed for ... days.**

Dear Mr. Thomas,
We have sent you the products for one month;however, we haven't received any payment from your company.
Firstly, we do value our cooperation with your company. We'd like to express our situation for you. Unfortunately, we ***will not be able to send*** you any products before we make sure the payment is completed.
Please submit your payment ***promptly***.
We look forward to your early reply.

Faithfully,
Emily Jovi
Forever Co., Ltd.

SEND

 中譯

主旨：您的貨款已延期……天

湯馬仕先生您好：
我們一個月前已將您的產品送出，但是至今尚未收到貴公司任何款項。
首先，我們珍惜與貴公司合作的關係。這是我們要表達的處境。不幸的是，在確認您完成付款之前，我們將**不會再寄**任何商品給您。
請**馬上**付款。
期待您早日回覆。

誠摯地，
艾蜜莉‧喬維
永遠股份有限公司

照著抄～ Email 簡單搞定！　　　　　　　　　　— ⤢ ✕

範例2

Title : Your payment has been delayed for ... days.

Dear Sirs,

We had written to you to remind you that we haven't received any of your payment.

We do want your business and hope to continue to serve you. The accepted ***payment methods*** are check, Visa, MasterCard, or money order. We shall be glad if you can send us a ***check*** as soon as possible to balance the amount. We appreciate an immediate reply.

Yours faithfully,
Adam Ryan

SEND　　　　　　　　　　　　　　　　　　　A ⎘ ⇔ ☺

中譯

主旨：您的貨款已延期……天

先生您好：

我們已經寫信提醒您，目前我們尚未收到您的付款。

我們在乎您的生意，也希望能繼續替您服務。

我們接受**付款方式**為：支票、Visa、萬事達卡或匯票。如果您能儘快以**支票**付款，讓我們抵銷帳務，我們將十分高興。

您的盡速回覆，我們不勝感激。

忠實地，
亞當・萊恩

① 這封信提醒您付款是於 2021 年 7 月 20 日截止。

The letter is a reminder that your payment was due on July 20th, 2021.

② 您是我們的尊榮客戶。

You are the privileged customer to us.

③ 請用信用卡或支票付款。

Please pay with credit card or check.

④ 很遺憾您並沒有做出回應。

It is regrettable that you haven't sent us any reply.

⑤ 請利用郵件提交。

Please submit it by mail.

⑥ 我們希望您付款方面不再有任何拖延情況。

We hope that you would submit the payment without any further delay.

⑦ 我很高興能在 7 月 20 號之前收到您的款項。

We are glad to receive your payment before July 20th.

⑧ 收到您的付款前，我們將不再寄送任何商品給您。

Before receiving your payment, we won't send any merchandise to you.

24【回應】催繳貨款通知

照著抄 ～ Email 簡單搞定！

Re : Your payment has been delayed for ... days.

Dear Mrs. Jovi,
Please accept my sincere apology for the late payments.
This late payment was due to an issue with
communication between our departments. We will
be sending the payments by April 30th.
Moreover, this shall ***never happen again*** in future.
We appreciate your patience and understanding.

Faithfully,
Ken Thomas

SEND

中譯

回覆：您的貨款已延期……天

喬維女士您好：
請接受我因延遲付款致上誠摯歉意。因為我們**部門之間的溝通問題**，而產生這個問題。我們將於 4 月 30 日之前付款。
此外，以後**再也不會發生**此問題。
感謝您耐心配合和理解。

誠摯地，
肯‧湯馬仕

Re : Your payment has been delayed for ... days.

Dear Mr. Ryan,
We are sincerely sorry for the delay in payment. I apologize for any inconvenience caused you. We have included ***the check for the full amount***.
We apologize again for the delay.
Thank you so much for your consideration
We are very thankful that you reply me quickly.

Yours faithfully,
Gary Smith

SEND

回覆：您的貨款已延期……天

萊恩先生您好：

對於付款延遲事件，我們深表歉意。不便之處，在此至上我深深的歉意。我們付上**全額支票**。

造成逾期付款，我們再次表示歉意。

非常感謝您的體諒。

謝謝您迅速回覆。

忠實地，

蓋瑞‧史密斯

Email 這樣寫也行！

① 對於未付款，我們深表歉意。

We sincerely apologize for not paying your payment.

② 我們寫此信表達本公司延遲付款的歉意。

We are writing this letter to apologize for the late payment.

③ 您會於 5 月 30 日之前收到本公司款項。

You will receive my payment before May 30th.

④ 我明白 6 月 1 日之前須支付款項。

I understand I was to make payments by June 1st.

⑤ 我保證以後不會再發生這種情況。

I promise that it shall never happen again in future.

⑥ 對於逾期未付的 200,000 元款項，我深表歉意。

I sincerely apologize over the late payments in depth of $200,000.

⑦ 非常感謝您的耐心和理解。

Thank you so much for your patience and understanding.

⑧ 我保證此事永遠不會再發生。

I promise that it shall never happen again.

PART3
婉拒請求

因各家手機系統不同，若無法直接掃描，仍可以（https://tinyurl.com/2ah57jay）電腦連結雲端下載，一貼搞定！

Part 3. 婉拒請求

01 婉拒報價

照著抄 ～ Email 簡單搞定！

範例 1

Title : We cannot lower the price anymore.

Dear Mr. Charles,

Thank you very much for your email of November 21st.
Unfortunately, I am afraid that we cannot make a better offer than the one we suggested to you. We feel that it is ***the most favorable one presently***.

We hope you will be able to accept our offer after reconsideration.

Awaiting for your reply.

Yours sincerely,
John Brown

SEND

主旨：我們無法再降低價格

親愛的查理斯先生：

感謝您在 11 月 21 日的來信。

不幸的是，我們恐怕不能再提供更低的價格。這已經是**目前最優惠的價格**了。

希望您們能再重新考慮一下，接受我們的該項報價。

等候佳音。

您誠摯地，

約翰・布朗

照著抄 ～ Email 簡單搞定！

Title : We cannot lower the price anymore.

Dear Mr. Johnson,

In response to your last letter, perhaps you may think our price is a little high. Actually, the price is indeed our **minimum**; I am sorry I cannot lower it any more.

You know that **the cost of raw material has been going up** since last year. Therefore, the cost of the finished product is increasing and our profit is becoming smaller.

We sincerely hope you could reconsider our price.

Yours truly,
Brad Madden
ABC Co.

SEND

中譯

主旨：我們無法再降低價格

強森先生您好：

謹以此信回覆您上一封信。或許您覺得我們的價格偏高，但事實上，這個價格的確是我們的**最低價**，很抱歉我們不能再降價了。

您知道自從去年開始，**原物料的價格一直上漲**，產品的成本也一直增加，我們的利潤就越來越少了。

我們真誠地希望您能夠重新考慮我們的價格。

您真誠地，
布萊德·梅登
ABC 公司

Email 這樣寫也行！

① 很抱歉，我們不能給您所希望的折扣。

Unfortunately, we cannot give you the discount you requested for the goods.

② 我們所有商品都已經降價 15% 了。

We have already marked all prices down by 15%.

③ 我們只能降價百分之 5，不能再多了。

We cannot do more than a 5% reduction.

④ 我們不同意降價要求，因為價格已降至最低點。

We cannot grant the reduction you ask, because the price has already been cut as far as possible.

⑤ 這是我們的最低價，我們拒絕再降價。

The price is our minimum; we refuse to lower it any more.

⑥ 我們必須拒絕您降價 10% 的要求。

We have to decline your request for a 10% reduction.

⑦ 我們通常是不降價的。

We usually don't give any discount.

⑧ 我們不能滿足您降價的要求。

We can't reduce the price as you required.

02【回應】婉拒報價

範例 1

Re : We cannot lower the price anymore.

Dear Mr. Brown,
We thank you for your letter dated 22nd November. I am writing from the offices of ABC Co.
To inform you of our **acceptance** of the price your offered after reconsideration.
Please let us know your proposed schedule as soon as possible.
For any more information, please feel free to reach out on this number 123-4567.
Awaiting for your reply.

Yours faithfully,
Bill Charles

SEND

回覆：我們無法再降低價格

親愛的布朗先生：

感謝您方 11 月 22 日的來信。我謹代表 ABC 公司寫此信給您。

經重新考慮後，我方**接受**貴公司報價，特此通知。

請儘快告訴我們您的計劃表。

如需更多資訊，請撥打 123-4567 聯繫。

期待您的回覆。

您誠摯地，

比爾·查理斯

Re : We cannot lower the price anymore.

Dear Mr. Madden,
I have received your letter dated 3rd May.
I am glad to inform you that I am pleased to **accept** the price which you have offered.
In order to process **the purchase order**, please supply some documents.
Please refer to the attached information for more details.
We look forward to doing business with you!

Best Regards,
Jack Johnson

SEND

回覆：我們無法再降低價格

梅登先生您好：
我方已收到您 5 月 3 日的來信。
很高興在此通知您，我方願意**接受**您的報價。
為了處理**採購訂單事宜**，請提供一些文件。
詳情請參閱附件資料。
期待與您有業務往來！

您真誠地，
傑克·強森

Email 這樣寫也行！

① 我方已收到您的來信。

I have received the letter that you have sent.

② 我方要求您安排會議來處理採購事宜。

We request you to arrange a meeting with us in order to process the purchase order.

③ 經重新考慮，貴公司報價已被接受。

Please be advised that your price has been accepted after reconsideration.

④ 我方很高興通知您報價已獲核准。

We are glad to inform you that your price has been approved.

⑤ 很抱歉通知您我們不同意貴公司的報價。

We are sorry to inform you that we cannot grant the price you offer.

⑥ 期待您在這方面的積極回應。

Looking forward to your positive response in this regard.

⑦ 貴方能降價百分之 10 以上嗎？

Can you do more than a 10% reduction?

⑧ 我們非常樂意討論將來業務往來之可能性。

We will be pleased to discuss the possibility of doing business in the future.

03 拒絕退款

Title : Because of... we cannot offer you refunds.

Dear Mr. Cruise,

I am so sorry to hear that a quarter of the goods were damaged in the harbor of your country.

We **have told** you that you must pack the goods in wooden cases in case they should be damaged during the transportation. Therefore, we cannot refund you the money for the losses because it is clear that **it has nothing to do with us**.

Thank you for your understanding.

Yours sincerely,
Julia Laura

SEND   A ⬧ ⊖ ☺

主旨：因為……我們無法退款

親愛的克魯斯先生：

很抱歉聽說您有四分之一的貨物在貴國港口被損壞。

我們**已經告訴過**您要用木箱把這些貨物裝起來，以防它們在運輸期間發生毀損。因此，我們無法為您的損失退款，因為此事**顯然與我們沒有關係**。

感謝您的體諒！

您誠摯地，
茱莉亞‧蘿拉

照著抄 ～ Email 簡單搞定！　　　　　　　　　　— ⤢ ✕

範例2

Title : Because of... we cannot offer you refunds.

Dear Mr. White,

We have received your claims dated July 16th in which you asked for US$650 refund for damage caused by **_heavy rainfall_** in the harbor of your country.

Sorry to tell you that we cannot refund in this case as our t erm is **_FOB_**.

Do sympathize with you, but you should turn to **_the insurance company_** for indemnity.

Yours sincerely,

Bob Smith

SEND　　　　　　　　　　　　　　　　　　A 📎 🔗 ☺

中譯

主旨：因為……我們無法退款

親愛的懷特先生：

收到貴公司 7 月 16 日的索賠信，要求賠償在貴國港口因**大雨**導致貨物損壞的損失金額 650 美元。

很抱歉這種情形下無法退款，因為我們的交易條件是**船上交貨**。

雖然很同情貴公司的遭遇，但您應該向**保險公司**尋求賠償。

您誠摯地，

鮑伯・史密斯

① 這次我們無法給您退款。

We are unable to refund your money this time.

② 對不起，我們對此愛莫能助。

I am so sorry that we cannot help you with that.

③ 我們不會對因天氣引起的損失負責。

We will not be responsible for the losses caused by the weather.

④ 建議您向其他相關部門請求賠償。

I suggest you turn to other related departments for compensation.

⑤ 很抱歉，我對此無能為力。

I am very sorry that we can do nothing about this.

⑥ 很遺憾您有部分貨物被損壞了。

I very much regret that part of your goods was damaged.

⑦ 很抱歉這事我無法幫您。

I am sorry to say that I cannot be of any assistance to you about that.

⑧ 由於此事與我們無關，因此我們無法給您退款。

We cannot refund you the money for it has nothing to do with us.

04 【回應】拒絕退款

 範例 1

Re : Because of... we cannot offer you refunds.

Dear Mrs. Laura,

We have received your letter that you cannot refund us the money for the losses because it is clear that it has nothing to do with you.

Unfortunately, we **won't be able to accept** the result.

Please notify me as soon as possible with an opening in your schedule so that we can **arrange a meeting**.

Thank you for your understanding.

Yours sincerely,

Sam Cruise

SEND   A ↕ ⊝ ☺

 中譯

回覆：因為……我們無法退款

親愛的蘿拉女士：

本公司已收到您的來信，表示貴公司不能退還我方損失的錢，因為明顯與您方無直接關。

很遺憾，我方**不能接受**此結果。請儘快通知您的行程，以便**安排一次會議協調**。

感謝您的體諒！

您誠摯地，

山姆‧克魯斯

Re : Because of... we cannot offer you refunds.

Dear Mr. Smith,

We are in receipt of a declining refund regarding the referenced reasons. This letter is to inform you that we understand your concern. Nevertheless, we ***still have some questions*** regarding damage caused by heavy rainfall in the harbor of our country.

Please do not hesitate to contact me if you need additional information.

Yours sincerely,

Marvin White

SEND   A ▯ ⊖ ☺

回覆：因為……我們無法退款

史密斯先生您好：

我們收到了您方拒絕退款的原因。這封信是為了告知，我們理解貴公司的考慮。然而，關於我國港口因大雨造成的貨物損失，我們還**有一些疑問**。

如果需要更多資訊，請隨時與我聯絡。

您誠摯地，

馬爾文‧懷特

Email 這樣寫也行！

① 我們閱讀了貴公司合約條款，我們深知本公司有權全額退款。

We read your terms and conditions, and we are well aware that our company is entitled to a full refund.

② 您應該對因船運引起的損失負責。

You shall be responsible for the losses caused by the shipment.

③ 根據退款政策，我將可獲得全額退款。

According to the refund policies, a full refund will be granted.

④ 我們希望您在這方面迅速採取行動。

We hope you take prompt action in this regard.

⑤ 感謝您對此事的關注，我們期待您的答覆。

Thank you for your attention to this matter, and I look forward to your reply .

⑥ 請查閱附加檔案以供參考。

Please find the attached file for your reference.

⑦ 請盡速寄郵件到 3838@ks5200.com.tw 通知我。

Please notify me at 3838@ks5200.com.tw as soon as possible.

⑧ 如果需要更多資訊，請隨時寫信給我們。

Please write to us anytime if you need more information.

05 拒絕更改交易條件

照著抄 ～ Email 簡單搞定！

範例 1

Title : We don't accept alteration of trade terms.

Dear Mr. Redfield,

We are terribly sorry to inform you that we have to decline your request to alter our terms of exchange.

If you find our terms are not in accordance with your requirements, we might suggest you try ***seeking other suppliers***.

We wish to have another opportunity to cooperate with you next time.

Yours sincerely,
Doris Roberts
BT Co.

SEND

 中譯

主旨：我們無法接受交易條款的更動

尊敬的雷德菲爾德先生：

非常抱歉地告訴您，我們不得不拒絕您想要更改交易條件的要求。

如果您覺得我們的條款和您要求的不一致，我們建議您不妨試著再找**其他供應商**。

希望下次我們還有機會合作。

您誠摯地，
朵莉絲‧羅伯茲
BT 公司

照著抄 ～ Email 簡單搞定！

Title : We don't accept alteration of trade terms.

Dear Sir or Madam,

We are sorry to learn that you are not very satisfied with our trade terms. However, we cannot accept your changes on the terms.

We still believe that is our best terms of exchange we can offer. Our trading terms and conditions ***have been widely accepted by most suppliers***.

Please contact us if you wish to accept our trade terms after reconsideration.

Yours sincerely,
Adam Foster
NEC Co.

SEND

主旨：我們無法接受交易條款的更動

敬啟者：
很遺憾得知您對我方的交易條件不太滿意。然而，我方不能接受您對交易條件的更改。
我們仍然相信這是我方能夠提供的最好的條件。**大多數的供應商都已廣泛採納**我方之交易條件。
如果您再次考慮後決定接受我們的交易條件，請與我們聯繫。

您真誠地，
亞當‧福斯特
NEC 公司

① 很抱歉，我們無法變更我們的交易條件。

We are sorry that we can't change our trade terms.

② 請告知我方，您是否願意再考慮一下這些交易條件。

Please inform us if you can reconsider these terms.

③ 您說您需要與我們再協商一下產品、價格、交易條件等條款。

You said that you want to negotiate with us on prices, delivery schedule, and purchase terms.

④ 您說您應該獲得更好的交易條件。

You told us you need to get a better possible deal.

⑤ 報價單中，我方已報出最好的交易條件。

We have quoted our best terms in the attached price lists.

⑥ 我已經盡力為您與供應商洽談貿易條件。

I've done my best to negotiate the trade terms with the supplier for you.

⑦ 我們的產品在這個地方很受歡迎。

Our products are very popular in the area.

⑧ 我們不能放寬基本的交易條件。

We cannot loosen the basic terms of the transaction.

06【回應】拒絕更改交易條件

照著抄～ Email 簡單搞定！ — ↗ ✕

範例 1

Re : We don't accept alteration of trade terms.

Dear Mrs. Roberts,

We are regret to learn that you have declined our request to alter our terms of exchange.

The letter is to inform you that we **will seek** other suppliers.

We hope that you will understand our concern.

We are look forward to collaborating with you next time.

Yours sincerely,

Leo Redfield

SEND A ⬚ ⊖ ☺

 中譯

回覆：我們無法接受交易條款的更動

尊敬的羅伯茲女士：

非常遺憾得知您們拒絕我公司想要更改交易條件的要求。

這封信是通知貴公司我們**會再找**其他供應商。本公司希望您瞭解我們的考量。

希望下次我們還有機會合作。

您誠摯地，

里歐‧雷德菲爾德

Re : We don't accept alteration of trade terms.

Dear Mr. Foster,

We are sorry to learn that you cannot accept our changes on the terms.

Since your trading terms and conditions have been widely accepted by most suppliers, we *are not fully satisfied with* them.

We would be really grateful to you if you could make this addition in the contract.

We look forward to discussing the changes on the terms. I prefer if we *have a meeting* on May 2nd.

Please confirm if that is convenient to you.

Yours sincerely,
Lisa Davis

SEND   A 🖉 ⊖ ☺

回覆：我們無法接受交易條款的更動

福斯特先生您好：

很遺憾得知您方不能接受我方對條件之更改。

雖然貴公司的貿易條件已被多數供應商廣泛接受，然而我方**無法完全滿意**。

如果貴公司能在合約中新增這此項，我們將不勝感激。

期待討論交易條件修正內容。希望我們能在 5 月 2 日**開會**。

請確認是否方便。

您真誠地，
麗莎‧戴維斯

Email 這樣寫也行！

① 請安排會議進行價格、交貨時間表和交易條件等條款協議。

Please arrange a meeting to negotiate with us on prices, delivery schedule, and purchase terms.

② 謝謝貴公司就此情況與我們聯繫。

Thank you for contacting us regarding the situation.

③ 期待著發掘進一步的合作機會。

We look forward to exploring further possibilities for us to do business together.

④ 請告知我方，您是否願意再考慮一下這些交易條件。

Please notify me at if you reconsider these terms.

⑤ 請問有可能放寬基本的交易條件嗎？

Is it possible to loosen the basic terms of the transaction?

⑥ 不便之處，敬請原諒。

We are sorry for the inconvenience caused to you.

⑦ 當我們比較所有供應商時，這些條款將會優先考慮。

These trade terms will be favorably considered when we compare from all of our suppliers.

⑧ 感謝您抽出寶貴時間重新考慮我們合約中的條款。

We appreciate your taking the time to reconsider these terms to our agreement.

07 拒絕提早交貨

範例 1

Title : We can only make the delivery as scheduled.

Dear Mr. Smith,

Thank you for your email requesting an **early delivery** of your goods.

I am sorry to tell you that we cannot advance the date of delivery any more. Though it sounds harsh, as you know, it usually **takes us two weeks to get the goods ready**. It's really impossible to deliver the goods in such short notice. Thank you very much for your understanding.

Yours sincerely,
Bob Hill

SEND

中譯

主旨：我們只能如期交貨

親愛的史密斯先生：

謝謝您的來信要求**提前出貨**。

雖然聽起來有點不近人情，但我還是要告訴您我們無法再將交貨日期提前。您是知道的，我們**備貨通常需要兩個星期**。我們真的沒辦法在如此短的時間交貨。感謝您的體諒！

您誠摯地，
鮑伯‧希爾

照著抄 ～ Email 簡單搞定！

範例 2

Title : We can only make the delivery as scheduled.

Dear Mr. Reynolds,

Thank you for your email requesting an early delivery of the goods.

We have checked our delivery schedule. However, we find there is no possibility to advance your delivery. It usually **takes three weeks** to finish the whole process.

Thank you for your understanding.

Yours sincerely,

Peter Lawson

SEND   A ⎥ ⬭ ☺

主旨：我們只能如期交貨

親愛的雷諾茲先生：

謝謝您的來信要求提前出貨。

我們已查看了發貨進度，但沒法提前供貨給您。完成整個流程通常**需要三週的時間**。

感謝您的體諒！

您誠摯地，

彼得・勞森

Email 這樣寫也行！

① 交貨日期不能再提前了。

We cannot advance the delivery date any earlier.

② 我已經查看了我們的生產進度。

I have checked our production schedule.

③ 我們現在沒辦法出貨給您。

We see no way of moving up your delivery now.

④ 非常抱歉，我們不能提前交貨。

I am very sorry that we cannot advance the time of delivery.

⑤ 我們無法加速生產，提前交貨。

We cannot step up production to advance the time of delivery.

⑥ 我們已經盡最大的努力交貨了。

We have done our best to deliver the goods.

⑦ 我們無法將交貨日期提前。

We cannot advance the date of delivery.

⑧ 我們無法接受您的要求，提前交貨。

We cannot accept your request for making an earlier shipment.

08 【回應】 拒絕提早交貨

Re : We can only make the delivery as scheduled.

Dear Mr. Hill,

With due respect it is stated, you made a request for early delivery of your goods.

Unfortunately, you cannot deliver the goods in such short notice.

If you cannot advance the date of delivery, we may need to cover up *the additional cost*.

We will be looking forward to your reply regarding this urgent matter.

Yours sincerely,

Tommy Smith

SEND

 中譯

回覆：我們只能如期交貨

希爾先生您好：

據我方所知，本公司提出交貨日期提前的要求。

很遺憾，貴公司無法在這麼短的時間內交貨。

但是如果您方不能提前交貨，我們可能需要支付**額外費用**。

我們期待著您對此緊急事件的答覆。

感謝體諒！

您誠摯地，

湯米・史密斯

Re : We can only make the delivery as scheduled.

Dear Mr. Lawson,

We have received your letter this morning. Indeed, we very much **regret** to hear that.

Please urgently reconsider this decision. Moreover, we will pay with the additional cost of urgent submission.

We would be highly obliged to hear from you within a week.

Thank you so much for your consideration and understanding.

Yours sincerely,

Tony Reynolds

SEND　　　　　　　　　　　　　　　　　　　Ａ 🖉 ⊖ ☺

回覆：我們只能如期交貨

親愛的勞森先生：

我們今天早上收到了您的來信。事實上，得知此答案我們深感**遺憾**。

請盡速重新考慮這項決定。此外，我們將支付貴公司提前出貨的額外費用。

如能在一周內收到您的來信，我們將不勝感激。

非常感謝您的關心和理解。

感謝您的體諒！

您誠摯地，

湯尼・雷諾茲

Email 這樣寫也行！

① 我們要求提前交貨，因為有足夠充分的理由。

We would request for earlier delivery because we have compelling reasons for doing so.

② 如能提前交貨，我們將不勝感激。

We will be grateful for early delivery.

③ 請盡最大努力提早交貨。

Please do your best to deliver the goods much earlier.

④ 我們要求提前交貨。

We request for making an earlier shipment.

⑤ 我們期待您的積極和立即回應。

We look forward to your positive and timely response.

⑥ 請問有可能將交貨日期提前嗎？

Is it possible to advance the date of delivery?

⑦ 您方若能提前交貨，我方將不勝感激。

It will be kind of you to release the supply of goods in advance.

⑧ 呼籲貴方儘快交貨以避免支付更多額外費用。

It's an appeal to make the delivery soon to avoid more cost.

09 拒絕延緩交貨日期

範例
1

Title : Please deliver the goods on time.

Dear Mr. Blake,

I am sorry that we **cannot accept** your request for delay in delivery.

Our project is **in great need of these building materials**, otherwise we cannot complete the task. If it is impossible for you to deliver them **on time**, we shall have to cancel the order.

We are sorry to cause you any inconvenience. Thank you for your understanding.

Yours sincerely,
Henry Taylor
CON Build Company

SEND   A 🖉 ⌇ ☺

 中譯

主旨：請如期交貨

親愛的布萊克先生：

很抱歉，我們**無法接受**您要求交貨延遲的請求。

我們的工程**急需這批建築材料**，否則我們無法完工。如果您無法**按時**交貨，我們只好取消訂單。

非常抱歉給您帶來的不便！感謝您的理解。

您誠摯地，
亨利·泰勒
CON 建築公司

照著抄 ～ Email 簡單搞定！

Title : Please deliver the goods on time.

Dear Mr. Wilson,

I regret to learn that you cannot deliver the goods at the set time and wish to delay some days. In that case, I might have to say we cannot accept the request. In accordance with our contract, once you cannot deliver the goods on time, you must be **held responsible for all the losses** caused by the delay in delivery of the goods. That is not a small sum.

I honestly hope that you could think it over and try your best to deliver our goods on time.

Yours sincerely,
Emily Cage
WOW Co.

SEND

主旨：請如期交貨

敬重的威爾森先生：

很遺憾得知您不能在規定時間內交貨並且希望能延遲幾天。如果是那樣的話，我們恐怕不能接受這個請求。根據合約，一旦貴方不能按時交貨，貴方必須**賠償我方因延遲交貨而造成的一切損失**。這可不是個小數目。

我真誠地希望貴方能仔細考慮，竭盡全力按時交貨。

您真誠地，
艾蜜莉‧凱基
WOW 公司

① 我們不能接受您交貨延遲的要求。

We cannot accept your requirement to postponing the delivery.

② 延遲將會造成我們很大的不便。

The delay will cause great inconvenience to us.

③ 我們仍希望貴公司能在規定時間內交貨。

We still hope you can deliver the goods at the set time.

④ 我們被告知您無法按時交貨。

We were informed that you could not deliver the goods on time.

⑤ 對不起，我們不能再等了。

We are so sorry we cannot wait any longer.

⑥ 希望您們可以瞭解目前的情況。

We hope you can understand the current situation.

⑦ 如果您還是堅持的話，我們將不得不取消訂單。

If you still insist on that, we will have to cancel the order.

⑧ 我們將要被迫取消這次訂單。

We will be forced to cancel this order.

10【回應】拒絕延緩交貨日期

Re : Please deliver the goods on time.

Dear Mr.Taylor,

I have received your letter of April the 20th. Since you cannot accept the request, we have equipped our departments with *more number of staffs*.

Moreover, we will make every effort to deliver these building materials *on time*. Please don't cancel the order.

We are sorry to cause you any inconvenience.

Yours sincerely,

Ward Blake

SEND   A 🖇 ⊝ ☺

回覆：請如期交貨

親愛的泰勒先生：

我方已經收到您四月二十日的來信。由於您方不能接受此項要求，本公司已為我們部門分配**更多員工**。

此外，本公司將盡一切努力**按時**交付此批建築材料。請勿取消訂單。

十分抱歉造成貴公司的不便！

您誠摯地，

沃德・布萊克

範例 2

Re : Please deliver the goods on time.

Dear Mrs. Cage,

With all my sincere respect, I am writing this letter of apology to you for the inconvenience that we have caused. In the light of our **excellent business relationship**, we will hold responsible for delivering the goods on time.

We hope you will continue to choose us in the future

We would appreciate your support.

Yours sincerely,

Scott Wilson

SEND　　　　　　　　　　　　　　　　A 📎 🔗 🙂

 中譯

回覆：請如期交貨

敬重的凱基女士：

對於造成您的不便，我謹致上最誠摯的敬意。鑑於兩間公司**良好的業務關係**，我方竭盡全力按時交貨。

希望貴公司未來繼續選擇本公司。

感謝您的支持。

您真誠地，

史考特‧威爾森

176

Email 這樣寫也行！

① 對可能發生的延遲，我們明白並深表歉意。

We are aware and very sorry for the delay that may occur.

② 我們將盡一切努力防止以後發生此種情況。

We will do anything to prevent this from happening in future.

③ 在仔細考慮我們的請求之前，請勿做出任何決定。

Please don't make any decisions before you have carefully considered your request.

④ 對於延遲將造成貴公司很大不便表示歉意。

We apology the delay will cause great inconvenience to you.

⑤ 請告知您是否要取消訂單。

Please advise us on whether you would like to cancel your order or not.

⑥ 我們明白更改交貨日期可能會帶給您不便。

We understand the change of delivery date will probably inconvenience.

⑦ 我方會盡我們所能保持如期交貨。

We do our best to always deliver your goods as scheduled.

⑧ 如果您能答應我方要求，我們將不勝感激。

We would be grateful if you would comply with our request.

11 拒絕取消訂單

範例 1

Title : We are not able to accept cancellations.

Dear Mr. Kennedy,

We are writing to inform you that we have received your email of December 15th requesting to cancel the order of No. SK 143728.

However, I am afraid that we are unable to accept such a cancellation, as we have already **had the goods shipped**. We most sincerely hope you will afford us your consideration. Thanks a lot!

Yours truly,

Daniel Bush

SEND

 中譯

主旨：我們無法接受取消

親愛的甘迺迪先生：

謹以此信通知貴方，我方已經收到您在 12 月 15 日的來信，信中要求取消訂單號碼 SK143728 。

然而，我們無法接受該項訂單取消，因為**已經出貨**了。

我們誠摯地希望您能諒解。

非常感謝！

謹致問候，

丹尼爾·布希

照著抄 ～ Email 簡單搞定！

範例 2

Title : We are not able to accept cancellations.

Dear Mr. Clark,

I feel sorry for hearing that you want to cancel the order NO. 257803. As a matter of fact, no change or cancellation can be made once the order is confirmed.

I wonder what made you make such a decision. Is there anything wrong with our product? I hope that you can provide me with some ***reasonable explanation***.

Your prompt reply is urgently awaited.

Yours sincerely,
Kevin Jones
MOV Co.

SEND

主旨：我們無法接受取消

親愛的克拉克先生：

很遺憾聽說您想要取消編號 257803 的訂單。事實上，訂單一經確認後是不能更改或取消的。

我想知道您為什麼做出這樣的決定。我們的產品有任何問題嗎？誠摯地希望您能給我一個**合理的解釋**。

煩請您儘快回信。

您真誠地，
凱文・瓊斯
MOV 公司

Email 這樣寫也行！

① 非常抱歉，我們無法撤銷訂單。

To my deep regret, we cannot cancel the order.

② 貨物已在昨天按您的要求出貨了。

The goods were shipped yesterday as you required.

③ 訂單無法取消，因為已經出貨了。

The order cannot be canceled for the goods are on the way.

④ 取消訂單將違反合約規定。

To cancel the order will violate our contract.

⑤ 我方將要求貴公司賠償訂單取消可能導致的損失。

We would ask you to cover any loss, which might be caused as a result of the cancellation of the order.

⑥ 產品已經在生產中了。

The items are already on the production line.

⑦ 我們上週已經按照合約出貨了。

We were under contract to deliver the goods last week.

⑧ 收到您的郵件後，我們就立即執行訂單了。

After receiving your email, we executed the orders promptly.

12【回應】拒絕取消訂單

照著抄 ～ Email 簡單搞定！

 範例 1

Re : We are not able to accept cancellations.

Dear Mr. Bush,

We have received your letter of December 16th. You are unable to accept such a cancellation since you have shipped the goods.

Therefore, we are writing to inform you that we **will not cancel** the order.

We apologize for any inconvenience that may have been caused.

Thank you for your prompt reply.

Yours truly,
Cole Kennedy

SEND

 中譯

回覆：我們無法接受取消

布希先生您好：

貴公司於 12 月 16 日之來函已知悉。由於已經發貨，故貴公司不能接受取消訂單。

因此，我們寫信通知您，我們**不會取消**訂單。

造成您方不便，我們深表歉意。

謝謝您的及時答覆。

謹致，

柯爾．甘迺迪

Re : We are not able to accept cancellations.

Dear Mr. Jones,

We are aware of the order is cancelled the charged are unable to refunded.

However, we request you to cancel the order as we **have already purchased** them from your company in March.

We would discuss our cancellation over **the phone**.

Please don't hesitate to contact me directly at any time.

Thank you for understanding the matter.

Yours sincerely,

Hayes Clark

SEND

回覆：我們無法接受取消

親愛的瓊斯先生：

我們理解取消訂單，是無法進行退款。

但是，我方要求貴公司取消訂單的原因，是因為我們在三月時，**已經向貴公司購買**此商品。我們會**在電話中**討論訂單取消事宜。

請隨時直接與我聯絡。

感謝您的諒解。

您真誠地，

海斯 · 克拉克

Email 這樣寫也行！

① 為商品誤訂一事，我們在此致上誠摯歉意。

We apologize sincerely to you for making a mistake in the purchased goods.

② 我知道您已經在行程中騰出時間，討論訂單。

I know that you have made time for this order in your schedule.

③ 我們部門內部有些溝通不良。

There has been some miscommunication within our departments.

④ 對於造成不便，我們深表歉意。

We apologize for all inconvenience that you have faced.

⑤ 發現問題後，我們就立即取消訂單了。

After we figured out the problem, we cancelled the orders promptly.

⑥ 我理解如果取消訂單將違反合約。

I know if we cancel the order, it will violate our contract.

⑦ 很抱歉我們要取消訂單。

Kindly accept our apology for cancelling the order.

⑧ 不便之處請見諒。

We are incredibly sorry for all the inconvenience caused.

PART 4
售後服務

因各家手機系統不同，若無法直接掃描，仍可以（https://tinyurl.com/3vzrt9ye）電腦連結雲端下載，一貼搞定！

Part 4. 售後服務

01 寄送銷售合約

照著抄～ Email 簡單搞定！

範例 1

Title : We have sent the contract of... on (date).

Dear Mr. Hanks,

I would like to inform you about the sales contract.

I **sent** the sales contract we agreed upon, dated August 1st yesterday.

After receiving it, please read it **carefully**.

If you have any questions regarding your contract, please do not hesitate to contact me at 111-1111.

Yours respectfully,

Cindy Lee

SEND

主旨：我們會在……時候把……的合約寄給您

漢克斯先生您好：

我想通知您銷售合約一事。

我在昨天已經將 8 月 1 號協議好的合約**寄出**。

收到合約後，請**仔細**閱讀。

如果合約方面有任何疑問，請不吝撥打 111-1111 與我聯絡。

恭敬地，

李欣蒂

照著抄 ～ Email 簡單搞定！

Title : We have sent the contract of... on (date).

Dear Mrs. Thomas,

I am writing to tell you we appended a copy of your sales contract for 20 pieces of furniture.

Please ***signed*** under seal and accepted August 10th, 2021 after reading the contract carefully.

Thank you for your consideration.

Sincerely yours,

Meg Hanks

SEND A 📎 🔗 😊

主旨：我們會在……時候把……的合約寄給您

親愛的湯瑪仕女士：

寫這封信的目的是告訴您，我們附上一份 20 件家具的訂購合約。

仔細閱讀合約後，請**蓋上印章**，並在 2021 年 8 月 10 日簽名。

感謝您的深思熟慮。

誠摯地，

梅格 • 漢克斯

Email 這樣寫也行！

① 我們想藉此機會表達我們對貴公司的感謝。

We would like to take this opportunity to convey our appreciation for your company.

② 我們要提醒您關於合約一事。

We would like to remind you about the contract.

③ 下列條款已經進行更動。

The following takes place the changes in terms.

④ 如果您有任何疑問，請讓我們知道。

If you have any queries, please let us know.

⑤ 簽名之前，請先閱讀合約。

Please read the contract before signing it.

⑥ 對您的體諒我們將不勝感激。

Your consideration will be appreciated.

⑦ 5 天前，我寄了一份銷售合約給您。

I sent the sales contract five days ago.

⑧ 請寄電郵或傳真給我們。

Please write an email or fax to us.

02【回應】寄送銷售合約

 照著抄 ~ Email 簡單搞定！ ― ⤢ ✕

範例1 **Re : We have sent the contract of... on (date).**

Dear Mrs. Lee,

I received the sales contract we agreed upon, dated August 3rd yesterday.

I will read it careful today. If I have any questions regarding my contract, I will contact you today.

If I accept the contract with all the terms and conditions included, ***I will send it back to you tomorrow***.

Should you have any questions, please feel free to contact us.

Yours respectfully,
Alex Hanks

SEND   A 🎤 🔗 ☺

 中譯

回覆：我們會在⋯⋯時候把⋯⋯的合約寄給您

李女士您好：
我已於昨天 8 月 3 日收到協議好的合約。
我會在今天仔細閱讀此合約。如果合約有任何問題，我會於今天聯絡你。
如果我方接受合約上包含所有條款和協議，**明天將會把合約寄回給您**。
有任何疑問，請隨時與我聯繫。

謹上，
艾力克斯 · 漢克斯

範例 2

Re : We have sent the contract of... on (date).

Dear Mr. Hanks,

We regret to inform you that we have not received a copy of our sales contract for 20 pieces of furniture by you.

We need to see the copy of my sales contract by August 6th.

If you **look into the matter at the earliest**, it will be a great help. Therefore, we request you to resend us a copy of our sales contract.

Thanks again for all your help.

For for any further clarifications, please do not hesitate to contact me.

Sincerely yours,

Judy Thomas

SEND

 中譯

回覆：我們會在⋯⋯時候把⋯⋯的合約寄給您

親愛的漢克斯先生：

很遺憾地通知您，我們尚未收到您 20 件家具的訂購合約。

我們必須於 8 月 6 日之前收到訂購合約。

如果您**儘早查明此事**，對本公司助益良多。因此，我方要求您將訂購合約重寄給我們。

感謝您的協助。

如果有進一步說明，請不吝與我聯絡。

誠摯地，

茱蒂 ‧ 湯瑪仕

Email 這樣寫也行！

① 我們將在明天討論合約中的部分內容。

We will discuss a section of the contract tomorrow.

② 如果對合約有任何疑問，請盡速回電。

If you have any questions about the contract, call me back at your earliest.

③ 我們公司將會接受合約上包含的所有條款和協議。

We would accept the contract with all the terms and conditions included.

④ 我們想更改合約中的付款條款。

We would like to change the payment terms of the contract.

⑤ 如果有更多問題，請隨時與我聯絡。

For any further questions, please feel free to contact me.

⑥ 請用快遞將訂購合約寄給我們。

Please send the sales contract to us by express.

⑦ 我們要求您盡速將訂購合約重寄給我們。

We request you to send us a copy of out sales contract again as soon as possible.

⑧ 從收到訂購合約已經過了一星期了。

We have received the sales contract for a week.

03 說明標記要求

範例

Title : Making sure our understating of ... is on the same bases.

Dear Sir or Madam,

I am writing to confirm one thing.

As we know, CE Marking is also called the "***Passport to Europe***"; it is ***an important measure of goods***.

Please be sure all the products I ordered have CE Marking ***affixed to*** them.

Thank you for your attention.

Best Regards,
Sally Stone

SEND   A ⬚ ⬚ ⬚

 中譯

主旨：確保我們對……的理解是一樣的

先生、女士您好：

寫這封信是想確認一件事。

正如我們所知道的，CE 標記也被稱為**「歐洲護照」**，它**是商品的重要標準**。

請確認所訂購的產品皆須**加上** CE 標記。

謝謝您的留意。

誠摯地，

莎莉 · 史東

照著抄 ～ Email 簡單搞定！

範例 2

Title : Making sure our understating of ... is on the same bases.

Dear Mrs. Gibson,

I am writing to tell you what CE Marking is.

CE Marking, also called the Passport to Europe, is a ***symbol of safety***. While some people use the term CE Mark, ***CE Marking*** is actually more correct.

For further information, please call the office at 388-3838.

I look forward to hearing from you soon.

Sincerely,

Frank Thomas

SEND   A ⌇ ⇔ ☺

 中譯

主旨：確保我們對……的理解是一樣的

親愛的吉勃遜女士：

我寫信告訴您何謂 CE 標記。

首先，它是**安全象徵**。第二呢，它也被稱為歐洲護照。第三，有些人會用 CE 標誌（CE Mark），但是，CE 標記（**CE Marking**）則更正確。

想知道更多資訊，請撥打我的辦公室電話：388-3838。

期待您盡速回覆。

誠摯地，

法蘭克 · 湯瑪仕

Email 這樣寫也行！

① CE 標記對產品而言是非常重要的。

CE Marking is very important to products.

② 您想知道更多關於 CE 標記的內容嗎？

Do you want to know more about CE Marking?

③ 另一方面，CE 標記是一項重要基準。

On the other hand, CE Marking is an important measure.

④ 我認為 CE 標記的說法更正確。

I think CE Marking is more correct.

⑤ 我想解釋一下為什麼 CE 標記非常重要。

I would like to explain why CE Marking is so important.

⑥ 如果您不明白何謂 CE 標記，您能問我以獲取更多資訊。

If you don't understand what CE Marking is, you may ask me for more information.

⑦ 請注意 CE 標記非常有用處。

Please be aware that CE Marking is very useful.

⑧ 下訂單之前，您最好多了解這個名詞。

It'd better to understand the term before you place an order.

04【回應】說明標記要求

範例
1

Re : Making sure our understating of ... is on the same bases.

Dear Mrs. Stone,

This is in response to your letter dated April 25, 2021concerning all the products you ordered have CE Marking affixed to them.

We understand that CE Marking is also called the "Passport to Europe" and it is an important measure of goods; therefore, we will ***pay attention to it***.

Thank you for your notification.

Should you have any question, please contact us by phone 09xx-xxx-xxx, Monday ~ Friday, from 9am to 6pm.

Best Regards,
Kasen Miller

SEND

回覆：確保我們對……的理解是一樣的

史東女士您好：

寫這封信是回覆關於 2021 年 8 月 25 日收到您來信，確認您所訂購的產品皆加上 CE 標記。

我們了解 CE 標記亦被稱為「歐洲護照」，而且它是商品的重要標準。所以我們會**非常留意**。

謝謝您的通知。

如果有任何問題，請在週一到週五，早上九點到下午六點，撥打 09xx-xxx-xxx 與我們聯絡。

誠摯地，

凱森 · 米勒

範例2 **Re : Making sure our understating of ... is on the same bases.**

Dear Mr. Thomas
I will take this good opportunity to thank you for your information about CE Marking.
After reading your letter, I learn more about CE Marking. In fact, it is not a quality indicator.
I would like to know more about *self-certification process*. What stages does it consist of?
We can *talk though the phone* with these questions.
Thank you for your patience.

Sincerely,
Bina Gibson

SEND

回覆：確保我們對……的理解是一樣的

親愛的湯瑪仕先生：
我想藉此機會謝謝您告知我何謂 CE 標記。
閱讀過這封信後，我學到更多關於 CE 標記的資訊。事實上，它並非質量指標。
我想知道更多關於**自行認證的程序**。包含哪幾種步驟呢？
我們可以**透過電話**解釋這些問題。
感謝您的耐心。

誠摯地，
碧娜 · 吉勃遜

Email 這樣寫也行！

① CE 標記是一種認證標誌嗎？

Is CE Marking not a certification mark?

② 我想透過電話詢問您更多關於 CE 標記的資料。

I would like to ask you more information about CE Marking by phone.

③ CE 標記有些明確規則。

There are some certain rules underlying CE Marking.

④ 我們理解 CE 標記是商品的重要標準。

We understand CE Marking is an important measure of goods.

⑤ CE 標記的說法並非官方用語。

CE Mark is not the official term.

⑥ 我真的想知道更多關於 CE 標記的資訊。

I really want to know more about CE Marking.

⑦ 謝謝您清楚的解釋。

Thank you very much for your clear explanation.

⑧ 請解釋一下為何 CE 標記之重要。

Please explain why CE Marking is so important.

05 建議用信用狀付款

照著抄 ～ Email 簡單搞定！

範例
1

Title : We would like to pay by L/C.

Dear Mr. Keeves,
We ***would like to place an order*** of 200 pieces of 18K
gold ring (3-1/8ct.t.w.) at your price of $4000 each, for
shipment on April 10th.
Moreover, we propose to pay by ***a 30-day letter of
credit***.
If you agree to all of the conditions, please send your contract
to us.
We appreciate your support.

Sincerely,
Sean Corner

SEND   A ⋃ ⊝ ☺

主旨：我們想以信用證付款

李維先生您好：
我們上星期已收到您的報價。
我們**想跟您下訂單**：200 只 18K 的金戒指（3-1/8ct.t.w.）
價格每只 4000 元，4 月 10 日送達。
此外，我們提議用 **30 天的信用狀付款**。
如果您同意我們所提的條件，請把合約寄給我。
非常感謝您的支持。

真誠地，
史恩 · 寇勒

照著抄 ～ Email 簡單搞定！

範例2

Title : We would like to pay by L/C.

Dear Mrs. Wu,

We have placed an order three days ago.

We *would like to change the terms of payment*. In fact, we suggested to change the terms of payment from D/A at sight to L/C at sight.

If we can settle the terms of payment soon, it will help us greatly.

Please take it into consideration.

We look forward to your prompt reply.

Faithfully,
Sam Spring

SEND

 中譯

主旨：我們想以信用證付款

親愛的吳女士：

我們在 3 天前下了訂單。

不過，我們**想改變付款方式**。事實上，我們建議將付款方式由承兌交單匯票，改成開立信用狀付款。

如果我們能儘快確定付款方式，將對我們助益良多。

請加以考慮。

我們期待著您迅速回應。

真誠地，

山姆 · 史步林

Email 這樣寫也行！

① 我們很抱歉，我們不能用匯票付款。
We are sorry we cannot pay by money order.

② 您想用什麼方式付款？
What is the mode of payment you wish to pay?

③ 希望我們今天能解決付款方式。
Hopefully, we can settle the terms of payment today.

④ 讓我們來討論付款方式。
Let's discuss the mode of payment.

⑤ 我能理解您們將無法接受延後付款。
I understand you won't accept payment on deferred terms.

⑥ 如果您同意，我們將會很感謝您。
If you are agreeable, we will be appreciative.

⑦ 如果您接受信用狀付款，對我們幫助很大。
If you accept L/C, it will help us a lot.

⑧ 附上公司的簡介和我的名片。
We enclose the company's profile and my business card.

06【回應】建議用信用狀付款

照著抄 ～ Email 簡單搞定！

範例1

Re : We would like to pay by L/C.

Dear Mr. Corner,

I am writing in response to the letter I received yesterday.
You would like to place an order of 200 pieces of 18K gold
ring (3-1/8ct.t.w.) at our price of $4000 each, for shipment on
April 10th.

Moreover, you will pay by a 30-day letter of credit.

We are happy to inform you of **_our acceptance_** of all of
the conditions. We will send the contract to you tomorrow.
We look forward to doing business with you!

Sincerely,
Ken Keeves

SEND   A ⬚ 🔗 ☺

中譯

回覆：我們想以信用證付款

寇勒先生您好：

寫這封信的目的是回覆您昨天收到的來信。

貴公司想訂購：200 只 18K 的金戒指（3-1/8ct.t.w.）。價格每只 4000 元，4 月
10 日送達。

再者，貴公司將用 30 天的信用狀付款。

我們很高興通知您，**本公司已同意**這些條款，我們將於明天將合約寄出。

期待與您有業務往來。

真誠地，

肯 · 李維

範例 2

Title : We would like to pay by L/C.

Dear Mr. Spring,

I am writing to inform you of ***our acceptance*** of the change the terms of payment.

You would change the terms of payment from D/A at sight to L/C at sight.

Please let us know of any issues as soon as possible.

If you any more questions, please feel free to contact me at xxx-xxxx.

We look forward to hearing from you.

Faithfully,

Jennifer Wu

SEND

中譯

回覆：我們想以信用證付款

史步林先生您好：

謹在此通知您，**本公司接受**更改付款方式。

您可以將付款方式從由承兌交單匯票，改成開立信用狀付款。

有任何問題請盡速與我聯絡。

如果還有其他問題，請隨時撥打 xxx-xxxx 與我聯繫

期待您的回應。

真誠地，

珍妮佛・吳

Email 這樣寫也行！

① 如果您同意用信用狀付款，我們將把合約寄給您。

If you agree to pay L/C at sight, we will send our contract to you.

② 我們這星期可以安排會議來討論付款方式。

We can schedule a meeting sometime this week to discuss the mode of payment.

③ 信用狀是種普遍的付款交易方式。

A Letter of Credit seems to be a popular method of payment transaction.

④ 有任何問題，請不吝告知。

Please let me know if there are any issues.

⑤ 如果您接受即期付款，請馬上告知本公司。

If you accept D/A, please let us know as soon as possible.

⑥ 我們將同意接受延後付款。

We will accept payment on deferred terms.

⑦ 很抱歉我方無法同意。

We are sorry that we are not agreeable.

⑧ 請盡速解決付款方式。

Please settle the terms of payment as soon as possible.

07 過期帳項的催款單

範例 1

Title : We haven't received your payment of... yet.

Dear Mr. Woods,
I am writing to inform you that your payment is two months **overdue**.
As per our agreement, you had to pay by August 25th.
However, we still haven't received any payment from you.
We would like to continue to serve you, but **you must pay within 20 days as agreed**.
After the payment goes through, we will handle your order immediately.
We look forward to your prompt reply.

Sincerely,
Elisa White

SEND

主旨：我們尚未收到您的付款

伍茲先生您好：
我以此郵件通知您，您的應付款項已**逾期** 2 個月。
依照協議，您必須在 8 月 25 日前付款。然而，我們至今仍未收到您任何付款。
我們願意繼續替您服務，但請**務必在 20 天內付完應付款項**。
一旦收到您的款項，我們會立即處理您的訂單。
期待您的迅速回覆。

誠摯地，
艾莉莎 · 懷特

照著抄 ～ Email 簡單搞定！

範例 2

Title : We haven't received your payment of... yet.

Dear Mr. Anderson,

We have not received any payment of your account. As you know, the following items totaling $90,000 are still open in your account.

We would like to know your *plans for paying* your account.

I am sorry to tell you that you must settle it *within a week*. Otherwise, we will be forced to take other measures to solve the problem.

Yours truly,
Ella Brooke

SEND

中譯

主旨：我們尚未收到您的付款

艾德森先生您好：

我們尚未收到您的帳戶內的款項。如您所知，您的帳戶欠款總計為 9 萬。

我們想了解您**付款的計畫**。

很遺憾地告訴您，您必須在**一星期內**解決。否則，我們將採取其他的方式來處理。

真誠地，
艾拉・布魯克

Email 這樣寫也行！

① 收到帳單後，請記得付款。

Please remember to send payment on receipt of the letter.

② 我們希望您即早處理。

We hope it may have your early attention.

③ 我們想聽聽您的解釋。

We should welcome an explanation from you.

④ 事實上，您的帳戶仍有欠款。

In fact, you account is still unpaid.

⑤ 我們將再給您一次機會解決。

We will give you a further opportunity to solve it.

⑥ 我們知道延遲付款是有原因的。

We understand there are some reasons for delay in payment.

⑦ 我們堅持要求您即刻付款。

We urgently request that you pay immediately.

⑧ 請了解我們將不會運送任何貨物給您。

Please realize that we won't send you any goods.

08【回應】過期帳項的催款單

Re : We haven't received your payment of... yet.

Dear Mrs. White,

I received your notification from your company that my payment is two months overdue.

I am sorry for my late payment. I will pay within 20 days **as agreed**.

I'm sorry for the inconvenience.

Once again, thank you for your consideration of my situation.

Sincerely,
Daniel Woods

SEND　　　　　　　　　　　　　　　A 🔗 ☺

 中譯

回覆：我們尚未收到您的付款

懷特女士您好：

茲收到貴公司通知，表示我方應付款項已逾期 2 個月。

對於延遲付款深感抱歉。我會**依約**在 20 天內付完應付款項。

抱歉造成貴公司之不便。

再次感謝您體諒目前情況。

誠摯地，

丹尼爾 · 伍茲

Re : We haven't received your payment of... yet.

Dear Mrs. Brooke ,

I am in receipt of your letter dated March 20. I sincerely apologize over the late payments in depth of $90,000.

In fact, I am so sorry I **have not been able to clear the balance**.

I will settle the problem by March 26. I promise that this situation shall never happen again.

Thank you for being patience with this matter.

Yours truly,
Alex Anderson

SEND   A 🖉 ⊖ ☺

回覆：我們尚未收到您的付款

布魯克女士您好：

我方已收到您 3 月 20 日之來信，對於逾期欠款總計 9 萬元，我深表歉意。

實際上，很抱歉**目前無法清償款項**。

我將在 3 月 26 日之前解決此問題。我保證此種情況將不再發生。

感謝您對此事的耐心配合。

真誠地，

艾力克斯 ‧ 艾德森

Email 這樣寫也行！

① 我已收到貴公司逾期催款函。。

I've received your letter of my late payment.

② 遲繳的款項將在四月一號前繳交。

The late payment amounts will be paid by April 1st.

③ 我們將在十天內付款。

We will pay the payment within 10 days.

④ 麻煩請用手機與我聯絡。

Kindly get back to me through my cell phone.

⑤ 對於延遲付款一事請見諒。

Kindly receive my sincere apologies for being late in paying the payment.

⑥ 事實上，我們很遺憾延遲繳款。

In fact, we are so regretful for delay in payments.

⑦ 請再給我公司一次機會解決問題。

Please give us a further opportunity to solve the problem.

⑧ 未來這種情形將不會重演。

This situation will not happen again in future.

09 要求按承兌交單付款

範例
1

Title : We would like to pay by D/A.

Dear Mrs. Silver,

We are grateful to do business with you since we have been your loyal customer for many years.

This time, we would like to pay under the documents against acceptance due to various reasons.

We really hope that you will still be willing to cooperate with us.

Please ***check our financial standing with our bankers***.

Sincerely,
Fiona Smith

SEND

中譯

主旨：我想以承兌交單的方式付款

席維爾女士您好：

承蒙與您有業務往來，多年來我們一直是貴公司的忠實顧客。

這一次，由於某些原因，我們要求按承兌交單付款。

我們由衷希望您願意與我們合作。

請向與我們合作的銀行調閱財務狀況。

真誠地，

費歐納 ・ 史密斯

照著抄 ～ Email 簡單搞定！

範例 2

Title : We would like to pay by D/A.

Dear Mr. Stone,

We are a bookstore in LKK City.

Although we believe that there is a possibility of sales, we ***cannot totally count on this***. Therefore, we are requesting payment by documents against acceptance (D/A). Should you have any questions, please feel free to contact us.

Faithfully,
Paula Williams

SEND

中譯

主旨：我想以承兌交單的方式付款

史東先生您好：

我們是位於 LKK 商城的書店。

雖然我們相信自己在銷售方面能達到目標，但我們**不能全倚賴這點**。

因此，我們要求承兌交單（D/A）為付款條件。

如果您有任何疑問，請隨時與我們聯繫。

真誠地，
寶拉 ‧ 威廉斯

① 我們要求按承兌交單付款。

We request to pay documents against acceptance terms.

② 如果您有任何問題，請馬上聯繫我們。

If you have any questions, please contact us immediately.

③ 請同意我的建議。

Please agree to my proposal.

④ 請同意我們按承兌交單付款。

Please agree us to pay under documents against acceptance.

⑤ 我們感謝您的幫助。

We do appreciate your help.

⑥ 我們期待儘速聽到您的回覆。

We look forward to hearing from you as soon as possible.

⑦ 隨函附上的文件副本，僅供您參考。

Enclosed herewith the copies of the documents for your reference.

⑧ 隨函附上詳細資料。

Detailed information is enclosed herewith.

10【回應】要求按承兌交單付款

 Re : We would like to pay by D/A.

Dear Mr. Simpson,
We received your letter of August 30th, 2021.
In practice, we have considered your request for delivery of furniture on documents against acceptance terms.
We are ***agreeable*** to your proposal.
If you have further questions, please let us know by calling us or sending us an email.

Best Regards,
Steve Steward

SEND　　　　　　　　　　　　　　　　A ⑈ 🔗 ☺

回覆：我們想以承兌交單的方式付款

親愛的辛普森先生：
我在 2021 年 8 月 30 日收到您的來信。
事實上，我們已經考慮您按承兌交單付款的要求。
而我們最後**同意**您的建議。
如果您有進一步的問題，請打電話或發送電子郵件給我們，讓我們知悉。

誠摯地，
史蒂夫 ‧ 史都德

Re : We would like to pay by D/A.

Dear Mrs. Jackson,

First, we are informing you that we received your letter on January 12th, 2021.

After taking it into consideration, we regret to inform you that we cannot agree to your request.

We have checked your *financial standing* with your bankers, and we *cannot accept* your proposal.

We are sorry about that.

We wish you have a great success.

Best Regards,

Jessica Jane

SEND

回覆：我們想以承兌交單的方式付款

親愛的傑克遜女士：

首先，我們來信通知您，我們於 2021 年 1 月 12 日，收到您的來信。

經過深思熟慮後，遺憾地通知您，我們無法同意您要求的付款方式。

經過查閱和您往來銀行的**財務狀況**後，我們決定**不能接受**此提案。

甚感遺憾。

祝您成就非凡。

誠摯問候，

潔西卡 ・珍

Email 這樣寫也行！

① 我們在 2021 年 10 月 22 號收到您的來信。

We are in receipt of your letter of October 22nd, 2021.

② 我們認為您將成功地達到令人滿意的銷售額。

We do think you will succeed in achieving a satisfactory amount of sales.

③ 我們認為貴公司涉及金融風險。

We consider your company that involves a financial risk.

④ 如果您有其他建議，請通知我們。

If you have another proposal, please contact us immediately.

⑤ 我們需要知道您的公司和財務狀況的詳細資料。

We need to know more information about your company and financial standing.

⑥ 我們很抱歉必須拒絕您的提議。

We are sorry that we must refuse your proposal.

⑦ 我們很高興地通知您，您的提議通過了。

We are pleased to inform you that your proposal is agreeable.

⑧ 期待收到您的消息。

Looking forward to learning from you soon.

11 說明包裝要求

範例 1

Title : Please pack the good as we request in the mail.

Dear Mr. Morris,

I am writing to indicate the ***packaging***.

Since packaging has a close bearing on ***sales and promotion***, we do care about how to package our items perfectly.

We pay great attention to packaging, so please do so carefully.

Enclosed here is packaging declaration.

Thank you for your time.

Sincerely,

Emma Black

SEND   A 🔗 ☺

 中譯

主旨：請按照郵件裡所提的要求來包裝商品

親愛的莫里斯先生：

我寫這封信的目的是要說明**包裝**。

由於包裝對產品**銷售和推廣**有很大的關聯，因此我們很介意該如何才能完美包裝。

我們非常重視包裝，所以請務必謹慎包裝。

隨函覆上包裝敘述。

感謝您寶貴時間。

真誠地，

艾瑪 ・ 布蕾克

Title : Please pack the good as we request in the mail.

Dear Mrs. Brown,

We are writing to inform you to have the goods packaged as per our instruction.

As we know, a great packing that ***catch buyers' eyes*** will help us raise the sales. Hence, we would like to explain the ***packing declaration***.

Please package as follows.

A. Ensure the packages are intact.

B. Pack in such a way as to protect the goods moisture.

C. It'd better to use large containers and cardboard boxes to pack the goods.

Thank you for your carefulness.

Sincerely,

James Rose

SEND

主旨：請按照郵件裡所提的要求來包裝商品

親愛的布朗女士，

我們以書面通知您，請務必按照我們的指示包裝商品。

誠如我們所知，好的包裝能成功**抓住消費者的目光**，且將有助我們提高銷售。因此，我們想解釋一下**包裝流程**。

請按照以下重點包裝。

A. 確定包裝的十分完善。

B. 請用防水的材質包裝。

C. 使用大型容器和紙板箱包裝商品會更好。

謝謝您的細心協助。

真誠地，

詹姆士 · 羅斯

Email 這樣寫也行！

① 我想表達我的關切。

I would like to express my consideration.

② 您應該按照包裝說明來包裝貨物。

You should pack as the packing declaration.

③ 請按照我們的說明來包裝。

Please pack the goods as per our instruction.

④ 確定這個商品包裝是防震的。

Ensure the product to be well protected against shock.

⑤ 具時尚感的包裝有助於銷售推廣。

The fashionable design of packing is good for promotion.

⑥ 您要避免不良包裝。

You have to avoid poor packing.

⑦ 記得寫上「小心搬運」這些字。

Remember to mark wording, "Handle with Caution."

⑧ 如果您有任何建議，請和我的助理凱西聯繫。

If you have any suggestion, please contact my assistant, Kathy.

12 【回應】包裝要求

範例 1

Re : Please pack the good as we request in the mail.

Dear Mrs. Black,
I am writing to let you know that we have read your letter of the packaging.
I've read the packaging declaration, and we will **pay attention to it**.
We understand the packaging has a close bearing on sales and promotion, so we will pack your items carefully.
Thank you for bring this point to our attention.

Sincerely,
Willy Morris

SEND   A ↕ ⊖ ☺

 中譯

回覆：請按照郵件裡所提的要求來包裝商品

親愛的布蕾克女士：
謹在此通知貴公司，我們收到您關於包裝之信件。
我已閱讀包裝說明，我們對此方面會**多加留意**。
我們深知包裝對產品銷售和推廣息息相關，因此我們會小心謹慎地包裝您的商品。
感謝您提醒此項重點。

真誠地，
威力 · 莫里斯

Re : Please pack the good as we request in the mail.

Dear Mr. Rose,

Thank you so much for your information regarding the packaging.

We will do our best to package as follows.

A. Ensure the packages are intact.

B. Pack in such a way as to ***protect the goods moisture***.

C. It'd better to use large containers and cardboard boxes to pack the goods.

Your packing tips show us the most important points to follow in order to catch a buyer's eye.

If you have any ideas, please feel free to contact me directly via phone: xxxx-xxx-xxx.

Sincerely,
Jenny Brown

SEND   A ✎ ⊖ ☺

回覆：請按照郵件裡所提的要求來包裝商品

羅斯先生您好，

非常感謝您提供包裝相關資訊。

我們將盡力按照以下指示包裝。

A. 確定包裝的十分完善。

B. 請用**防水**的材質包裝。

C. 使用大型容器和紙板箱包裝商品會更好。

您的包裝指示，闡明成功抓住消費者的目光的重點。

有任何想法，請隨時撥打 xxxx-xxx-xxx，直接與我聯繫。

真誠地，
潔妮 · 布朗

Email 這樣寫也行！

① 我們寫信是為了回覆您於 2021 年 1 月 15 日寄給我們的電郵。

We are writing to you in response to the email that you sent us on January 15, 2021.

② 謝謝您聯繫我們，所有建議都讓我們覺得非常實用。。

Thank you for contacting us with your suggestions, which are all useful.

③ 我們同意的時尚包裝將吸引潛在客戶的目光。

We agree that stylish packaging will attract the attention of potential buyers.

④ 實際上，優質包裝是預防商品損壞的關鍵。

In fact, quality packaging is a key when it comes to preventing damage.

⑤ 我們明白包裝對於商品推廣很重要。

We understand that packaging is important in the promotion of products.

⑥ 如果有任何建議，請隨時與我聯繫。

Please do not hesitate to contact me if you have any suggestion.

⑦ 本公司會按照包裝說明來包裝商品。

We will pack as the packing declaration.

⑧ 如果您之後有其他想法，請將它們寄給我們。

If you have additional ideas in the future, please send them along to us.

13 要求分期付款

範例1

Title : I would like to pay by monthly installments.

Dear Mr. Dickson,

Please consider this letter as my request for an agreement to pay for my *piano* in *installments*.

The price of my piano is ninety thousand dollars. I plan to pay fifteen thousand dollars per month.

Please feel free to call me at 02-111-1111 at any time.

Most sincerely,
Rita Brown

SEND

主旨：我想以分期付款的方式

狄更生先生您好：

請考慮我這封信所提及的，想以**分期付款**支付我買**鋼琴**的費用的要求。

我的鋼琴要價 9 萬元。我打算每月支付 1 萬 5 千元。

請隨時撥 02-111-1111 與我聯繫。

最誠摯地，
瑞塔 ‧ 布朗

照著抄 ～ Email 簡單搞定！

範例 2

Title : I would like to pay by monthly installments.

Dear Mrs. Robison,

Thank you for reading my proposal to pay the account by monthly installments.

I hope my monthly installments are acceptable. ***The schedule is made below***.

July 1st: $10,000

August 1st : $10,000

September 1st: $10,000

October 1st : $10,000

November 1st : $10,000

December 1st: 10,000

Your agreement will be appreciated.

Please contact me at 02-888-8888.

Yours truly,

Allen Roberts

SEND

主旨：我想以分期付款的方式

親愛的羅賓斯女士：

感謝您閱讀我按月分期付款的提議。

我希望您能同意我分期付款的提案。**時間表如下。**

7 月 1 日：$10,000　8 月 1 日：$10,000

9 月 1 日：$10,000　10 月 1 日：$10,000

11 月 1 日：$10,000　12 月 1 日：$10,000　.

若您能同意，我將十分感激。

請與我聯絡，電話為：02-888-8888。

誠摯地，

亞倫 · 羅勃茲

Email 這樣寫也行！

① 我將於 8 月開始付款。

I am scheduled to start the payment in August.

② 我寫這封信是為了要求分期付款。

I am writing to request for installment payments.

③ 我對分期付款協議很感興趣。

I am interested in making an installment payment agreement.

④ 我想用分期付款支付我購買的產品。

I would like to pay my product installments.

⑤ 鋼琴要價 9 萬元。

The piano costs ninety thousand dollars.

⑥ 請閱讀我下列的付款時間表。

Please read the schedule I made below.

⑦ 請告訴我，我提案被拒絕的原因。

Please tell me the reasons why my proposal was refused.

⑧ 我很感激您的善意。

I appreciate your kindness.

14【回應】要求分期付款

照著抄 ～ Email 簡單搞定！ — ⤢ ✕

範例 1

Re : I would like to pay by monthly installments.

Dear Mrs. Brown ,
I am writing with reference to your inquiry on March 10 2021 regarding your monthly installment payments.
I am happy to inform you that we have ***accepted your application***.
You can pay $15,000 per month as the schedule you listed in the letter.
If you have any questions, please contact me in writing at the number xxx-xxxx.
Your cooperation in this matter is appreciated.

Yours sincerely,
Karry Dickson

SEND   A ▮ 🔗 🙂

 中譯

回覆：我想以分期付款的方式

布朗女士您好：
謹以此函告知，我們已收到您於 2021 年 3 月 10 日寄來有關於分期付款的要求。
很高興通知您，本公司**已通過您的申請**。
請按照信函中的時間表，每月支付 1 萬 5 千元。
請撥打 XXX-XXXX 與我聯繫。我會盡速回覆您的來信。
感謝您的合作。

最誠摯地，
凱瑞 · 狄更生

Re : I would like to pay by monthly installments.

Dear Mr. Roberts
This letter is an notification that your payment plan has been approved based upon policy set by Happy Company.
You will agree to the payment installments plan as prescribed below.
Your schedule is made below.
July 1st: $10,000
August 1st : $10,000
September 1st: $10,000
October 1st : $10,000
November 1st : $10,000
December 1st: 10,000
Moreover, you agree to pay $10,000 per month **starting July**. This amount will be collected on the 1st of each month.
Thank you for your prompt response to this letter.

Yours truly,
Eva Robison

SEND   A ⓘ 🔗 ☺

回覆：我想以分期付款的方式

親愛的羅勃茲先生：
此信是根據《快樂公司》政策，批准您分期付款之通知。
本公司同意您分期付款的計畫。
時間表如下。
7 月 1 日：$10,000；8 月 1 日：$10,000；9 月 1 日：$10,000 ；10 月 1 日：$10,000
11 月 1 日：$10,000； 12 月 1 日：$10,000
此外，**從 7 月份開始**，每月您需支付一萬元。款項將在每月的 1 日從您的帳戶收取。
謝謝您的迅速回覆。

誠摯地，
伊娃 · 羅賓斯

226

Email 這樣寫也行！

① 寄出這封信是關於您在 3 月 10 日詢問所致。

This letter is sent to you in reference with the inquiry you made on March 10.

② 您下列的付款時間表已經通過了。

The payment schedule you made below has been approved.

③ 您付款計畫被拒絕有兩個原因。

There are two reasons why your payment plan has been refused.

④ 請確認並回覆此確認函。

Please reply with acknowledgement of this confirmation letter.

⑤ 請撥打 xxx-xxxx 與我聯繫，以便安排其他付款計劃。

Please contact me at xxx-xxxx so we can arrange for another payment plan.

⑥ 請將此信視為您每月分期付款的確認函。

Please consider this letter as the confirmation for your monthly installments as well.

⑦ 我將及時回覆您的來信。

I will respond to your letters in a timely manner.

⑧ 您將於 7 月 1 日開始付款。

You are scheduled to start the payment in July 1st.

15 延遲付款

範例 1

Title : May we have an extension on the payments of...

Dear Mr. Silver,

We have been a loyal and faithful client of your company for the past 4 years.

We have always made prompt payments.

Unfortunately, we are unable to make our payment on time this month due to some *unforeseen circumstances*.

We plan to remit the payment *by the end of month*.

Please contact me at 888-8888 if you have any questions.

Respectfully yours,

Vic Laure

SEND   A 🖉 🔗 ☺

 中譯

主旨：請問能否延期……的付款時間

席歐維先生您好：

在過去 4 年我們一直是貴公司的忠誠客戶。

我們付款一向迅速。

不幸的是，這個月由於一些**意外**，使我們無法如期付款。

我們計畫**月底**前付款。

如有疑問，請撥打 888-8888 與我聯繫。

真誠地，

韋克 · 賴拉

照著抄 ～ Email 簡單搞定！

範例 2

Title : May we have an extension on the payments of...

Dear Mr. Red,

I am regretfully writing to request an extension on my payments.

Due to unforeseen circumstances, I am experiencing immediate ***cash flow problems***.

Therefore, I will be unable to pay before August 31st.

Thank you in advance for your consideration.

Kind regards,

Lisa Hilton

SEND

中譯

主旨：請問能否延期……的付款時間

雷德先生您好：

很遺憾我必須要求延遲付款。

由於一些無法預知的情況，我目前有些**現金問題**。

因此，我 8 月 31 日前將無法付款。

先感謝您的體諒了。

誠摯地，

麗沙・西爾頓

① 對此麻煩我們深感抱歉。

We are very sorry for the trouble.

② 因為有一些原因，我們必需延期付款。

There are some reasons why we got deferred payment.

③ 感謝您的關心。

Thank you for your attention.

④ 抱歉造成不便。

Sorry for your inconvenience.

⑤ 我一向是您的忠實顧客。

I am always your loyal customer.

⑥ 我在準時付款方面有困難 。

I have difficulty in paying on time.

⑦ 我們應該在 7 月 12 日付款。

We were supposed to pay on July 12th.

⑧ 對不起打擾您了。

I am sorry to disturb you.

16 【回應】延遲付款

照著抄 ～ Email 簡單搞定！

範例 1

Re : May we have an extension on the payments of...

Dear Mr. Laure,

We have received your request on August 1st for the extension of your payments. We understand you will be unable to make your payment on time due to some unforeseen circumstances.

You have been a loyal and faithful client of our company for the past 4 years. Hence, we are pleased to inform you this request **has been approved**.

If you require any further assistance in this matter, please contact me directly on the phone number 1234567.

We look forward to a prompt response.

Yours Truly,
Sean Silver

SEND

中譯

回覆：請問能否延期……的付款時間

賴拉先生您好：

我們已於 8 月 1 日收到您的延遲付款之要求。我們理解這個月由於一些意外狀況使貴公司無法如期付款。

過去 4 年貴公司一直是本公司的忠誠客戶。因此，我們很高興通知您，此請求**已獲批准**。

針對此問題，若您需要其他協助，請直接撥打 1234567 與我聯繫。

期待您的迅速回應。

真誠地，

史恩 ・ 席歐維

範例 2

Re : May we have an extension on the payments of...

Dear Mr. Hilton,

Thank you for contacting me to request an extension on the payment terms.

Unfortunately, we are unable to accommodate your request at this time after reviewing your circumstances.

We are really sorry for the *denial* of your request this time.

Thank you in advance for your prompt attention to this matter.

Kind regards,
Kevin Red

SEND

回覆：請問能否延期……的付款時間

西爾頓先生您好：

感謝您與本公司聯繫，要求延遲付款期限。

很遺憾，審核過您的情況後，我們無法核准您的要求。

對於此次申請**被拒絕**，我們深感抱歉。

在此先感謝您關注此事。

親切的問候，誠摯地，

凱文 ‧ 雷德

Email 這樣寫也行！

① 我們收到您要求延期付款的申請函，此筆款項原於 8 月 31 日付款。

We received your request letter to have an extension on the payment, which is supposed to be paid on August 31st.

② 如果您能在 8 月 31 日之前付款，我們將不勝感激。

We would appreciate it if you send the payment before August 31st.

③ 您成為本公司忠實顧客很多年了。

You have now been our customer for many years.

④ 請盡速處理付款事宜。

Please deal with the payment immediately.

⑤ 您要求延遲付款因為某些原因而遭到拒絕。

Your request for having an extension on the payments was denied because of some reasons.

⑥ 希望您能找到另一種解決方式來處理付款。。

We are hoping that you can find another solution on the payments.

⑦ 請告知我們必需延期付款的原因。

Please write the reasons why you have to defer your payment.

⑧ 對於您的請求遭拒，我們深感抱歉。。

We are really sorry if your request will be denied.

17 索賠處理

照著抄 ～ Email 簡單搞定！

範例 1

Title : I want to ask for a refund.

Dear Mr. Cruise,

We placed an order last week, but we found one carton of damaged goods.

We will return the carton to you today. We thought the carton might have been damaged by ***careless handling***.

Enclosed is a detailed claim.

Please contact us once you receive this letter.

We look forward to your prompt reply.

Yours Faithfully,

Donny Jones

SEND   A 🔗 😊

 中譯

主旨：我想要求退款

親愛的克魯斯先生：

我們在上週向貴公司下了訂單，但我們發現有箱貨物受損了。

今天，我們將把箱子寄回。我們認為箱子貨物受損，是因為**包裝過程不慎**，才會造成損壞。

隨信附上要求細節。

當您收到這封信後，請與我們聯繫。

我們期待您迅速回應。

誠摯地，

唐尼 • 瓊斯

照著抄 ～ Email 簡單搞定！

 範例 2

Title : I want to ask for a refund.

Dear Sir or Madam,

I am writing to express my disappointment to you.

I have been your loyal customer for the past two years.

Recently, I received two tables from your company.

Unfortunately, they were both ***damaged***.

I was expecting a better quality and service from your company. Therefore, I decided to return them for ***a full refund***.

I have been purchasing furniture from you before without any trouble. I hope to receive your explanation and refund ***immediately***.

I look forward to hearing from you.

Sincerely,

Linda Green

SEND

 中譯

主旨：我想要求退款

先生、女士您好：

我寫這封信目的是表達我對貴公司感到失望。

過去 2 年我一直是您的忠實客戶。最近，我收到貴公司寄來的 2 張桌子。不幸地是，它們是**破損的**。

我期待貴公司提供更好的品質和服務。因此，我決定退貨，並**全額退款**。

我已經跟您們買過許多家具，從來沒發現過任何問題。我希望您能說明，並**立即**退錢。

我期待您的回覆。

真誠地，

琳達 • 格林

Email 這樣寫也行！

① 我寫信來是因為對您們的產品不滿。

I am writing to complain your products.

② 在過去 3 年，我一直向您們購買家具。

I have been purchasing your furniture for the past three years.

③ 我最近收到貴公司一張壞掉的桌子。

I recently received a damaged desk by your company.

④ 我上星期把毀損的那箱商品寄回您們公司。

I returned one carton of damaged goods to you last week.

⑤ 請確認您的貨物是完好的才寄給我。

Please ensure that your goods are in perfect condition before they are sent out.

⑥ 如需更多資訊，請隨時打電話給我。

For further information, feel free to call me.

⑦ 事實上，我希望您能提供更高品質和更好服務。

In fact, I expect a higher quality of goods and service from you.

⑧ 請隨時打 888-1688 與我聯繫。

Please contact me anytime at 888-1688.

18【回應】索賠處理

範例 1

Re : I want to ask for a refund.

Dear Mr. Jones,

We received your request for a refund of one carton of damaged goods.

If the carton might have been damaged by careless handling, we will be issuing you a refund as soon as we have completed **the necessary paperwork**.

If you have further information, please don't hesitate to provide that. We hope that you will be able to enjoy our products in the future.

Thank you for your understanding.

Yours Faithfully,
Tommy Cruise

SEND

 中譯

回覆：我想要求退款

親愛的瓊斯先生：

我們收到您整箱貨物受損的退款要求。

如果是因為包裝過程不慎，才會造成損壞，我們將在完成**必要文書作業**後立即退款給您。

如果有更多資訊，請隨時提供給我們。

希望您將來還能繼續喜愛本公司產品。

感謝您的理解。

誠摯地，

湯米 · 克魯斯

照著抄 ～ Email 簡單搞定！

 Re : I want to ask for a refund.

Dear Mrs. Green,

We have received your letter of March 5. We would like to take this opportunity to thank you for shopping with us. We take all customer requests seriously. Indeed, we do our best to help our customers.

We are really sorry that your tables were damaged. The tables have been damaged by ***careless handling*** after we checked them. Hence, we take full responsibility for the mistake, and will be able to ***accommodate your request for a full refund***.

If you have any questions, we invite you to call us immediately at xxx-xxxx.

Sincerely,
Neil Cook

SEND

主旨：我想要求退款

格林女士您好：

我們已經收到您 3 月 5 日的來信。我們藉由此機會感謝您在本公司購物。我們認真對待所有顧客要求。事實上，本公司盡力為顧客提供任何協助。

對於您桌子破損深表歉意。經過檢查後，因為**搬運不慎**而損壞。因此，我們對此疏忽承擔全部責任，並**同意全額退款要求**。

如有任何疑問，歡迎您立即致電 XXX-XXXX，與我們聯絡。

真誠地，
倪爾 · 庫克

Email 這樣寫也行！

① 謹在此通知您，您的退款要求並未通過。

I am informing you that your refund request has been rejected.

② 我們重視您的反饋，並期待為您服務。

We value your feedback and look forward to serving you.

③ 我很抱歉您們對我們商品不滿。

I am sorry that you complained our products.

④ 我們未來會提供更高品質和更好服務。

We would provide a higher quality of goods and service in the future.

⑤ 如果您需要進一步協助，並寄信至 123@coldmail.com.tw 與我們聯繫。

If you need further assistance, you may contact us at 123@coldmail.com.tw.

⑥ 請隨時撥打 xxx-xxxx 與我聯繫。

Please feel free to call me at xxx-xxxx.

⑦ 我們將無法退還您的款項。

We won't be able to refund your purchase price.

⑧ 感謝您提供本公司服務的機會。

Thank you for providing us with the opportunity to be of service to you.

PART5
客訴與回覆

因各家手機系統不同，若無法直接掃描，仍可以（https://tinyurl.com/b2bwmana）電腦連結雲端下載，一貼搞定！

Part 5.
客訴與回覆

01 投訴延遲交貨

範例1

Title : The shipment is delayed.

Dear Mr. Donald,

Your shipment was scheduled to be handled at the end of June; however, yesterday you informed me that you wanted to postpone this shipment to July 16th 2010.

I feel the strong need to remind you that we are ***in urgent need*** of the goods. The given date is too late to accept. ***You'd better proceed with this shipment at once***, or else we have to cancel this deal.

Yours sincerely,
Ron Miller

SEND

主旨：延期交貨

親愛的唐納德先生：

貴方的出貨原本排定在 6 月底，但是昨天您告知我欲將出貨日想延至 2010 年 7 月 16 日。

我必須提醒您，我們現在正**急需**這批貨物。您們給的時間太晚了，讓人無法接受。**您們最好馬上進行出貨**，否則我們將取消本次交易。

您誠摯地，

羅恩．米勒

照著抄 ～ Email 簡單搞定！

Title : The shipment is delayed.

Dear Ms. Kitty,

Your delivery of purchasing order No. 0702065 was scheduled to be handled at the end of May. You postponed this shipment to June 5th, 2021, because of uncompleted accessories. But now you want to postpone it again. We are in urgent need of these goods and ***will not accept any excuse this time***. Please proceed with this shipment at once, andlet me know ***when*** it will arrive at our factory.

If there are any other problems, please do not hesitate to contact me now.

Yours sincerely,

Andy Lee

SEND

A

主旨：延期交貨

敬愛的凱蒂小姐：

訂單編號 NO. 0702065 的出貨原本排定在 5 月底。因為配件未完成而將之延遲到 2021 年 6 月 5 日，但是現在您又想延遲交貨日期。我們急需這批貨物，這次我們**不再接受任何理由**。請立刻進行出貨，並讓我知道貨物**何時**抵達我們的工廠。

如果有任何問題，現在就請與我聯絡。

您真誠地，

安迪・李

Email 這樣寫也行！

① 您們已經拖延出貨一週了。

You have postponed the shipment for one week.

② 所有毛衣的交貨期都將延後一個月。

All of the delivery of sweaters will be postponed for one month.

③ 交貨期不能拖延超過 5 天。

The delivery cannot be postponed for over five days.

④ 如果您可以接受三週以後的交貨期，我們就不再跟您議價。

If you can accept the delivery schedule of three weeks later, we will not negotiate your offer.

⑤ 我們只接受因惡劣天氣而引起的延遲出貨。

We only accept the delayed delivery caused by bad weather.

⑥ 這些產品會延後至明天才到我們的公司。

These products will be postponed until tomorrow to reach us.

⑦ 因為主要零件缺貨而將延後出貨。

There will be a delayed shipment caused by shortage of some main components.

⑧ 延遲交貨已經造成我方莫大的不便。

Late delivery has caused a huge inconvenience on our side.

02【回應】投訴延遲交貨

照著抄 ～ Email 簡單搞定！

範例1

Re : We are sorry about the delayed shipment.

Dear Mr. Robert,

I would like to apologize for the delay in shipping your order.
Due to **excessive demand** last month, it seems impossible for us to process all the orders in time.
However, we sent your order **earlier this morning**, and we are sure you will receive them by tomorrow.
Please accept our sincere apologies again for any inconvenience we have caused you.
Thank you very much for your consideration.

Yours truly,
NEC Co.

SEND   A ⬦ 🔗 🙂

中譯

回覆：對於延期交貨，我們深感抱歉

親愛的羅伯特先生：

我想要對此次的交貨延遲道歉。由於上個月**訂單過多**，我們不太可能及時完成所有的訂單。

不過您的貨品我們已於**今天早上**寄出，相信您將於明天之前收到貨品。

給您造成任何不便，請再次接受我們真誠地歉意。

非常感謝您的諒解。

您真誠地，
NEC 公司

Re : We are sorry about the delayed shipment.

Dear Mr. Karl,

Please accept our heartfelt apologies for the late delivery of goods to your company.

The delay resulted from **a minor malfunction in our inventory system**. However, we have had it resolved now. Your shipment will be sent out **this afternoon**. We are sure you will get them tomorrow.

We hope that you will forgive our minor mistakes and we can continue our cooperation.

Yours sincerely,
KS Co.

SEND   A ╎ ⌐ ⊙

回覆：對於延期交貨，我們深感抱歉

親愛的卡爾先生：

對於此次出貨日期延遲，請接受我們真誠地道歉。

此次延遲是由於我們的**存貨系統出了一點小故障**，但是現在問題已經解決了。您的貨物我們將於**今天下午**發出。我們確信您能在明天收到它們。

希望您能原諒我們小小的過失並且能與敝公司繼續合作。

您真誠地，
KS 公司

Email 這樣寫也行！

① 對於延遲交貨，我感到非常抱歉。

I am really sorry for delaying delivering your products during transportation.

② 我們會儘快寄出您訂購的貨物。

We will send the goods you ordered as soon as possible.

③ 對於此次延遲出貨，請接受我們真誠地道歉。

Please accept our whole-hearted apologies for delaying delivery of your goods.

④ 我為我們出貨過程中的疏忽向您誠心地道歉。

Please accept my sincere apology for our carelessness during the shipment.

⑤ 延遲您的出貨日期我感到非常抱歉。

I am so sorry for delaying the goods you ordered.

⑥ 對於延遲交貨給您帶來的不便我感到很抱歉。

I apologize for the inconvenience caused by the late delivery of goods.

⑦ 我們保證這樣的延遲不會再發生。

We are sure such delay won't happen again.

⑧ 我們一定會跟守時的運輸公司合作。

We will certainly cooperate with a punctual freight company.

03 投訴商品寄送錯誤

範例 1

Title : The goods you sent were incorrect.

Dear Mr. Smith,

It is the second time that I have received the **incorrect items** from your company.

To tell you the truth, I am so angry at that because I have to call your staff and assist them in taking these items back once again. It really **takes me a lot of time**. I think that other buyers will feel anger, too.

What if you received incorrect items?

I hope that you can take care of this at once and I am looking forward to your reply.

Yours sincerely,
John Roberts

SEND

主旨：您寄出的商品是錯的

親愛的史密斯先生：

我已經第二次收到您們公司**寄錯**的物品了。

說實話，我對此很生氣。因為這意味著我又要再次打電話聯繫您們的工作人員，協助他們把物品拿回去。**這很浪費我的時間**。若是其他買家也一定會感到生氣吧。

如果您也收到寄錯的物品，您又會怎麼樣呢？

希望您能立刻處理這件事。期待回覆。

您誠摯地，
約翰‧羅伯特

照著抄 ～ Email 簡單搞定！

Title : The goods you sent were incorrect.

Dear Sirs,

I am writing to express my dissatisfaction with your service. I received the shipment on July 15th, and found that you sent the wrong item again.

In fact, I am disappointed that you sent the wrong item again. This is the third time that your company has made the mistake.

I must ***insist on canceling*** my order this time. I will return the package within three days.

I regret that we were unable to complete this order.

Sincerely,
Shelly Stone

SEND

主旨：您寄出的商品是錯的

敬啟者：

我寫這封信的目的是為了表達我對您的服務感到不滿。我在 7 月 15 日收到商品，但是發現您們又寄錯商品。

事實上，我對您們又寄錯品項感到失望。這已經是貴公司所犯的第三次錯誤。

這次我非常**堅持取消**此次的訂單。三天內我會寄回包裹。

很遺憾無法完成這次訂單。

真誠地，
雪莉·史東

① 我並沒有在週六的時候訂購這些東西。

I don't think I ordered these items on Saturday.

② 您一定是將貨物送錯地方了。

You must have delivered the goods to the wrong place.

③ 我希望下次不要再收到這樣的東西了。

I do not hope to receive such things next time.

④ 請儘快處理這件事情。

Please take care of this as soon as you can.

⑤ 希望類似的事情不要再發生了。

I hope such thing will not happen again.

⑥ 恐怕您得先檢查一下地址才行。

I am afraid that you have to check the address first.

⑦ 寄送錯誤確實造成了很大的不便。

The wrong delivery really caused great inconvenience.

⑧ 我決定取消這次的訂購。

I decide to cancel my order this time.

04【回應】商品寄送錯誤的道歉

照著抄 ～ Email 簡單搞定！

 Re : Apology for the incorrect goods delivery.

Dear Mr. Rogers,

We feel terribly sorry for delivering the wrong model to you. We sent *the right one* to you today and you should receive it within two days.

We guess that it must bring you great trouble because of our fault. We hereby express our deep sorry for this error and guarantee that we will prevent such thing from happening again.

We are sorry again for any inconvenience it may cause you.

Yours sincerely,
John Barker

回覆：為寄錯商品而道歉

親愛的羅傑先生：

給您送錯了貨品型號，我們感到非常地抱歉。我們已於今天將**正確的型號**寄送給您了，您應該在 2 天之內就可以收到。

想必我們的疏失給您帶來不小的麻煩，在此我們對這樣的錯誤表示深深的歉意。我們保證會避免再次發生這樣的事情。

給您帶來不便，再次表達我們的歉意。

您誠摯地，
約翰‧巴克

Re : Apology for the incorrect goods delivery.

Dear Mr. Black,

In your email, you said that what you ordered was Model WZ-250, but instead what you received was Model WZ-205. This ***is a typing error on our part***. I apologize to you for our carelessness and promise you that it will not happen again.

I will send you the correct shipment at ***our expense*** on Saturday.

If any questions, please contact me.

Yours sincerely,

Bill Diamond

SEND

Ａ 📎 🔗 ☺

回覆：為寄錯商品而道歉

敬愛的布萊克先生：

您在郵件中說您訂購的型號是 WZ-250，而您卻收到了 WZ-205。這是我們的**打字錯誤**。我在此為我們的疏忽大意向您致歉，並保證此類事情不再發生。

我會在本週六將正確的貨物寄去給您，其運費**由我方支付**。

如果有什麼問題的話，請聯絡我。

您真誠地，

比爾‧蒙德

Email 這樣寫也行！

① 這是我們運送上的疏失。

It is a mistake on the part of our shipping.

② 就這件事情，我們想聽聽您的意見。

We would like to know your opinion regarding this matter.

③ 我們正期待您的迅速回覆。

We are looking forward to your earliest reply.

④ 這是我們作業上的一個疏失。

This due to a clerical error on our part.

⑤ 請儘快將正確的貨物寄給我。

Please send the right goods to me as soon as possible.

⑥ 這批錯誤的貨物遞送對我們的業務影響很大。

This delivery of wrong goods affects our sales greatly.

⑦ 您希望我以對方付運費的方式寄回工廠嗎？

Do you want me to send it back to your factory at your cost?

⑧ 貨物寄送錯誤已經使我們經理非常不愉快！

The delivery of wrong goods has caused our manager to be very unhappy!

05 投訴商品數量短少

範例 1

Title : There is a shortage of goods...

Dear Mr. Miller,

Our goods just reached us several minutes ago. However, we found a **shortage** in quantity because only **two thirds of them** were received.

I do not think your workers are careful enough to check our goods before shipping. I hope you can tell me the exact reason and send the rest as soon as you read this.

We look forward to your early reply.

Yours sincerely,
Kate Smith

SEND

中譯

主旨：商品數量有缺

親愛的米勒先生：

貨物在幾分鐘前到達了。然而，我們發現貨物數量**短缺**，我方僅收到訂單**三分之二的貨物**。

我覺得您們的工作人員在裝運之前並沒有仔細地進行清點。希望您看到郵件後能告知確切原因並將剩餘的貨物寄來。

期待早日回覆。

您誠摯地，
凱特‧史密斯

照著抄 ～ Email 簡單搞定！

範例2

Title : There is a shortage of goods...

Dear Mr. Johns,

Your delivery of order No. 52063 just reached us a few hours ago. However, only 500 boxes were received.

We want to know the reason and when other goods can be sent out. As to **the freight cost caused, it will be at your cost**.

We look forward to receiving the rest as soon as possible.

Yours sincerely,
Iris Yang

SEND

 中譯

主旨：商品數量有缺

敬愛的約翰斯先生：

訂單編號 52063 在幾個小時前已經到達我們公司，然而我們只收到了 500 箱貨物。

請告知原因，並告訴我們其他的貨物何時可以寄過來。至於因此**所產生的運費將由您們支付**。

期待能儘速收到其餘的貨物。

您真誠地，

愛麗絲 ‧ 楊

Email 這樣寫也行！

① 總計短少了 260 公斤。

The total amount of shortage is 260 kgs.

② 這批貨物的短少導致我們要延遲交貨。

The shortage of this shipment caused us to delay the delivery.

③ 請儘快將短缺的貨物寄出。

Please deliver the remaining part of shortage goods as soon as possible.

④ 如果交貨有短缺，請務必通知我。

Please inform me if there are any shortages of your goods.

⑤ 我們想知道您們將如何賠償我們的損失。

We want to know how you will compensate our loss.

⑥ 這次的短缺起因於貴公司員工的粗心大意。

The shortage is caused by your employee's carelessness.

⑦ 您們經常性的貨物短缺是無法被接受的。

The shortage of your usual delivery cannot be accepted.

⑧ 您能否接受我們在下次出貨時補足剩下的部份？

Is it possible for us to re-supply the remaining part in next delivery?

06【回應】投訴商品數量短少

照著抄 ～ Email 簡單搞定！　　　　　　　— ⤢ ✕

範例 1

Re : There is a shortage of goods...

Dear Mrs. Smith,

Thank you for your letter. We are sorry to learn you have observed a shortage.

It seems to have occurred due to **the negligence of some newly staffs**. In spite of the fact that our consignments are checked twice before packing, this mistake has still occurred.

The inconvenience so caused is regretted.

Yours sincerely,
Mark Miller,

SEND　　　　　　　　　　　　　　　　　A ‖ ⊖ ☺

回覆：商品數量有缺

史密斯女士您好：

謝謝您的來信。得知發生短缺現象，我們深感抱歉。

此狀況發生原因似乎是因為**一些新進員工的疏失**。儘管我們貨物在包裝前已經過檢查兩次，但這個錯誤依然存在。

造成貴司的不便，我們深感遺憾。

您誠摯地，

馬克 · 米勒

Re : There is a shortage of goods...

Dear Mrs. Yang,

We thank you for your letter dated 10th July.

We are sorry to learn that you have received 500 boxes
instead of 600 boxes. **_100 boxes have already sent out_**
and will arrive there on 16th July.

Our company would like to address your concerns further.

We regret for the inconvenience caused.

Yours sincerely,

Alan Johns

SEND　　　　　　　　　　　　　　　　　　A ⏿ ⊖ ☺

回覆：商品數量有缺

敬愛的楊女士：

感謝您 7 月 10 日的來信。

我們很遺憾得知您只收到 500 箱，而不是 600 箱。 我們**已經寄出 100 箱**，將會
在 7 月 16 日抵達貴處。

本公司希望進一步解決您的疑慮。

對此造成不便，我們深表遺憾。

您真誠地，

艾倫 ‧ 約翰斯

Email 這樣寫也行！

① 我們很訝異得知貴司收到貨物短缺。

We are surprised to learn that you have received shortage of goods.

② 我們感謝您 7 月 10 日寄來相關資訊信件。

We thank you for the information contained in your letter dated 10 July.

③ 我們已經在 7 月 12 號將其餘短缺的貨物寄出。

We have delivered the remaining part of shortage goods on July 12th.

④ 這次的短缺起因於本公司同仁的粗心。

The shortage is caused by our staff's carelessness.

⑤ 我們對於貨物短缺造成的不便感到遺憾。

We regret for the inconvenience caused.

⑥ 如果交貨仍有短缺，請隨時通知我。

If there are still any shortages of your goods, please don't hesitate to inform me .

⑦ 我們已經將問題回報公司。

We have now referred the matter to our company.

⑧ 我們對於貨物短缺很抱歉。

We are sorry for the shortage of our delivery.

07 投訴商品瑕疵

 照著抄 ～ Email 簡單搞定！　　　　　　　　　— ⤢ ✕

範例 1

Title : Some goods are defective in order...

Dear Mr. Brown,

We are glad to inform you that your delivery has arrived at our company on time. However, on the other hand, we found some **defects** of some goods. I am afraid no customers would like to buy them.

Attached are some pictures for your reference, and please transfer this information to your related department.

Your prompt reply will be highly appreciated.

With best regards,
Bob Hill

SEND　　　　　　　　　　　　　　　　　　　A ◊ ⊖ ☺

 中譯

主旨：這批訂單的商品有一些有瑕疵

敬愛的布朗先生：

我們很高興地通知您的貨物已經按時抵達我們公司。然而，我們發現其中一些商品是有**瑕疵的**，恐怕沒有顧客會願意購買這些商品。

附上一些照片供您參考，並請將這些資訊轉交給您們的相關部門。

您若能的快速回覆，我們會很感謝。

誠摯的祝福您，
鮑伯 ‧ 希爾

照著抄 ～ Email 簡單搞定！ — ⤢ ✕

Title : Some goods are defective in order...

Dear Mr. John,

I really appreciate you deliver these goods on time. However, I found some of these vases broken in the boxes and also some defective ones. I do not know whether you will **replace** them or just **refund** the money.

If you want to check them, I have attached some pictures for your reference.

I am looking forward to your reply.

Yours sincerely,
Bill Peterson

SEND   A ⇩ ⌇ ☺

主旨：這批訂單的商品有一些有瑕疵

親愛的約翰先生：

我們十分感謝您按時交貨了。然而，我發現一些花瓶在箱子裡有破損，還有一些瑕疵品。我不知道您們是打算給我們**更換**貨物呢？還是直接**退錢**？

如果您們想確認破損情況的話，我已經有附上一些照片供您參考。

期待您的回覆。

您真誠地，

比爾 · 彼得森

Email 這樣寫也行！

① 這批貨物的損壞起因於我方員工的粗心大意。
The damage of this cargo is caused by our employee's carelessness.

② 這些損壞的貨物讓我們感到非常苦惱。
The damage goods already made us very annoyed.

③ 這批貨物的損壞導致我們延遲客人的交貨日期。
The damage of the goods caused delayed delivery to our customer.

④ 我們想知道您們會在何時、何種方式賠償我們的損失。
We want to know how and when you will compensate our loss.

⑤ 我們認為運費必須由您方支付。
We think freight charge must be on your account.

⑥ 我們覺得瑕疵品太多了。
We feel that there are too many defective items.

⑦ 恐怕您必須再等幾天才能將其餘的貨物交齊。
I am afraid that you need to wait for few days longer for us to deliver the remaining goods.

⑧ 我們發現有將近 15% 的包裝已破損。
We found that nearly 15% of the package is broken.

08【回應】投訴商品瑕疵

照著抄～ Email 簡單搞定！

範例 1

Re : Some goods are defective in order...

Dear Mr. Hill,

We are sorry to learn that you have received some defective good.

In spite of the fact that we checked carefully before packing the goods, the mistakes were still made. We assure you that this **will not be repeated**.

I will **transfer this information to our related department** and reply to you as soon as possible.

We regret for the inconvenience caused.

Yours faithfully,
Roger Brown

SEND

回覆：這批訂單的商品有一些有瑕疵

敬愛的希爾先生：

本公司很遺憾得知您收到的一些商品有瑕疵。

儘管我們在貨物整箱之前仔細檢查過，但仍然出錯。 我們向您保證**不會再犯**。

我會**將此這些資訊轉交給我們的相關部門**，並儘速向您回覆。

對此造成的不便，我們深表遺憾。

誠摯的祝福，

羅傑‧布朗

Re： Some goods are defective in order...

Dear Mr. Peterson,

Thank you for bringing the matter to our notice. We regret to learn that you have received some broken goods.

We are arranging to ***refund your money***; therefore, ***return*** those broken vases and defective ones to us.

We assure you that this will not be repeated.

Yours faithfully,
Tom John

SEND

回覆：這批訂單的商品有一些有瑕疵

親愛的彼得森先生：

謝謝您提醒我們注意此事。 得知您收到了一些貨物有瑕疵，我們深感遺憾。

我們正在安排**退款**；因此，麻煩將那些碎掉和有瑕疵的花瓶**寄還**給我們。

我們向您保證不會再犯。

您真誠地，

湯姆 · 約翰

Email 這樣寫也行！

① 我們已經收到您 12 月 20 日寄來的信。

We have received your letter dated 20th December.

② 我們將會更換這些產品。

We will replace them.

③ 請扣除相關運費。

Please deduct the freight charges incurred on you.

④ 我們確保您將來提供最好的服務。

We assure you of our best service in the future.

⑤ 我們正安排更換這些瑕疵品。

We are arranging to replace the defective goods.

⑥ 謝謝您讓我們注意到這個問題。

Thank you for having called our attention to this matter.

⑦ 對於造成的不便，我深感歉意。

I apologize for the inconvenience caused to you.

⑧ 我們會盡快與您連繫。

We will contact you shortly.

09 匯款延遲的道歉

照著抄 ～ Email 簡單搞定！   — ⤢ ✕

範例 1

Title : We are sorry for the late payment.

Dear Mr. White,

I am terribly sorry for the 10-day *delayed remittance* to you. I think there is no point in finding any excuse for this. The reason why we delay it is that *the sales volume of our wines has dropped* during this economic downturn. I do hope that you can understand it.

I ensure that you will receive the remittance on time in the future. Thank you for your understanding and patience.

Yours sincerely,
Jack Seltzer

SEND   A 🖊 🔗 ☺

主旨：對於延期付款感到很抱歉

親愛的懷特先生：

非常抱歉我們逾期 10 天才能付清帳款。我無法為此找藉口。我們之所以**延遲匯款**是因為在這次的經濟低迷中，我們的**葡萄酒銷量驟減**。希望您能理解。

我保證以後您會準時收到匯款。謝謝您的理解和耐心。

您誠摯地，
傑克·薩爾茨

照著抄～ Email 簡單搞定！

Title : We are sorry for the late payment.

Dear Mr. Wright,

I am terribly sorry for 12-day delayed remittance to you. This is because **the photocopiers are not yet sold**, nor are they likely to be for some time. Anyway, please accept our sincere apology.

I ensure that it will not happen in the future. I appreciate your understanding and forgiveness.

Yours faithfully,
Bob Jones

SEND

主旨：對於延期付款感到很抱歉

親愛的賴特先生：

非常抱歉我們逾期 12 天才能付清帳款。由於**影印機尚未售出**，近期也難有可能售出。不管怎樣，請接受我們誠摯地歉意。

我保證以後再也不會發生這樣的事情了。非常感謝您的諒解。

您真誠地，

鮑伯‧瓊斯

Email 這樣寫也行！

① 這麼晚才給您匯款，我們感到非常抱歉。

We are terribly sorry for remitting you so late.

② 對於匯款延遲我們感到非常抱歉。

We feel very sorry for the late remittance.

③ 非常感謝您的理解。

Thank you very much for your understanding.

④ 我們的貨物目前還未賣完。

So far our goods have not been sold out.

⑤ 不管怎樣，請接受我們誠摯地歉意。

Anyway, please accept our earnest apology.

⑥ 請接受我們對於此次匯款延遲的真心道歉。

Please accept our sincere apology for this late remittance.

⑦ 我們保證這樣的延遲不會再發生。

We are sure that such delay won't happen again.

⑧ 今後我們會盡最大努力避免匯款延遲。

We will try our best to avoid late remittance from now on.

10【回應】匯款延遲的道歉

照著抄 ～ Email 簡單搞定！ — ⤢ ✕

範例 1

Re : We are sorry for the late payment.

Dear Seltzer,

I am contacting you for the following reason. At present, we cannot fulfill the request of your late payment.

Our account department needs to prepare ***the balance sheet for the accounted month***, so please contact us immediately. We will discuss this matter further.

We look forward to receiving your payment by July 20th at the very latest. Hope to get a prompt reply from you.

Yours sincerely,
Steve White

SEND   A Ⅱ 🔗 ☺

中譯

回覆：對於延期付款感到很抱歉

薩爾茨先生您好：

本公司基於以下原因與您聯繫。 目前，我們無法同意貴司匯款延遲的要求。

我們會計部門需要準備**編制月份資產負債表**，所以請立即與我們聯絡。我們將進一步討論這件事。

我們期待在 7 月 20 日之前收到您的付款。希望盡快得到回覆。

您誠摯地，
史帝夫·懷特

Re : We are sorry for the late payment.

Dear Mr. Jones,

I am replying to your letter dated October 15 in which you requested the late payment.

We are sorry for not having replied earlier.

We have appreciated the good business relationship we have had with your company, so we *agree to this request*.

Please let me know if you have any questions.

Yours faithfully,
Adam Wright

SEND

回覆：對於延期付款感到很抱歉

親愛的瓊斯先生，

我寫信回覆您於 10 月 15 日的來信，信中您提到要求匯款延遲。

很抱歉沒早點答應。

本公司對和貴公司之間彼此的商業關係良好深感謝意，因此我們**同意此要求**。

若有任何問題，請告知。

您誠摯地，

亞當‧賴特

Email 這樣寫也行！

① 我寫信的目的是回覆您的來信。

I am writing to you in reply to your letter.

② 我們相信延遲付款問題很快能獲得解決。

We trust that the late payment problem will soon be resolved.

③ 對於匯款延遲我們感到非常不便。

We feel inconvenient for the late remittance.

④ 請盡最大努力避免匯款延遲。

Do your best to prevent the late payment.

⑤ 我們期待繼續維持商業關係。

We look forward to a continued business relationship.

⑥ 我們接受貴司對於此次匯款延遲的真心道歉。

We accept your sincere apology for this late remittance.

⑦ 期待接到您迅速地回覆。

Looking forward to receiving your prompt reply.

⑧ 請即刻與我聯繫。

Please do not hesitate to contact me.

11 商品毀損的道歉

照著抄 ～ Email 簡單搞定！

範例 1

Title : We are sorry for the damaged items.

Dear Mr. Smith,

We are very sorry to hear that certain goods were **damaged** in the shipment. Our director instructed us to take care of it very carefully the moment he got the news.

Therefore, could you please tell us **all the details**? The more we know, the faster we can respond.

Your assistance will be greatly appreciated, and we look forward to your early reply.

Yours sincerely,
John Diamond

SEND

 中譯

主旨：對於毀損的商品我們感到很抱歉

親愛的史密斯先生：

運往貴公司的貨物出現了商品**毀損**，我們感到十分抱歉。我們主管一聽到這個消息就指示我們要好好處理這件事。

因此可以告知我們**全部的詳情**嗎？我們瞭解得越多，回覆就越快。

如果您方能儘早回覆，我們將不勝感激。

您誠摯地，

約翰‧戴蒙

照著抄 ～ Email 簡單搞定！

範例2

Title : We are sorry for the damaged items.

Dear Ms. Robert,

We are extremely sorry to hear that the glass you ordered was broken during transportation.

We have instructed the shipping company to handle them very carefully, but something obviously went wrong *in the containers*.

Please wait while I am *negotiating* with the shipping company about how to settle the matter best.

Yours truly,
Mary Brown

SEND

 中譯

主旨：對於毀損的商品我們感到很抱歉

親愛的羅伯特女士：

得知您訂購的玻璃製品在運輸中毀損一事，我們感到非常遺憾。

我們曾指示船運公司要多加小心，但顯然在**貨櫃**中出了一些問題。

我方正在與船運公司進行**交涉**，如何好好地解決此事，這段時間請您等待我們的回覆。

您真誠地，

瑪麗·布朗

① 我們保證這樣的失誤再也不會發生。

We promise that such error will not happen again.

② 我們當然會為您更換貨品。

We will certainly exchange your goods.

③ 對於此次您的貨品毀損，請接受我們誠摯地道歉。

Please accept our whole-hearted apologies for damaging your products.

④ 給您造成不必要的麻煩我感到很抱歉。

I make an apology for causing you unnecessary trouble.

⑤ 對於運輸中損傷了您的貨物我向您道歉。

I do apologize for damaging your goods during the transportation.

⑥ 我們會儘快解決此事。

We will settle the matter as soon as possible.

⑦ 為我們運輸中的疏忽向您誠摯地道歉。

Please accept my sincere apology for our carelessness during the shipment.

⑧ 非常抱歉毀損了您訂購的貨物。

I am so sorry for damaging the goods you ordered.

12 【回應】商品毀損的道歉

照著抄 ～ Email 簡單搞定！　　　　　　　　— ⟋ ✕

範例 1

Re : We are sorry for the damaged items.

Dear Mr. Diamond,

I have received the package, but we would like to bring it to your knowledge that *five of them* were damaged.

I am sending broken items back to you with this letter. Please settle the matter as soon as possible.

We look forward to your early reply.

Your sincerely,

Bill Smith

SEND　　　　　　　　　　　　　　　　　　A ⋃ ⟨⟩ ☺

 中譯

回覆：對於毀損的商品我們感到很抱歉

戴蒙先生您好：

我已經收到包裹，但是我們讓您知道，其中有**五件商品**已經毀損。

我會將毀損商品寄還給您。請儘快解決這件事。

我們期待您盡速回覆。

您誠摯地，

比爾・史密斯

Re : We are sorry for the damaged items.

Dear Mrs. Brown,

Thanks for your letter. We were expecting a perfect delivery, but it was not what we expected. We are sorry that we cannot wait for your negotiation with the shipping company.

If you **fail to replace** these broken items in the next week, we will **cancel** this order. Please improve your services in the future.

We are looking for your response.

Yours truly,

Alce Robert,

SEND

回覆：對於毀損的商品我們感到很抱歉

親愛的布朗女士：

謝謝您的來信。我們期待完美交貨，然而這並非我們所期望。很抱歉，我們無法等待您方與船運公司談判的結果。

如果您**無法**於下週前**更換**這些毀損商品，我們將**取消**此訂單。今後請改善您的服務。我們期待您的回信。

您真誠地，

艾莉絲・羅伯特

Email 這樣寫也行！

① 最近我已經收到訂購商品。

We have got my order recently.

② 檢查過包裹後，發現我們訂購的玻璃製品已毀損。

I have checked the package, and found the glass we ordered was broken.

③ 運送中造成的商品毀損，我們深感不滿。

We are not satisfied with damaging our goods during the transportation.

④ 期待在下週收到新的商品 。

We are looking forward to receiving the new products within the next week.

⑤ 請在下週內更換那些毀損商品。

Please replace these broken items in the next week.

⑥ 請儘快解決此問題。

Please solve this matter on urgent.

⑦ 我們期待您的回覆。

We are looking for your reply.

⑧ 請隨時撥打 0800-000-000 與我聯繫。

Please feel free to contact me on my number 0800-000-000.

13 開錯發票的道歉

範例 1 **Title : Sincere apology for the wrong invoice.**

Dear Mr. King,
I am writing to apologize to you for issuing an incorrect invoice. As you said, the sum on it is $2500 instead of $2700. It is not your fault, but entirely our own.
We ***promise to revise the sum and deliver a right one to you at once***.
Please inform us when you receive it.
Thank you very much for your kind assistance!

Yours sincerely,
Susan Lee

SEND

主旨：對於錯誤的發票，致上最深的歉意

親愛的金先生：

此信是為開錯了發票向您道歉。正如您所說的，上面的金額應該是 2500 美金而不是 2700 美金。這不是您的問題，完全是我們自己的過錯。

我們**保證修改金額並立刻將正確的發票寄送給您**。

請您收到的時候告知我們一聲。非常感謝您的幫助！

您誠摯地，

蘇珊‧李

Title : Sincere apology for the wrong invoice.

Dear Mr. Cruise,

I am deeply sorry to tell you that, as you pointed out, we have made a mistake on our invoice NO. 6751258. I do apologize for any inconvenience it may cause.

We have remedied the situation by ***issuing a new invoice***, which will be sent to you by ***express delivery*** today.

We have taken measures to ensure that such error will not happen again.

Yours sincerely,
WT Co.

SEND

主旨：對於錯誤的發票，致上最深的歉意

親愛的克魯斯先生：

非常抱歉告訴您，正如您指出的，發票編號 6751258 出了錯，為此給您帶來不便我在此向您道歉。

我們已經改正此次錯誤，**重開了一張發票**，會在今天用**快遞**將發票寄出。

我們已經採取措施來保證此類錯誤不再發生。

您真誠地，
WT 公司

① 我們立刻給您重開發票。

We will issue the invoice for you at once.

② 您的發票的確是開錯了。

Your invoice was indeed in error.

③ 我們今天已經將正確的發票寄給您了。

We have delivered the right invoice to you today.

④ 我們會竭盡所能地杜絕此類錯誤發生。

We will make every effort to avoid such errors.

⑤ 對於開錯發票，我們向您真誠地道歉。

We do apologize for issuing the wrong invoice.

⑥ 我們保證這樣的錯誤不會再發生。

We promise that such mistake will not happen again.

⑦ 對於發票上的錯誤我們感到非常抱歉。

We feel terribly sorry for the error on the invoice.

⑧ 對於可能給您帶來的不便，請接受我們真誠地道歉。

Please accept our sincere apology for the inconvenience that may have been caused.

14【回應】開錯發票的道歉

範例 1

Re : Sincere apology for the wrong invoice.

Dear Mrs. Lee,

I am writing to inform you that we received the wrong invoice today.In fact, I have received the letter that you sent me regarding the wrong invoice.

Please revise the sum and deliver a right one to us at once. I would appreciate it if you could please reply **_as soon as possible_**.

I look forward to receiving your invoice.

Yours sincerely,
Mark King

SEND　　　　　　　　　　　　　　　　A ⌀ ⊝ ☺

中譯

回覆：對於錯誤的發票，致上最深的歉意

親愛的李女士：

寫這封信是通知您，我們今天收到錯誤發票。事實上，我也收到您寄給我關於開錯發票的信。

請修改金額並**盡速**寄給我們。如果您能儘快回復，我將不勝感激。

期待收到您的發票。

您誠摯地，

馬克・金

Re : Sincere apology for the wrong invoice.

To whom it may concern,

This letter is in reference to the apology for the wrong invoice letter that had been sent to us on 12th July, 2021.

We are writing to inform you that we have accepted your apologies. Please send us the **correct invoice** as soon as possible. In the future, we expect that such a mistake will never happen.

We look forward to your reply.

Yours sincerely,
Tommy Cruise

SEND   A ‖ ⟨⟩ ☺

回覆：對於錯誤的發票，致上最深的歉意

敬啟者：

這封信是關於 2021 年 7 月 12 日，您寄給我們因發票開錯的道歉信。

我們寫信通知您，我們接受您的道歉。請盡速將**正確發票**寄給我們。未來，我們期望此類錯誤不再發生。

我們期待著您的答覆。

您誠摯地，

湯米‧克魯斯

Email 這樣寫也行！

① 我方因為以下問題聯繫您。

I am contacting you for the following question.

② 請盡速將正確的發票寄給我們。

Please deliver a right voice to us as soon as possible.

③ 請盡力避免發生這樣的錯誤。

Please make every effort to avoid such mistakes.

④ 對於造成的不便，我們接受您們真誠地道歉。

We've accepted your sincere apology for the inconvenience.

⑤ 如果貴司能在兩天內寄出正確發票，我們將不勝感激。

We would appreciate it if you would send the correct invoice within two days.

⑥ 以後請更注意防止發生這樣的錯。

Please pay more attention to prevent such mistakes in the future

⑦ 請採取措施來保證此類錯誤不再發生。

Please take measures to ensure that such error will not happen again.

⑧ 期待您的立即回覆。

Looking forward to your prompt reply.

PART 6
公告通知

因各家手機系統不同，若無法直接掃描，仍可以（https://tinyurl.com/4z8rxhpj）電腦連結雲端下載，一貼搞定！

Part 6. 公告通知

01 樣品寄送通知

範例 1

Title : [Notification] Samples have been sent.

Dear Mr. Schofield,

I am advising you that the **samples** you requested were shipped this morning by Federal Express.

I have attached **a price list** and **color swatches**, too.

Please inform me as soon as they are delivered. Thank you very much.

I am looking forward to your earliest feedback.

Yours sincerely,

Benny Stone

DB Co.

SEND

主旨：〔通知〕樣品已寄出

親愛的斯科菲爾德先生：

在此通知您索取的**樣品**已經於今天早上委託聯邦快遞寄出。

我把**價格表**和**顏色樣本**也附在裡面。如果收到貨物，請即時通知我。非常感謝！

期待您的回覆。

您真誠地，

班尼‧史東

DB 公司

照著抄 ～ Email 簡單搞定！ — ⤢ ✕

 Title : [Notification] Samples have been sent.

Dear Sirs,

Thank you very much for your letter of April 11th.
We are pleased to send you all samples, which you requested, by another air mail. Please do not hesitate to place your ***initial order*** if our samples meet your satisfaction. We are ready to serve you at any time.
I should be grateful if you respond soon.

Yours sincerely,
Sandra Brown
I O U Company

SEND   A 🖉 🔗 ☺

主旨：〔通知〕樣品已寄出

敬啟者：

感謝您 4 月 11 日之來函。

本公司已透過另一航空郵件送上您所需之各種樣品。請勿猶豫惠賜**首筆訂單**。如此次寄送之樣品供試滿意，本公司隨時為您服務。

若蒙早日賜覆則不勝感謝。

您真誠地，

珊卓‧布朗

I O U 公司

Part 6. 公告通知 | 287

Email 這樣寫也行！

① 樣品一旦作好，我們就會馬上寄給您。

Once the swatches are made, we will send you at once.

② 我們今天早上已經寄出您要的樣品了。

We have shipped the sample this morning.

③ 我們已經透過聯邦快遞把您要的樣品寄給您了。

We have shipped the sample you requested by Federal Express.

④ 只要您有需要，樣品會立即寄去。

Sample will be present to you immediately upon request.

⑤ 如果樣品到達，請馬上通知我們。

Please inform us as soon as they arrived.

⑥ 我們寄送的樣品 3 個工作日即可送到。

The samples we sent will reach you within 3 working days.

⑦ 我等著您的回覆。

I am waiting for your feedback.

⑧ 我們正在寄送樣品，徵求顧客意見。

We are sending out samples in the hope of receiving comments.

02【回應】樣品寄送通知

照著抄～ Emgil 簡單搞定！

 Re : [Notification] Samples have been sent.

Dear Mr. Stone,

I am writing to let you know how delighted I was to receive my samples I requested.

I've received the samples this morning. I am **satisfied** with their quality. I would like to **place an order later this week**.

Thank you very much.

Looking forward to doing good business with you.

Yours sincerely,

Jay Schofield

SEND   A ⁞ ⊖ ☺

回覆：〔通知〕樣品已寄出

史東先生您好：

寫信是為了告知您，很高興收到索取的樣品。

我在今天早收到樣品。對樣品的品質感到**滿意**。我想**這星期晚點會訂購**。

非常感謝您。

期待與您建立良好業務關係。

您真誠地，

杰‧斯科菲爾德

Re : [Notification] Samples have been sent.

Dear Mrs. Brown,

Thank you very much for your samples. We are pleased to receive all samples this morning.

We are **interested** in the new products including reasonable prices. Additionally, we need a **salesman** to help us out with our questions about your new products.

We will then place an order later.

I will appreciate prompt response.

Yours sincerely,
Mark Jordan

SEND

回覆：〔通知〕樣品已寄出

布朗女士您好：

非常感謝您的樣品。我們很高興今天上午收到所有樣品。

我們對合理價格的新產品**有興趣**。另外，我們需要**業務人員**來幫助我們解決新產品的問題。

我們稍後會下單。

對於您的迅速回覆，深感謝意。

您真誠地，

馬克‧喬丹

Email 這樣寫也行！

① 今天下午我們已收到貴司寄來的樣品。
We've received your samples this afternoon.

② 請以便宜的價格提供我們這項商品。
Please make this product available to us at a meager price.

③ 歡迎隨時與我聯繫。
You are always the most welcome to contact us.

④ 我今天已經收到您寄出的樣品了。
I have received the samples today.

⑤ 我們想知道更多關於產品和價格的細節部分。
We'd like to know more details about the product and pricelist.

⑥ 期待佳音。
Looking forward to a favorable reply.

⑦ 感謝您的時間和體諒。
Thank you for your time and consideration.

⑧ 我希望貴方能緊急處理這張訂單。
We hope that you treat this order with urgency.

03 通知客戶價格調整

範例 1

Title : Price adjustment notification.

Dear customers,

I am writing this letter to inform you we have adjusted price for our products.

About **40 % of our products price are increased**.

I apologize for the inconvenience. You can please visit our website for more information and the details.

Thanks for your understanding.

Sincerely,

Roger Smith

Winner Furniture

SEND

A

中譯

主旨：價格調整通知

親愛的客戶：

寫這封信是想通知您，本公司的商品已經調整價格。

大約有四成的商品都調漲。

對於您的不便，我深表歉意。想了解更多資訊和細節方面，請參考我們的官網。

感謝您的體諒。

真誠地，

羅傑‧史密斯

勝利者家具

照著抄 ～ Email 簡單搞定！　　　　　— ⤢ ✕

範例2　**Title : Price adjustment notification.**

Dear customers,

Please accept this letter as notification of a pricing adjustment which will be effective on December 31st, 2021.

We do regret we have to make such a decision. ***A summary of price changes*** is attached with this email.

Should you have any questions, please feel free to contact Mr. Brown at 0900-000-000.

Yours truly,
Neil Simpson

SEND　　　　　　　　　　　　　　　A ⋃ ⊖ ☺

主旨：價格調整通知

親愛的客戶：

這封信是定價調整通知，將於 2021 年 12 月 31 日起生效。

我們很遺憾必須做此決定。電子郵件內的附加檔是**價格調整的清單總覽**。

如您有任何疑問，請隨時和布朗先生聯繫，電話是 0900-000-000。

謹致，
尼爾‧辛普森

Email 這樣寫也行！

① 我們想對您的全然體諒表示感謝。

We'd like to thank you for all your understanding.

② 我們提供您公司高規格服務。

We provide you with our high quality.

③ 如果有任何需要替您服務之處，請讓我們知道。

Please let us know if there is anything we can do for you.

④ 2022 年 1 月 1 日起價格將全面調整。

The new price will take effect from January 1st, 2022.

⑤ 附件是我們新的價格清單。

Enclosed is our new price list.

⑥ 感謝您了解，關於價格調漲的確是有其必要性。

Thanks for your understanding that this price increasing is certainly necessary.

⑦ 我們感謝您理解我們做出此決定的原因為何。

We appreciate you understand the reasons for our decision.

⑧ 想知道更多資訊，請撥辦公室專線號碼 111-1111。

For further information, please contact our office at 111-1111.

04【回應】通知客戶價格調整

 照著抄 ～ Email 簡單搞定！

範例 1

Re : Price adjustment notification.

Dear Mr. Smith,

We have come to know about your notification of increasing the price for our products.

We respect your concerns. However, we are keeping the cost down because of the company's policies. I would like to ***cancel the order which was placed earlier*** this week. The order number is 5438A.

Hope you understand our concerns.

Warm Regards,
Fanny Tyler

SEND

中譯

回應：價格調整通知

親愛的史密斯先生：

我們已收到貴公司商品調漲價格的通知。

我們尊重您的想法。然而，由於公司的政策，我們正致力於降低成本。因此我方**想取消本週稍早前的訂單**。訂單編號是 5438A。

希望您能理解我們的顧慮。

感謝體諒。

真誠地，
芬妮・泰勒

範例 2

Re : Price adjustment notification.

Dear Mr. Simpson,

We have received your letter of price adjustment dated October 1st. We have been a longtime customer of your company. We are disappointed to see that you have raised your price.

Moreover, we **can't find** a summary of price changes attached with this email.

If you would like to discuss with me, please **feel free to contact me**.

Looking forward to your positive response.

Yours truly,

Willy Thomas

SEND   A ⎗ ⊝ ☺

中譯

回應：價格調整通知

親愛的辛普森先生：

已知悉貴公司 10 月 1 日寄來的訂價調整。我們是貴公司的老客戶。

看到您提高價格，我們深感失望。

另外，我們在電子郵件內**找不到**價格調整的清單。

如果想和我討論這方面問題，請**隨時與我聯絡**。

期待您的積極回覆。

謹致，

威力‧湯瑪斯

Email 這樣寫也行！

① 已收到貴公司 10 月 1 日寄來的調價通知。

I've received your letter of October 1st in regard to the price adjustment notification.

② 我很遺憾得知貴公司調高價格。

I was sorry to know that you have increased your prices.

③ 我認為這可能是個錯誤決定。

I believe that it may be a mistake.

④ 我想與您討論這類情況。

We'd like to discuss this situation with you.

⑤ 一看到這封信，請將新的價格清單寄給我。

Please send your new price list once you've received this letter.

⑥ 我要求請您取消我方訂單。

I request you to cancel my order.

⑦ 我負擔不起這樣的價格。

I can no longer afford these prices.

⑧ 很抱歉造成您的不便。

I am sorry for the inconvenience caused.

05 人員變動通知

範例 1

Title : Personnel shifting announcement.

Dear Colleagues,

We are very pleased to announce, effective from today, the appointment of Stephen Browne as Chief Information Officer to our company.

Mr. Browne possesses **ten years of experience in the information technology sector** and his extensive knowledge and experience will bring invaluable asset to our company.

Please join us in welcoming Mr. Browne to our company!

Yours faithfully,
Daniel Lincoln

SEND   A ⏐ ⊖ ☺

 中譯

主旨：人事調動公告

各位同事：
我們非常高興地宣布，本公司的資訊部總監將由史蒂芬‧布朗先生擔任，當日生效。
布朗先生在**資訊技術**方面擁有**長達 10 年的相關工作經驗**。他豐富的知識和閱歷將會為公司帶來不可估量的價值。
請大家一起為布朗先生加入我公司致以熱烈的歡迎！

您真誠地，
丹尼爾‧林肯

照著抄 ～ Email 簡單搞定！

範例 2

Title : Personnel shifting announcement.

Dear Sir or Madam,

As you know, Mr. Turner has been promoted to Sales Manager for our New Zealand office. As a result, Mr. Smith will be your new Account Executive. Mr. Smith has been working in our Sales Department for more than four years and *is experienced in computer-related products* like yours. We believe he will do an excellent job in servicing your account.

If you have any questions, please feel free to ask him.

He will contact with you in these few days.

Willy Bullock
Candia Company

SEND

中譯

主旨：人事調動公告

敬啟者：

如您所知，特納先生已經調升為紐西蘭分公司的業務經理。因此史密斯先生將成為服務貴公司的業務專員。史密斯先生在本公司業務部服務 4 年多了，對於貴公司這樣的**電腦相關產品經驗十分豐富**。

相信他會做得更好。

如有任何問題，請儘管與他聯繫。

他這幾天將會與您聯絡。

威力・布拉克
甘地亞公司

① 我非常榮幸向大家宣布一個任命通知。

It is with great pleasure for me to announce an appointment.

② 我很高興地宣布安德里亞將被任命為我們的財務主管。

I am pleased to announce that Adrian will be appointed as our Chief Financial Officer.

③ 他擁有豐富的知識和經驗。

He has broad knowledge and rich experience.

④ 很高興宣布任命貝爾先生為總經理。

We are pleased to announce the appointment of Mr. Bell as our new General Manager.

⑤ 李教授已經在商學院任教 13 年了。

Professor Lee has served for 13 years in the Faculty of Commerce Institute.

⑥ 他將為我們公司創造無法估量的價值。

He will certainly be an invaluable asset to our company.

⑦ 班已為我公司服務了 20 年，將於本月退休。

Ben will be retiring at the end of this month after 20 years service.

⑧ 請大家為史密斯夫人加入我公司致以熱烈歡迎。

Please join us in welcoming Ms. Smith to our company.

06【回應】人員變動通知

範例 1

Re : Personnel shifting announcement.

Dear Mr. Lincoln,
It gives us immense joy in accepting the the appointment of
Stephen Browne of Chief Information Officer to our company.
We believe Mr. Browne's extensive knowledge and
experience **will lead** our company **more successful**.
Our confidence in his abilities means a great deal to us.
I'd like to welcome Mr. Browne to our company.

Yours faithfully,
Harry Freeman

SEND   A 🖉 ⊝ ☺

 中譯

回覆：人事調動公告

林肯先生您好：

我們非常高興地接受資訊部總監將由史蒂芬‧布朗先生擔任。

我們相信布朗先生豐富的知識和經驗**將帶領**本公司**大獲成功**。我們對他能力充滿信心，這點意義重大。

熱烈歡迎布朗先生加入本公司。

您真誠地，

哈利‧費里曼

Re : Personnel shifting announcement.

Dear Mr. Bullock,

We heard Mr. Smith will be your new Account Executive. Mr. Smith has been working in your Sales Department for more than four years. We believe that his experience in computer-related products are ***professional and knowledgeable***. We believe Mr. Smith can use his skills in making the service reach new heights.

We are looking forward to his reply.

Yours, truly
Doris Hansen

SEND   A ⓤ ⊖ ☺

回覆：人事調動公告

布拉克先生您好：

我們得知史密斯先生將擔任新的業務專員。史密斯先生在業務部工作了 4 年以上。

我們相信他在電腦相關產品的經驗**非常專業而且知識淵博**。

我們相信史密斯先生可以藉由技能使服務達到新高度。

我們期待他的答覆。

謹誌，

朵莉絲・韓森

Email 這樣寫也行！

① 他在會計部工作已經五年了。

He has been working in your Account Department for five years.

② 史密斯有善於和他人溝通的能力。

Mr. Smith has the ability to communicate well with people.

③ 我們很高興知道艾瑪將被任命為我們的總經理。

We are pleased to know that Emma will be appointed as our general manager.

④ 很高興得知您們已經任命羅伯特女士為經理。

We are pleased to know you have appointed Mrs. Roberts as your new manager.

⑤ 他將會替您們小組創造寶貴的價值。

He will be an invaluable asset to your team.

⑥ 他擁有非常豐富的經驗。

He has a huge amount of experience.

⑦ 瓊斯先生已經在快樂公司任職超過 10 年了。

Mr. Jones has served for over 10 years in the Happy Company.

⑧ 史密斯先生將是能完成任務的最佳人選。

Mr. Smith is going to be a best asset who can accomplish tasks.

07 公司搬遷通知

範例 1

Title : [Notification] Address information update.

Dear Customers,

We are pleased to announce that our company will **move to** International Building, Room 2317 at Futong Street from June 23rd, 2010.

Our email address remains unchanged and mail should now be addressed to Post Office Box NO.312.

On behalf of our company, I'd like to take this opportunity to express our gratitude for your continued support and attention.

Yours faithfully,
Stephen
BBC Corporation

SEND   A Ⓘ ⊖ ☺

主旨：〔通知〕更新地址

親愛的客戶：

我們很高興地宣布，本公司自 2010 年 6 月 23 日起將**遷往**富通街國際大廈 2317 室。

我們的電子信箱保持不變，郵件地址將變更為 312 號信箱。

我代表公司藉此機會，對各位一如既往的支持和關注表示感謝。

您忠實地，
史蒂芬
BBC 公司

照著抄 ～ Email 簡單搞定！ — ⤢ ✕

範例 2

Title : [Notification] Address information update.

Dear Sir or Madam,
This is to inform you that our company is going to move to a new place in Da-an District of Taipei on and after June 28th, 2010. The new address is as below:
KBS Company
7/F, No. 7, Zhong Xiao East Road Sec.4, Da-an District, Taipei City, Taiwan, R.O.C.
Phone number, fax number and email address are without change. ***Please revise your records*** and send all your new correspondence to the above new address.
Thanks and best regards.

Adam Brown
KBS Company

SEND   A ◊ ⌯ ☺

 中譯

主旨：〔通知〕更新地址

敬啟者：
茲通知各位本公司自 2010 年 6 月 28 日起將搬遷到臺北市大安區。新地址如下：
KBS 公司
臺北市大安區忠孝東路四段 7 號 7 樓
電話號碼、傳真號碼和電子信箱都保持不變。請**即時修改您的記錄**，並將信件寄送至新的地址。
感謝並致以最美祝福，

亞當‧布朗
KBS 公司

① 非常高興地宣布我們要搬到遠大大廈了。

I am very happy to announce that we are going to move to Yuan Da Building.

② 請記下我們的新地址。

Please remember our new address.

③ 我們的電子郵件沒變。

Our email address stays the same.

④ 感謝您繼續予以支持和幫助。

Thank you for your continued support and kind help.

⑤ 電話號碼並無變動。

Telephone number will not be changed.

⑥ 請保持聯絡。

Please keep in touch with us.

⑦ 我們要搬家了。

We are going to move.

⑧ 我藉此機會宣布搬遷通知。

We take the opportunity to make a relocation announcement.

08 【回應】公司搬遷通知

 範例 1

Re : [Notification] Address information update.

Dear Stephen,

Thank you so much for your announcement that our company will move to International Building, Room 2317 at Futong Street. We will send a letter to **Post Office Box NO.312** next time.

Additionally, We will support you at anytime.

Good wishes for your new office move.

Yours faithfully,
Stanley Jordan

SEND   A ⫶ 🔗 ☺

 中譯

回覆：〔通知〕更新地址

親愛的史帝芬：

非常感謝您通知我們，貴公司將搬到富通街國際大廈 2317 室。下次寄信我們將會寄到 **312 號郵政信箱**。

此外，我們隨時支持貴公司。

祝新辦公室搬遷愉快。

您忠實地，
史丹利‧喬丹

照著抄 ～ Email 簡單搞定！

Re : [Notification] Address information update.

Dear Mr. Brown,

We are happy to have received your letter of your new location. Your registered office address has change under: 7/F, No. 7, Zhong Xiao East Road Sec.4, Da-an District, Taipei City, Taiwan, R.O.C.

We will *update* our records as soon as possible.

If there are any questions regarding the change of your new address or information, *when can you best be reached?*

Thank you for your assistance.

With best regards,
Frank Jackson

SEND

回覆：〔通知〕更新地址

布朗先生您好：

我們很高興收到您的來信。貴公司辦公室地址更改如下：

臺北市大安區忠孝東路四段 7 號 7 樓

我們會即時**更新**您的記錄。

如果對新地址更改或資訊有任何疑問，請問**何時方便與您聯繫呢？**

謝謝您的協助。

誠摯祝福，

法蘭克・傑克森

Email 這樣寫也行！

① 之後我們信件會寄到您的新地址。

We will send all future communications to your new address.

② 寫這封信的目的是回覆貴公司住址資料更新。

I'm writing in response to your address information update.

③ 謝謝您的通知。

Thank you for your notice.

④ 我們將修改您們的記錄。

Our will make modify our records with you.

⑤ 我們將熟悉您的新地點。

We will get acquainted with your new location.

⑥ 謝謝您盡早通知。

Thank you very much for your early notification.

⑦ 我們很高興與您有業務往來。

We have enjoyed doing business with you.

⑧ 我們已經被告知貴公司已經搬到新大樓。

We have be advised that you have moved to a new building.

09 公司盤點通知

範例 1

Title : Stocktaking notification on (date).

Dear customers,

We would like to inform you that our *annual stocktaking* will be held from December 30th-31st, 2021. During this period, all of our *delivering and receiving operations will be stopped*. Therefore, we would not arrange any goods delivery to your warehouses except under special request by your Purchasing Department before December 22nd, 2021.

We will resume the normal delivering and receiving operations from January 2nd, 2022.

We apologize for any inconvenience caused.

Yours faithfully,
Sean Cage
SITONG Logistics Co.

SEND   A 🔗 ☺

中譯

主旨：於（日期）庫存盤點通知

親愛的客戶：

謹此通知本公司將於 2021 年 12 月 30 日至 31 日進行**年度盤點**，在這期間**所有送貨或收貨之運作都會停止**。因此，除非有特殊要求，我們不會安排運送任何貨物至您們的倉庫，請貴公司的採購部預先在 2021 年 12 月 22 日前告知，敝公司將另行安排。

此外，本公司將於 2022 年 1 月 2 日恢復營運。

不便之處敬請見諒。

您忠實地，
史恩．凱基
四通物流公司

照著抄 ～ Email 簡單搞定！　　　　　　— ⤢ ✕

範例 2

Title : Stocktaking notification on (date).

Dear readers,
Our store's **quarterly stocktaking** will be held from
September 28th-30th, 2021. In addition, we will resume
normal operations on October 1st, 2021, so please arrange
your purchase schedule well.
As it is **a long period** of stocktaking, we do apologize for
causing any inconvenience to you.
Thank you very much for your consideration and support.

Best regards,
Vicky Pitt
Haidian Book City

SEND　　　　　　　　　　　　　　　A 🖉 🔗 ☺

主旨：於（日期）庫存盤點通知

親愛的讀者：
本店將於 2021 年 9 月 28 日到 30 日進行**季度盤點**，並於 2021 年 10 月 1 日恢
復正常營業。請安排好您的購書時間。
由於此次盤點**時間較長**，我們對此次盤點給您帶來的任何不便表示深深的歉意。
非常感謝大家的理解和支持！

最誠摯地問候，
薇琪・彼特
海澱圖書商城

① 我們將於 12 月 28 日至 31 日進行盤點。

We are going to make an inventory from December 28th to 31st.

② 今日盤點，明日照常營業。

Stocktaking today, business as usual tomorrow.

③ 我們這家食品店每週盤點存貨。

Our food store took stock every week.

④ 倉庫暫停營業進行年度存貨盤點。

The warehouse is closed for the annual stocktaking.

⑤ 本商店每月盤點一次存貨。

The store makes an inventory of its stock once a month.

⑥ 我們對各類配件要每月盤點。

We make an inventory of all accessories every month.

⑦ 我們將於 2022 年 1 月 1 日恢復營運。

We will resume the normal delivering from January 1st 2022.

⑧ 如果造成任何不便，我們感到非常抱歉。

We are sorry if it may cause any inconvenience.

10 【回應】公司盤點通知

照著抄 ～ Email 簡單搞定！

範例 1

Re : Stocktaking notification on (date).

Dear Mr. Cage,

The purpose of this letter is to reply to your letter dated December 15th, 2021. It mentioned that all of our delivering and receiving operations will be stopped during this period. However, we will ***arrange some goods delivery to your warehouses on December 30th, 2021***.

Do not hesitate to contact me at 123-4567.

I'm looking forward to your prompt reply.

Yours faithfully,

Molly White

SEND   A 🖉 🔗 ☺

回覆：於（日期）庫存盤點通知

親愛的凱基先生：

此信目的是回覆您 2021 年 12 月 15 日的來信。信中提到這段期間貴公司所有送貨或收貨之運作都會停止。但是，我們將**安排 2021 年 12 月 30 日運送貨物到貴公司倉庫**。

請隨時撥打 123-4567 與我聯繫。

期待您迅速回覆。

您忠實地，

莫莉·懷特

Re : Stocktaking notification on (date).

Dear Mrs. Pitt,

I have received and read the letter which you have sent me regarding the stocktaking notification of September 18th, 2021.

I will arrange my *purchase schedule* well.

Thank you very much for your notification.

Wish you a good day.

Best regards,

Gary Thomas

SEND

回覆：於（日期）庫存盤點通知

彼特女士您好：

我已收到並閱讀您寄來貴公司 2021 年 9 月 18 日盤點的信。

我會安排好我的**採購計畫**。

非常感謝您的通知。

祝您天天開心。

最誠摯地問候，

蓋瑞‧湯瑪士

Email 這樣寫也行！

① 這封是回應您於 2021 年 9 月 15 日寄來的電子郵件。

This is in response to your email dated September 15th, 2021.

② 我們收到您於 2021 年 9 月 15 日寄來的盤點通知。

We received your letter of stocktaking notification dated September 15th, 2021.

③ 本封信的目的是為了回覆您於 2021 年 9 月 15 日的來信。

The purpose of this letter is to reply your letter dated September 15th, 2021.

④ 謝謝您提供的資訊。

Thank you for the information.

⑤ 您提供關於盤點的相關資訊非常有用。

The information you provided about inventory notification has been very helpful.

⑥ 我會記住這幾個重要日期。

I will keep these important dates in mind.

⑦ 我已經收到您寄來電子郵件的資訊。

I have received the information you sent in the email.

⑧ 貴公司盤點後我再去買書。

I will purchase books after your store's quarterly stocktaking.

11 公司暫停營業／破產通知

Title : [Notification] We will have a business suspension.

Dear Sir or Madam,

Our loving friends, we regret to inform you that our **business will be temporarily suspended** on November 11th due to bad state of operation.

However, we have made up our mind to **reopen after we make adjustments inside**. In other words, we are just saying goodbye for a while.

Thank you very much for always supporting us. Welcome the new-old friends' patronage!

Best wishes,
Emma Roberts
VOV Co.

SEND

中譯

主旨：〔通知〕我們將暫停營業

敬啟者：

親愛的朋友，很遺憾通知您，我公司由於慘澹的經營狀況，將於 11 月 11 號**暫停營業**。

不過我們已經下定決心在**內部調整後會重新開業**。換句話說，我們只是短暫的別離。

感謝各位一直以來對我們的支持。歡迎新老朋友再次光臨惠顧！

致以最美的祝福，

艾瑪‧羅伯茲

VOV 公司

Title : Bankruptcy declaration of ... company.

Dear Sir or Madam,
I regret to inform you that our company ***has gone bankrupt*** due to ***financial difficulties***.
We have applied to the court for bankruptcy and set up a liquidation group in accordance with the law.
We hereby remind all creditors to pay attention to the procedure in bankruptcy for your own sake.

Kenny Cruise
NO KIAN Company

SEND

中譯

主旨：……公司宣告破產

敬啟者：
很遺憾地通知您，由於**財務困難**，本公司**已宣告破產**。
我們已經向法院申請破產，現已成立清算小組進行清算資產。
提醒各位債權人，為了您們自己的利益，請對破產程序予以關注。

肯尼‧克魯斯
諾起亞公司

① 我們公司已進入破產狀態。

Our company is going into bankruptcy proceedings.

② 很遺憾地宣布我們已經破產了。

We regret to announce that we have gone bankrupt.

③ 我公司今日正式宣布破產。

Our corporation is officially emerging from bankruptcy today.

④ 要求全體員工嚴格遵守法律規定。

All workers are now required to strictly comply with the law.

⑤ 資產清算小組將會接管所有資產。

The liquidation team will take over all assets.

⑥ 任何人都不得隱匿、私分企業財產。

Everybody shall not conceal nor divide the business property.

⑦ 任何人都不得實施妨害破產清算的行為。

Everybody shall not implement any acts to hold back the liquidation.

⑧ 企業的法定代表人不得擅離職守。

Enterprise's legal representative in bankruptcy shall not be absent from duty.

12 【回應】公司暫停營業／破產通知

照著抄 ～ Email 簡單搞定！

 範例 1

Re : [Notification] We will have a business suspension.

Dear Mrs. Roberts,

I have read your letter dated 1st October 2021. I am sorry hear that your business will be temporarily suspended on November 11th due to bad state of operation.

Indeed, I have fond memories of your company.

We look forward to **resuming operations as soon as possible**.

Always support you.

Sincerely,
Amy Brown

SEND

 中譯

回覆：〔通知〕我們將暫停營業

羅伯茲女士您好：

我已閱讀您 2021 年 10 月 1 日的來信，對於貴店由於慘澹的經營狀況，將於 11 月 11 號暫停營業的消息，我們感到抱歉。

其實，我很喜愛您的公司。

我們期望貴公司**盡快恢復營業**。

永遠支持您。

誠摯問候，
艾咪·布朗

Re : Bankruptcy declaration of ... company.

Dear Mr. Cruise,

I'm sorry to learn that your company has gone bankrupt due to financial difficulties. I understand how frustrating this must have been for you.

I have **contacted an attorney**, Roger Thomas. He is hired to **protect my interests**. Because bankruptcy cases have many deadlines, my attorney will determine how to precede it.

If you have any further information, please contact Mr. Thomas at 0900-383838.

Best wishes,
Lisa Gere

SEND

回覆：……公司宣告破產

克魯斯先生您好：
很遺憾得知貴公司由於財務困難而宣告破產。我理解您的沮喪心情。
我已**聯繫律師**羅傑湯瑪士。聘請用他是為了**保護我的權益**。因為破產案件的截止日期很多，代表律師將決定如何進行破產程序。
如果您有任何其他資訊，請打 0900-383838 與湯瑪士先生聯繫。

謹致，
麗莎‧吉爾

Email 這樣寫也行！

① 很遺憾得知貴公司已進入破產狀態。

I am sorry to hear that your company is going into bankruptcy proceedings.

② 我會試著理解您的情況。

I would try to understand your situation.

③ 我很高興得知您們已下定決心內部調整後會重新開業。

I am pleased to know you have made up your mind to reopen after making adjustments inside.

④ 我的代理人會幫我解決問題。

My attorney isn't helping me out.

⑤ 很遺憾地貴公司已經破產了。

I regret to know that you have gone bankrupt.

⑥ 重新開幕之前請通知我。

Please inform me before you reopen your business.

⑦ 期待您重新開業。

Looking forward to you reopen your business.

⑧ 如果有其他關於貴店的消息，請讓我知曉。

Please let me know if you have any additional news about your store.

PART7

邀請函

因各家手機系統不同，若無法直接掃描，仍可以（https://tinyurl.com/8y8jnp6j）電腦連結雲端下載，一貼搞定！

Part 7.
邀請函

01 邀請出席新品展示會

照著抄 ～ Email 簡單搞定！　　　　　　　　　— ⤢ ✕

範例 1

Title : We will release a new product on (date).

Dear Sir or Madam,

We are delighted to inform you that our company will **hold a press release** for our new products on August 12th, 2021. We believe you will be attracted by some well-designed and **fashionable products**. We are really hoping you will visit us.

Sincerely,
Meg Twain

SEND

主旨：我們將在（日期）發表新產品

先生、女士您好：

很高興地通知您，本公司將在 2021 年 8 月 12 日，**舉行新聞發布會**，發表本公司的新產品。

相信您會被本公司精心設計的**時尚產品**吸引。由衷希望您撥空參與。

真誠地，

梅格·吐溫

照著抄 ～ Email 簡單搞定！ — ↗ ×

範例 2

Title : We will release a new product on (date).

Dear Mrs. Jordan,

Lucky Company is pleased to tell you that our company has scheduled to launch a new product next Friday.

We are hoping you to have a complete and close look at the new product. We therefore send you **an invitation and a pin number**.

After you fill out the registration form and enter the pin number, we will give you **a gift certificate**.

For further information, please confirm with Judy at 383-8538.

We look forward to see you then.

Wendy White

SEND

主旨：我們將在（日期）發表新產品

喬丹女士您好：

幸運公司很高興告訴您，本公司計劃將在下週五推出新產品。

我們希望您能完整並仔細地品味我們的新產品。因此，我們將寄給您**邀請函和密碼**。

填寫登記表之後，請輸入密碼，我們將會贈送給您**禮物兌換券**。

如需進一步資訊，請打 383-8538 跟茱蒂確認。

我們期待再次與您相見。

溫蒂‧懷特

Email 這樣寫也行！

① 我們將發表一個新的購物網站。

We are going to launch a new shopping website.

② 我們相信您會對新產品感興趣。

We believe you will be interested in some new products.

③ 如需要訂購單請與史密斯先生連絡。

For an order form, please contact Mr. Smith.

④ 發表會上將提供各項細節。

Details will be provided on the press release.

⑤ 新產品發表對於公司業務非常重要。

Upcoming product release is very important in our business.

⑥ 感謝您對本公司的忠誠。

Thank you for your loyalty.

⑦ 期待您的迅速回應。

I am looking forward to your early reply.

⑧ 我們業務人員已準備好與您聯繫。

Our salespeople are ready to keep in touch with you.

02 【回應】邀請出席新品展示會

 照著抄 ～ Email 簡單搞定！ — ⤢ ✕

Re : We will release a new product on (date).

Dear Mr. Twain
Thank you so much for inviting me to the press release for your new products on August 12th, 2021.
It sounds like really attractive. I believe your press will be successful.
Unfortunately, I will *go on a business trip* on August 11th. I won't be able to attend this press.

Sincerely,
Sean Brown

SEND

 中譯

回覆：我們將在（日期）發表新產品

吐溫先生您好：
非常感謝您邀請我 2021 年 8 月 12 日，舉行新產品的新聞發布會。
聽起來真的非常吸引人。我相信新聞發布會將會大獲成功。
遺憾地是，我將在 8 月 11 日**出差**。因此將無法參加這次新聞發布會。

真誠地，
史恩‧布朗

範例 2 Re : We will release a new product on (date).

Dear Mrs. White,

Thank you so much for sending me an invitation and a pin number.

I have been a loyal customer of your company since 2018. However, I have some problem for filling out the registration form. ***Obviously the PIN number didn't work.***

Please help me solve this problem in detail.

Looking forward to your reply.

Best wishes,

Emily Jordan

SEND   A 📎 🔗 😊

 中譯

回覆：我們將在（日期）發表新產品

親愛的懷特夫人：

非常感謝您寄來的邀請函和密碼。

自從 2018 年來，我一直是貴公司的忠實客戶。然而，我在填寫登記表時遇到了一些問題。**密碼顯然無法使用。**

請幫我詳細解決問題。

期待您的回覆。

誠摯祝願，

艾蜜莉‧喬丹

Email 這樣寫也行！

① 我很抱歉我已經在其他地方了。

I am sorry I am already committed elsewhere.

② 我相信出席者會被本公司精心設計的時尚產品吸引。

I'm sure the attendees will be attracted by some well-designed and fashionable products.

③ 我收到了貴公司新聞發布會的邀請。

I received your invitation to your company's press.

④ 密碼有問題。

There's something wrong with the pin.

⑤ 祝新聞發布會一切順利。

All the best with the press.

⑥ 我是貴公司多年的忠誠客戶。

I am a loyal customer for years.

⑦ 祝一切順利。。

Best of luck with everything.

⑧ 請盡快解決這些問題。

Please solve these problems as soon as possible.

03 邀請參觀貿易展覽會

範例 1

Title : We'd like to invite you to attend the ... event.

Dear Mr. Keith,

There is going to be *a trade show* coming in Seattle. The Trade Expo last year was a hit! We are hoping for an interesting and popular event this year.

We'd like to invite you to attend this event *next Friday at 11:00 a.m. at the Happy Center*.

Please kindly confirm your attendance by calling Mr. Wang or replying to this email.

Enclosed here is the information and invitation.

Best regards,
Willy Williams

SEND

主旨：想邀請您參加……活動

親愛的凱斯先生：

西雅圖將舉行**貿易展覽會**。去年的貿易展非常轟動！我們希望今年的展覽將會是有趣且受歡迎的活動。

我們想邀請您參加這次活動，時間是**下週五上午 11 點，在快樂中心**。

煩請致電給王先生，確認是否出席，或者回信給我們。

隨信附上資料和邀請函。

誠摯問候，
威力‧威廉

照著抄 ～ Email 簡單搞定！

Title : We'd like to invite you to attend the ... event.

Dear Mr. Cage

We proudly invite you to **the International Trade Expo at ABC Center**. The trade event will be held on October 14th, 2021.

There are over 300 booths in the center. We believe you will have a good opportunity to **find some companies you are interested in**.

Enclosed here are an invitation and a registration form. Please fill it out and send it back before September 30th, 2021.

Just call Emma at 0800-383-838 to confirm your attendance. For more information, don't hesitate to contact Mrs. Simpson at 987-6543.

Sincerely,
Jay Silverstone

SEND

主旨：想邀請您參加⋯⋯活動

親愛的凱吉先生：

我們榮幸地邀請您參加在 **ABC 中心舉辦的國際貿易博覽會**。貿易展覽會將在 2021 年 10 月 14 日開始。

中心內有超過 300 家展示攤位。我們相信這是您**找到感興趣公司**的絕佳機會。

隨信附上邀請函和登記表格。

請於 2021 年 9 月 30 日前填寫並寄回。

煩請撥打 0800-383-838 與愛瑪連絡，確認您出席時間。

欲了解更多資訊，請不吝與辛普森女士聯繫，電話如下：987-6543。

真誠地，

杰・席維斯史東

Email 這樣寫也行！

① 上次的貿易展廣受歡迎。

The Trade Expo last time was very popular.

② 我們感激您的出席。

Your present will be appreciated.

③ 請撥打 02-1234-5678 與我們確認。

Please confirm us by calling 02-1234-5678.

④ 隨信附上我們的公司資料。

Enclosed here is our company's profile.

⑤ 我們誠摯地想邀請您參加貿易展覽會。

We sincerely invite you to the Trade Expo.

⑥ 您絕對可以找到感興趣的公司。

You certainly can find some companies you are interested.

⑦ 請隨時與我聯繫。

Please feel free to contact me.

⑧ 需要更多資訊，請上本公司官網查詢。

For further information, please visit our website.

04【回應】邀請參觀貿易展覽會

 照著抄 ～ Email 簡單搞定！　　　　　　　　　　　─ ↗ ✕

範例1

Re : We'd like to invite you to attend the ... event.

Dear Mr. Williams,

Thank you very much for your invitation to the Trade Expo in Seattle. The Trade Expo last year was very successful and popular! I would like to attend, but unfortunately I **_have another event scheduled for the same day_**.

Hope we can meet in other Trade Expos.

Best regards,
Mark Keith

SEND　　　　　　　　　　　　　　　　　A ❘ ⌐ ☺

中譯

回覆：想邀請您參加……活動

親愛的威廉先生：

非常感謝您邀請我參加西雅圖貿易博覽會。去年的貿易展大獲成功並廣受歡迎！

我很想參加此活動，但是很遺憾我在**同一天已經安排了另一項活動**。

希望我們能在其他貿易博覽會上見面。

誠摯問候，

馬克‧凱基

照著抄 ～ Email 簡單搞定！

範例 2

Re : We'd like to invite you to attend the ... event.

Dear Mr. Silverstone,

Thank you for the kind invitation to the International Trade Expo at ABC Center. I **will be accepting the invitation**. I will have a good opportunity to find some companies I am interested in. I will fill out the registration form and send it back before September 30th, 2021. Moreover, I have call Emma to confirm my attendance on September 1st.

I look forward to the International Trade Expo.

Sincerely,
Fred Cage

SEND   A ⬙ ⊖ ☺

 中譯

回覆：想邀請您參加……活動

親愛的席維斯史東先生：

謝謝您邀請我參加在 ABC 中心舉辦的國際貿易博覽會。我將會**接受您的邀請**。我相信這會是我找到感興趣公司的大好機會。我會於 2021 年 9 月 30 日前填完登記表格並寄回。另外，我已於 9 月 1 號與愛瑪連絡，確認出席時間。

期待這場國際貿易博覽會。

真誠地，
弗瑞德‧凱基

① 感謝您邀請我參加貿易博覽會。

Thank you for inviting me to the Trade Expo.

② 然而，我將無法參加。

However, I will not be able to attend.

③ 我確定可以找到感興趣的公司。

I am sure I can find some companies I'm interested.

④ 我很想參加之後的活動。

I would love to attend future events.

⑤ 我很高興接受您的邀請。

I am pleased to accept your invitation.

⑥ 很高興收到您邀我參加國際貿易博覽會。

I was pleased to receive your invitation to the the International Trade Expo .

⑦ 去年的貿易展大獲成功。

The Trade Expo last year was a huge success.

⑧ 對於您邀請我參加 9 月 30 日星期三的聚會，甚感榮幸。

I accept with pleasure your kind invitation for Wednesday, September 30th.

05 邀請參加股東大會

照著抄 ～ Email 簡單搞定！

Title : [company] We are having annual stockholder meeting on (date).

Dear Shareholder,

It is our pleasure to invite you to ***the Annual Meeting of Stockholders*** on date January 12th, 2021 at the conference of the ***LKK Company***.

We'd like to ask for your presence on the meeting. If you will not be able to attend, please ***call*** Mr. Johnson or ***send us an email***.

Enclosed here is the information regarding the agenda. Please take some time to read it.

Thank you very much.

Sincerely yours,
Neil Washington

SEND

主旨：〔公司〕我們於（日期）召開年度股東大會

各位股東們您好：

我們很榮幸邀請您在 2021 年 1 月 12 號，前來參加 **LKK 公司的年度會議**。

敬邀您蒞臨會議。如果您無法出席，請**致電強納森先生**，或者**寄電子郵件**給我們。

隨信附上會議程序的相關資訊。請撥空閱讀。

十分感謝。

您真誠地，
尼爾·華盛頓

Title : [company] We are having annual stockholder meeting on (date).

Dear Fellow Shareholder,

We are pleased to invite you to the 2021 Annual Stockholders' Meeting.

This year's meeting will be held on Wednesday at 1:30 p.m. at Summer Hotel. We will focus on ***Summer Hotel's profits*** in 2020.

In case you are not able to attend the annual meeting, please ***send a representative***.

Faithfully,
Larry Golden

SEND

主旨：〔公司〕我們於（日期）召開年度股東大會

各位股東您好，

很高興邀請您參加 2021 年的年度股東大會。

今年的會議將於週三的下午一點半在夏季飯店舉行。會議內容將以**夏季飯店 2020 年的利潤**為主。

如果您不克出席年度股東大會，煩**請派代表**前來。

忠實地，
賴瑞‧高登

Email 這樣寫也行！

① 邀請您前來參加年度會議是我們的榮幸。

We have the pleasure to invite you to the annual meeting.

② 您的出席將是我們的榮幸。

Your presence will be our pleasure.

③ 我們榮幸地想請您參加會議。

We are proudly to invite you to the meeting.

④ 如果您需要了解更多相關議程，煩請寫信給我。

If you need more information regarding the agendas, please kindly write a letter to me.

⑤ 年度會議將在下週五舉行。

The annual meeting will be held next Friday.

⑥ 我們將把焦點放在投資一事。

We are going to focus on the investment.

⑦ 如果您不克出席，請先通知我們。

In case you won't attend the meeting, please contact us in advance.

⑧ 有任何疑問，請勿遲疑來信詢問。

If you have any questions, please do not hesitate to ask us by email.

06【回應】邀請參加股東大會

Re : [company] We are having annual stockholder meeting on (date).

Dear Mr. Washington,

I have already received your invitation. I am very pleased to **confirm** that I will be attending the Annual Meeting of Stockholders on date January 12th, 2021.

Indeed, I am hoping to be able to meet you on the 12th January, 2021.

All the best with the annual stockholder meeting.

Sincerely yours,

Brad Stone

SEND

回覆：〔公司〕我們於（日期）召開年度股東大會

華盛頓先生您好：

我已收到您的邀請。我非常愉快與您**確認**，將在 2021 年 1 月 12 日參加年度會議。

我期待能在 2021 年 1 月 12 日與您會面。

祝年度股東大會一切順利。

您真誠地，

布萊德・史東

Re : [company] We are having annual stockholder meeting on (date).

Dear Mr. Golden,

This is in ***response*** to the invitation at the 2021 Annual Stockholders'Meeting.

Indeed, I would love to come. However, I have other business meetings I need to attend on the same day.

Hence, I won't be able to attend the 2021 Annual Stockholders'Meeting. Mr. Roberts will go to the meeting ***instead of me***.

Please send me ***a summary of the annual stockholder meeting*** over the email.

Faithfully,
Vic Bullock

SEND

中譯

回覆：〔公司〕我們於（日期）召開年度股東大會

高登先生您好,

本封信是關於 2021 年年度股東大會邀請的**回覆**。

事實上,我非常想參與。但是,同一天我必須參加其他商業會議。

因此,我將無法參加 2021 年年度股東大會。羅伯特先生將會**代替我**參加會議。

用電子郵件將**年度股東大會摘要**寄給我。

忠實地,
維克‧布拉克

Email 這樣寫也行！

① 謝謝您邀請我前來參加年度會議。

Thank you very much to invite me to the annual meeting.

② 參加 2021 年的年度股東大會將會很棒。

It will be great to attend the 2021 Annual Stockholders'Meeting.

③ 我們非常高興地接受邀請。

With great pleasure we accept the invitation.

④ 由於我的行程繁忙，我將無法參加會議。

I won't be able to attend the meeting due to my busy schedule.

⑤ 很遺憾地通知您，我將無法參加 2021 年年度股東大會。

I regret to inform you that I won't be able to attend the 2021 Annual Stockholders'Meeting.

⑥ 我 1 月 12 日可能無法參加。

I'm afraid I can't make it on January 12th .

⑦ 我需要了解更多相關議程，請隨時撥打 0800-000-000 與我聯繫。

I need more information regarding the agendas, please feel free to contact me at 0800-000-000.

⑧ 我想知道更多關於投資一事。

I'd know more about the investment.

07 邀請參加公司周年慶

範例 1

Title : Sincerely invite you to attend our annual celebration.

Dear Sir or Madam,
You are kindly invited to attend the ***anniversary*** of DCC Company on Monday, October 28th, 2021.
We will have ***dinner and a dancing party*** at 6 p.m. The celebration will end at 9 p.m..
Please feel free to contact Anne at 0938-383-838 for more information.

Truly,
Jill Bieber

SEND   A̲ 📎 🔗 ☺

 中譯

主旨：誠摯邀請您參加我們的年度典禮

先生、女士您好：
恭請您出席 DCC 公司**周年慶**，時間為 2021 年 10 月 28 日，星期一，下午 6 點。
我們將有**晚宴和舞會**。慶祝活動將於晚上 9 點結束。
請隨時撥打 0938-383-838，和安妮聯繫，以獲取更多資訊。

誠摯地，
吉兒‧畢博

照著抄 ～ Email 簡單搞定！

範例 2

Title : Sincerely invite you to attend our annual celebration.

Dear Mr. Bullock,

PTT Company cordially invites you to attend our **5th anniversary celebration**. We'd like to share this special moment with you on Monday, August 12th, 2021.

The celebration will start at 5 p.m.. To show our thankfulness, you will receive **a special gift** and have **a delicious dinner**.

Thank you for supporting us and making the past five years so wonderful. We look forward to seeing you on Monday.

Sincerely yours,

Roger Rose

SEND

主旨：誠摯邀請您參加我們的年度典禮

親愛的布拉克先生：

PTT 公司誠摯地邀請您於下星期一，2021 年 8 月 12 日，前來參加我們 **5 周年的周年慶**。我們想與您分享這特別時刻。

慶祝活動將在下午 5 點開始。為了表示感謝，您將會收到一份**特別禮物**，並享用**美味的晚餐**。

感謝您對我們的支持，讓我們公司在過去 5 年來成長茁壯。我們期待在週一看到您。

您真誠地，

羅傑・羅斯

Email 這樣寫也行！

① 我們不希望您錯過這個場合。

We don't want to let the occasion pass without telling you.

② 我們相信公司的成長是因為您們的信任。

We well believe our growth is due to your (customers') trust in us.

③ 感謝您參與我們的成功。

Thank you for your participation in our success.

④ 我們想向您表現出我們的感激之情。

We want to express our appreciation.

⑤ 公司周年慶將在 5 點開始。

The anniversary of our company will start at 5 p.m..

⑥ 慶祝活動將會於 10 點前結束。

The celebration will end before 10 in the evening.

⑦ 我們感謝您的支持。

We appreciate your support.

⑧ 期待您與您分享意見。

I look forward to sharing ideas with you.

08【回應】邀請參加公司周年慶

範例 1

Re : Sincerely invite you to attend our annual celebration.

Dear Mrs. Bieber,

In reply to your invitation received October 1st, 2021. I would be pleased to meet you at the party. It will be my pleasure to come to the anniversary of DCC Company.

I'm planning a gift for you.

I look forward to **_discussing some projects_** with you.

Best regards,
Emma Cage

SEND   A 🔗 😊

回覆：誠摯邀請您參加我們的年度典禮

畢博女士您好：

出席 DCC 公司周年慶，時間為 2021 年 10 月 28 日，星期一，本封信是回覆您，我在 2021 年 10 月 1 日收到的邀請，很高興在聚會上能和您見面。出席 DCC 公司周年慶是我的榮幸。

我會為您準備禮物。

期待與您**討論一些專案**。

誠摯地，
愛瑪‧凱吉

照著抄 ～ Email 簡單搞定！　　　　　— ↗ ✕

Re : Sincerely invite you to attend our annual celebration.

Dear Mr. Rose,

Thank you very much for your thoughtful invitation to attend 5th anniversary celebration. I will definitely be at PTT Company on August 12th, 2021.

I *have a meeting at 3 p.m.*, so I am afraid I *won't be able to show up on time*.

I look forward to seeing you on Monday.

Sincerely yours,
Sandy Bullock

SEND　　　　　　　　　　　　　　　　A ⬙ ⬤ ☺

回覆：誠摯邀請您參加我們的年度典禮

羅斯先生您好：

非常感謝您誠心邀請我參加貴公司 5 周年的周年慶。我確定 2021 年 8 月 12 日會到 PTT 公司。

由於**下午 3 點要開會**，所以恐怕**無法準時出席**。

期待在星期一能見到您。

真誠地，

珊笛‧布拉克

Email 這樣寫也行！

① 非常感謝您邀我參加貴公司 5 週年周年慶。

Thank you so much for inviting me to your 5th anniversary celebration.

② 我想我會接受邀請。

I'd like to take this opportunity to accept the invitation.

③ 參加周年慶是我的榮幸。

It was a pleasure to participate in the celebration.

④ 我期待聽到您關於投資的想法。

I look forward to hearing your thoughts on the investments.

⑤ 祝您慶祝會愉快。

May you enjoy a wonderful celebration.

⑥ 我們非常興奮星期一能與您見面。

We are very excited about seeing you on Monday.

⑦ 我期待和您討論近期新聞。

I look forward to discussing current news with you.

⑧ 我正在為派對準備完美禮物。

I am planning a perfect gift for the party.

09 邀請進行合作

Title : We are looking for partnership.

Dear Mr. Hanks,

I am a general manager of SPP Company. I truly appreciate your interest in our products.

I am writing to **_formally extend an invitation_** for you to know more about our company and products. If you are **_interested in the investment_**, please contact me at 0900-888-888.

We look forward to meeting you in our company.

Best regards,
Gary Stone

SEND   A ⎘ ⇋ ☺

主旨：我們正在尋找合作夥伴

漢克先生您好：

我是 SPP 公司總經理。非常感謝您對我們產品感興趣。

我寫這封信的目的，是寄**正式的邀請函**給您，讓您更了解本公司和產品。如果您**有興趣投資**，請撥打 0900-888-888 與我聯繫。

我們期待與您在公司見面。

最誠摯問候，

蓋瑞‧史東

Title : We are looking for partnership.

Dear Sir or Madam,

We are *a famous exporter of bikes in Taiwan*. We are interested in *establishing a business partnership* with you.

If you are interested in cooperating with us, you are welcome to visit our company.

Please inform us of your visiting time so as we can make arrangements in advance.

Please feel free to ask questions by calling us or sending us an email.

I am look forward to your prompt reply.

Truly yours,
Vic Pitt

SEND   A ⬭ ⊖ ☺

主旨：我們正在尋找合作夥伴

親愛的先生、女士：

我們是**台灣著名的腳踏車出口商**。我們有興趣與您**建立合作關係**。

如果您有興趣與我們合作，歡迎您前來敝公司參觀。

請告知我們您前來參觀的時間，以便能讓我們能提前做出完善安排。

如有任何疑問，請隨時以電話、或電子郵件與我們聯繫。

期待您迅速回應。

真誠地，

維克‧彼特

Email 這樣寫也行！

① 我們很榮幸尋求和您有生意往來的機會。

We're honored to seek an opportunity of doing business with you.

② 我們公司地點在台北市，近 101 大樓。

Our company is located in Taipei city, near Taipei 101.

③ 我們有興趣要和您討論合作的可能性。

We are interested in discussing the possibility of doing business with you.

④ 我們期待您的回音。

We look forward to hearing from you.

⑤ 我們強烈鼓勵您多了解我們公司的資料。

We strongly encourage you to know more information about our company.

⑥ 我們感謝您的關心。

We thank you for your consideration.

⑦ 謝謝您提供資訊給我們。

Thank you for providing us the requested information.

⑧ 有任何疑問請致電給我。

Please let me know if you have any questions.

10【回應】邀請進行合作

範例1

Re : We are looking for partnership.

Dear Mr. Stone,

Thank you for your invitation for me to know more about your company and products.

We are interested in the investment after careful analysis.

Indeed, you have a good reputation in the industry.

We can ***hold a business meeting*** later this Friday.

Please contact me at 123-4567.

I am look forward to your prompt reply.

Best regards,

Adam Hanks

SEND

回覆：我們正在尋找合作夥伴

史東先生您好：

感謝您的邀請，讓我能更了解您的公司和產品。

經過仔細分析，我們有興趣投資。確實，您在業界聲名遠播。

我們可以在這個星期五**開商務會議**。請撥打 123-4567 與我聯絡。

期待您迅速答覆。

敬啟，

亞當‧漢克斯

照著抄 ～ Email 簡單搞定！   — ⤢ ✕

範例 2

Re : We are looking for partnership.

Dear Mr. Pitt,

Thank you for inviting us to visit your company. We have received some documents from your company.

Thank you for offering us the opportunity of cooperating with you. Before that, we request you to kindly provide us with ***a catalog of all your bike products***.

Indeed, we are looking forward to establishing a business partnership with you.

We hope to hear from you soon.

Truly yours,
Sonia Smith

SEND   A ◊ ⇔ ☺

中譯

回覆：我們正在尋找合作夥伴

彼特先生您好：

感謝您邀請我們參觀貴公司。我們已經收到貴公司的文件。

感謝您為我們提供合作的機會。在此之前，我們想請您提供我們**所有腳踏車產品目錄**。

事實上，我們期待與您建立業務合作關係。

期待您迅速回覆。

真誠地，

桑妮雅‧史密斯

Email 這樣寫也行！

① 我們對您的商業提案感興趣。

We are interested in your business proposal.

② 我們需要開一次商務會議，以免造成誤解。

We need to organize a business meeting to avoid any miscommunication.

③ 我們期待與您建立良好的合作關係。

We look forward to a good working relationship with you.

④ 請隨時與祕書聯繫。

Please feel free to contact my secretary regarding the proposal.

⑤ 這個月晚點我們可以開個會。

We can have a meeting later this month.

⑥ 請提供更多公司資訊給我。

Please provide me more information about your company.

⑦ 我們期待與您討論。

We are looking forward to discussing with you.

⑧ 一收到信請盡速致電給我。

Please contact me as soon as you receive this email.

11 接受邀請

照著抄～ Email 簡單搞定！　　　　　　　　— ⤢ ✕

範例 1

Title : I'm honored to work with you/join the occasion.

Dear Mrs. Jackson,
I am Gary Wang, sales manager of Season Corporation. I've read your **proposal** recently.
Due to **the growing demand for pleated fabrics**, we do need some new suppliers. I am interested in your proposal and may need to know more about your information. We should discuss it before July 31st.
For an easier way to contact me, please call 02-1234-5678.

Sincerely,
Gary Wang
Season Corporation

SEND　　　　　　　　　　　　　　　　　　A ♪ ⊖ ☺

主旨：我很榮幸能與您一起工作／參加這個場合

親愛的傑克森女士：
我是季節公司的銷售經理王蓋瑞。我最近拜讀過您的**提案**。
由於**皺摺布料的需求量逐漸增加**，我們的確需要些新的供應商。我對於您的提案很感興趣，我們想知道更多關於貴公司的資訊。讓我們在 7 月 31 日前討論這項合作。
便於聯繫我的方式，請撥打 02-1234-5678。

真誠地，
王蓋瑞
季節公司

Title : I'm honored to work with you/join the occasion.

Dear Mr. Harrison,

Thank you for your offer to join the anniversary celebration.

I'd be pleased to attend the event, and hopefully we could have some time to *share our ideas*.

I can't wait to spend this special time with you.

Looking forward to seeing you then.

Faithfully Yours,

Paul Kao

SEND

主旨：我很榮幸能與您一起工作／參加這個場合

親愛的哈里遜先生：

謝謝您邀請我參加周年慶。

很高興參與這次盛會，希望我們能撥空**分享彼此的意見**。

迫不及待想與您共度這特別時光。

期待再見到您。

忠實的，

保羅‧高

Email 這樣寫也行！

① 我上星期已經收到您的提案。

I received your proposal last week.

② 由於工人的需求增加，我們可能會同意您的建議。

Due to the growing demand for workers, we may accept your suggestion.

③ 我有些問題想當面向您討教。

I got some questions and hope to discuss with you in person.

④ 謝謝您撥冗和我們一起慶祝。

Thank you for taking your time to celebrate with us.

⑤ 很榮幸您能參加這個活動。

I am honored that you can attend the event.

⑥ 我等不及要和您會面。

I can't wait to meet with you.

⑦ 謝謝您大力相助。

Thank you for all your assistance.

⑧ 謝謝您的理解和為我們所做的一切。

Thank you for your understanding and everything you have done.

12【回應】接受邀請

Re : I'm honored to work with you/join the occasion.

Dear Mr. Wang,

I am writing this letter on behalf of Happy firm. I am pleased that you are interested in our proposal. We can have a business meeting on July 25th. If you need any details, please contact me before the meeting. Furthermore, we look forward to forming ***a long-term relationship***.

Looking forward to collaborating with you!

If you have any questions, please do not hesitate to contact me.

Faithfully Yours,
Molly Jackson

SEND　　　　　　　　　　　　　　　　　　　A 〗 ⊝ ☺

回覆：我很榮幸能與您一起工作／參加這個場合

王先生您好：

本封信代表快樂公司。很高興您對我們的商業提案感興趣。我們可以在 7 月 25 日召開商務會議。如果需要任何詳細資訊，請在會議前與我聯繫。此外，我們期待與您建立**長期的合作關係**。

期待與您的合作！

如有任何疑問，請隨時聯絡我。

忠實地，

莫莉・傑克森

照著抄 ～ Email 簡單搞定！

Re : I'm honored to work with you/join the occasion.

Dear Mr. Kao,

Since you have been kindly supported our company over the years, it gives us great pleasure to invite you to **the anniversary celebration**.

We are pleased to know that you will be able to attend the celebration. We can have some time to discuss some ideas. We look forward to seeing you.

Sincerely,
Dave Harrison

SEND

回覆：我很榮幸能與您一起工作／參加這個場合

親愛的高先生：

由於多年來您對本公司大力支持，因此很開心邀請您來參加**週年慶**。

很高興知道您將參加本公司周年慶。我們能花一些時間分享彼此的意見。

我們期待您的光臨。

真誠地，
戴福．哈里遜

Email 這樣寫也行！

① 如果您需要任何其他資訊，請隨時致電給我。

If you require any further information, please feel free to call me.

② 我們期待與您的合作。

We are looking forward to cooperating with you.

③ 很高興與您分享我的想法。

It's my pleasure to share my ideas with you.

④ 參加周年慶是我的榮幸。

I am honored that I can attend the the anniversary celebration.

⑤ 我期待有更多時間與您聚會。

I look forward to spending more time with you.

⑥ 如果您有其他疑問，請隨時與我們聯繫。

If you have any further queries , please do not hesitate to let me know.

⑦ 我們期待未來成功的合作關係。

We look forward to a successful working relationship in the future.

⑧ 謝謝您的支持。

Thank you for your support.

13 拒絕邀請

照著抄 ～ Email 簡單搞定！

範例 1

Title : I won't be able to join/show up at...

Dear Mrs. Ryan,

Thank you for your thoughtful invitation to **the Christmas party**. It would be my pleasure.

Unfortunately, I have already **committed to another engagement**, so I will be unable to attend. Otherwise, I certainly would be there.

I'd like express my regrets as well as my wishes.

May you enjoy a wonderful Christmas party.

Best Regards,

Anne King

SEND

 中譯

主旨：我無法參加／出現在……

萊恩女士您好：

感謝您貼心的邀請我出席**聖誕派對**。這是我的榮幸。

不幸的是，我已經**另外有約了**，所以我將無法參加這次盛會。否則，我一定會出席。

在此表達我的遺憾和祝福。

願您有美好的聖誕晚會。

最佳問候，

安妮・金

Title : I won't be able to join/show up at...

Dear Mr. Depp,

I really appreciate your kind invitation to your **opening ceremony**. I am honored by the invitation to participate in the ceremony.

I'd love to go and share in your happiness. Unfortunately, I will **go on a business trip** to Seattle that week, so I won't be here. I'd like to arrange some other time to meet with you when I return.

Wish you the great success at the ceremony.

Sincerely,
Thomas Madison

SEND   A 🖉 ⊖ ☺

 中譯

主旨：我無法參加／出現在……

親愛的戴普先生：

很感謝您盛情邀約我，前往參加您的**開幕儀式**。對於能受邀參加盛會，我備感榮幸。

我很樂意與您分享快樂。不幸的是，我那個時候將會到西雅圖**出差**，所以我將不在國內。當我回國時，我希望能再安排時間和您見面。

祝您典禮盛大成功。

真誠地，
湯瑪仕‧梅迪森

Email 這樣寫也行！

① 收到您的邀請是我的榮幸。
It is my pleasure to receive your invitation.

② 很抱歉我已經有約了。
I am sorry that I have made an engagement.

③ 希望您有個美好愉快的夜晚。
May you have a wonderful and happy night.

④ 我沒辦法參加明天的晚會。
I cannot attend the party tomorrow.

⑤ 很感激您的邀請，但是我無法去。
We appreciate you inviting us, but we cannot make it.

⑥ 我真的很想去，但是我要去紐約拜訪祖父母。
I'd love to go, but I will visit my grandparents in New York.

⑦ 當我回來時，我會與您聯繫。
When I return, I will contact you.

⑧ 希望您快樂成功。
Wish you all happiness and success.

14【回應】拒絕邀請

Re : I won't be able to join/show up at...

Dear Mrs. King,

I have received your letter, informing me that you are not able to attend to Christmas party. It was ***disappointing*** to know that you have already committed to another engagement.

Please ***feel free to contact me*** once you have received this email.

Best wishes for you.

Sincerely,

Judy Ryan

SEND　　　　　　　　　　　　　　　　　　A ▯ ⊖ ☺

回覆：我無法參加／出現在……

金女士您好：

我已經收到了您通知我不能參加聖誕節盛會的消息。得知您已經約好另一項活動，覺得**失望**。

收到此封電子郵件後，請**隨時與我聯繫**。

萬事如意。

誠摯問候，

茱蒂・萊恩

範例 2

Re : I won't be able to join/show up at...

Dear Mr. Madison,

I just received your letter today. I'm sorry that you won't attend the opening ceremony.

Indeed, I'd *like to share my happiness with you*.

I am looking forward to meeting you when you return.

Please *give me a call once you are back*.

Hope everything works out smoothly for you.

Sincerely,

John Depp

SEND   A ◊ ⊝ ☺

主旨：我無法參加／出現在……

親愛的梅迪森先生：

我今天收到您的來信。很遺憾您無法參加開幕儀式。

事實上，我**想與您分享我的喜悅**。

期待回來時能與您會面。

回來時請**打電話給我**。

祝您一切順利。

真誠地，

約翰‧戴普

① 很遺憾您不能參加我的開幕儀式。

I'm sorry you won't make it to my opening ceremony.

② 您一回國請打電話給我。

Give me a call once you've come back.

③ 希望我們盡速見面。

I hope we will meet soon.

④ 很遺憾知道您因為有其他商業會議而無法參加。

I am sorry that you won't be able to attend due to another business commitment.

⑤ 祝您一切順心。

Wish you all the way best.

⑥ 希望您 2021 年及以後都順心如意。

All the best to you in 2021 and beyond.

⑦ 希望您一切順利。

I hope everything is going well with you.

⑧ 您一收到電子郵件請和我聯繫。

Contact me once you have received this email.

PART8
祝賀&慰問

因各家手機系統不同，若無法直接掃描，仍可以（https://tinyurl.com/y3cnewa9）電腦連結雲端下載，一貼搞定！

Part 8.
祝賀&慰問

01 祝賀節日

照著抄 ～ Email 簡單搞定！

範例
1

Title : Holiday Greetings from...

Dear Mr. Brown,

During this **holiday season**, our company would like to take this opportunity to thank you for your business support over the last few years.

Since we have been working with each other for such a long time, we hope to **continue our cooperation** in the future.

I believe that we will certainly have **a promising future**.

With best wishes for a happy New Year!

Edmond

SEND   A 🔗 😊

中譯

主旨：來自……的節日問候

親愛的布朗先生：

欣逢**佳節**，在此藉由這個機會感謝您在過去幾年對本公司生意上的照顧。

我們已經合作許久，在此也希望未來能**繼續維持**彼此生意上的**合作**。

我相信我們一定會**生意興隆的**。

謹祝新年快樂，

艾德蒙

Title : Holiday Greetings from...

Dear Mr. Foster,

The Thanksgiving holiday is around the corner. We wish you lots of happiness for the upcoming year.

We have been good partners over last few years. We hope to continue our cooperation in the future since the relationship between our companies is close and great.

I believe that we will have a favorable future.

With best wishes for a Happy Thanksgiving.

Brad Brown

SEND　　　　　　　　　　　　　　　A ⑂ ⊖ ☺

主旨：來自……的節日問候

親愛的福斯特先生：

感恩節即將到來。我們希望您在未來一年裡能夠快樂順利。

我們過去幾年一直是關係融洽的合作夥伴。因為我們兩家公司的合作關係密切且良好，因此未來希望我們能繼續合作。

我相信我們未來能順利合作。

謹祝感恩節快樂！

布萊德‧布朗

Email 這樣寫也行！

① 祝賀新年。

A happy New Year to you.

② 請接受我誠摯的新年祝福。

Please accept my sincere wishes for the New Year.

③ 祝賀佳節。

Season's greetings.

④ 祝福您佳節愉快、新年快樂。

Season's greetings and best wishes for the New Year.

⑤ 祝賀新禧！

Best wishes for the year to come!

⑥ 謹祝新年快樂、大吉大利。

I hope you have a most happy and prosperous New Year.

⑦ 願佳節愉快伴您整年。

May the season's joy fill you all year round.

⑧ 願來年大發。

May great success in the coming New Year.

02【回應】祝賀節日

範例 1

Re : Holiday Greetings from...

Dear Edmond,

Please accept my heartiest greetings during this holiday season. We are very pleased with the quality of service and products your company provides.

Since we have been working with each other for such a long time, we look forward to continuing our good cooperation.

May the year ahead bring you good luck and happiness.

Eric Brown

SEND

中譯

回覆：來自……的節日問候

親愛的艾德蒙：

欣逢佳節，請接受我們最誠摯的問候。本司對於貴公司提供的服務和產品品質感深覺滿意。

因為我們已經合作許久，我們期待未來能繼續合作。

謹祝新年快樂和幸運。

艾利克・布朗

照著抄 ～ Email 簡單搞定！ — ⤢ ✕

Re : Holiday Greetings from...

Dear Mr. Brown,

I am glad to have received you email. It's November and the Holiday season is upon us. I wish all of you a very Happy Thanksgiving

I hope that we will have better cooperation in the coming days. I believe that we will have a promising future.

Warmest thanks and best wishes for a wonderful Holiday!

David Foster

SEND   A 🔗 ☺

 中譯

回覆：來自……的節日問候

親愛的布朗先生：

很高興收到您的電子郵件。現在正值十一月，我們的假期將至。我在此祝您們感恩節快樂。

希望我們在未來日子能有更好的合作。相信我們未來前景可期。

由衷感謝並誠摯祝福佳節愉快！

大衛・福斯特

Email 這樣寫也行！

① 祝您新年萬事如意。
Wishing you a Happy New Year.

② 恭喜發財！
May you come into a good fortune!

③ 祝您和家人佳節愉快。
Wishing you and your family a wonderful holiday season.

④ 希望新年祝福給您帶來歡樂。
New Year greetings to cheer you.

⑤ 祝您新年好運。
Wish you have a New Year filled with good fortune.

⑥ 新年快樂！
Have a happy New Year!

⑦ 願 2021 年是您最好的一年！
I hope 2021 is your best year yet!

⑧ 祝您新年快樂。
Wish you happiness in the year to come.

03 祝賀公司開業

範例 1

Title : Congratulations on your new firm.

Dear Mr. Wood,

Congratulations on the opening of your new company. You once worked with me for three years and always did a great job whenever our CEO gave you a task. In my eyes, you are an excellent man and I am sure you will ***make it another success in your career***.

I wish you a prosperous business!

Yours sincerely,
Steven

SEND

 中譯

主旨：恭喜您成立新公司

敬愛的伍茲先生：

恭喜您的新公司開業。您我曾共事三年，每次執行長給您的任務您都完成得很漂亮。在我眼裡，您是個非常優秀的人，我相信您一定能**再創事業高峰**。

祝您生意興隆！

您真誠地，
史蒂芬

Title : Congratulations on your new firm.

Dear Mr. Cage,

Congratulations on your new firm. I am certain that the new firm will be *a remarkable success*.

I believe that you have the advantage of experience and profession. I am pleased to see that you are always outstanding and successful. If any *positions open* up in the future, please bear me in mind.

Look forward to working together.

Best wishes,
Robin Gere

SEND

主旨：恭喜您成立新公司

親愛的凱吉先生：

恭喜您開新公司。我十分確定您的新公司將會**十分成功**。

我對您的經驗和專業優勢予以信任。我很高興地看到您的表現一直是如此優秀和成功。如果將來貴公司有任何**職缺**，請不吝找我。

期待共同合作。

誠摯祝福，

羅賓·吉爾

Email 這樣寫也行！

① 祝您生意興隆，買賣越做越好！

I wish you a prosperous business and continued development in our business!

② 祝您生意興隆！

May you succeed in business!

③ 祝您生意興隆。

With best wishes for your prosperity.

④ 您的生意很快就會興旺起來的。

Your business will become prosperous soon.

⑤ 我相信您和您的員工一定可以建立一個成功的事業。

I'm sure you, with your employees, can build a prosperous business.

⑥ 沒有良好的經營管理，事業就不會興旺發達。

No good management, no prosperous business.

⑦ 我相信您很快就能生意興隆的。

I believe it will be auspicious in the near future.

⑧ 恭禧您開拓新事業。

Congratulations on your new venture.

04【回應】祝賀公司開業

範例 1

Re : Congratulations on your new firm.

Dear Steven,

Thank you so much for congratulating me on my new company. I want to let you know how interesting it was working with someone like you.

It has been an honor working with a hard-working colleague like you. ***Thank you for all the support you have shown to me for the past years.***

I'll miss you and think of you.

I look forward to seeing you again soon.

Sincerely,
Gary Wood

SEND

中譯

回覆：恭喜您成立新公司

敬愛的史蒂芬：

非常感謝祝福我新公司的成立。我想讓您知道和您共事非常有趣。

與像您這樣努力工作的同事共事是我的榮幸。**感謝過去幾年裡，您對我提供的一切支持。**

我會想念並記著您。

期待再次會面。

真誠地，
蓋瑞・伍茲

378

照著抄 ～ Email 簡單搞定！　　　　　　　　　　　─ ⤢ ✕

範例 2

Re : Congratulations on your new firm.

Dear Mr. Gere,

I'm highly thankful to you for your kind letter congratulating me on my new firm. Reading your letter full of good words makes me happy.

If there are any **positions open,** you would be **my first choice**.

Thank you for the congratulations. I hope I will succeed in my new business.

I'm looking forward to working with you in the future.

Best regards,
Leo Cage

SEND　　　　　　　　　　　　　　　　　　　A 📎 🔗 ☺

回覆：恭喜您成立新公司

吉爾先生您好：

非常感謝您對我成立新公司的祝賀。閱讀充滿溢美之詞的信讓我很高興。

如果將來本司有任何**職缺**，您將會**是我的首選**。

謝謝您的祝賀。希望我能在新事業中獲得成功。

期待未來有機會合作。

誠摯祝福，
李歐・凱吉

Email 這樣寫也行！

① 謝謝您來信祝賀！

Thank You for sending me your congratulations!

② 對您的祝福深感謝意！

I feel glad that I received your blessings!

③ 我們很高興圍繞著祝福。

We feel glad to be surrounded by your blessings.

④ 謝謝您的支持。

Thank you for your support.

⑤ 我相信我新的事業將能大獲成功。

I ensure that my new business will be successful.

⑥ 感謝您祝賀我展開新事業。

Thank you so much for congratulating me on my new business.

⑦ 謝謝您充滿鼓勵的郵件。

Thank you for your encouraging email.

⑧ 收到這麼棒的祝福真好。

It was nice to receive such good wishes.

05 祝賀生日快樂

Title : Birthday congratulations

Dear Mrs. Jones ,

I am writing this letter to you for congratulating **on your birthday**.

Your birthday will be arriving next Tuesday, but I will go on my business trip this weekend. I 'm sorry to inform you that I **can't attend your birthday party**. I am thus giving my advance wishes to you.

Have a good time.

I wish you a hearty congratulation on your birthday.

Sincerely,

Vicky Pitt

SEND

主旨：生日祝福

瓊斯女士您好，

寫此封信是為了祝賀**您的生日**。

下週二是您的生日，但我這周末將要去出差。抱歉通知您，**無法參加生日派對**。

因此，在此謹向您致上最美的祝福。

玩得開心。

誠心誠意地祝您生日快樂。

真誠地，

薇琪‧彼特

Title : Birthday congratulations

Dear Emily,

I am writing this letter to you to wish you a very **happy birthday**.

Next Friday is your birthday. It's your 25 birthday. We've known each other for five years. You are one of my good partners. Your friendship has made my life so much easier.

If you're **planning to hold a party**, please don't hesitate to let me know.

I'm looking forward to your prompt reply.

Take care and enjoy your birthday.

Yours truly,
Sandra

SEND

主旨：生日祝福

親愛的艾蜜莉：

我正在寫這封信是為了祝妳**生日快樂**。

下星期五是妳的生日。25 歲的生日。我們已經認識了五年了，妳一直是我其中一個好夥伴。妳的友誼讓我的生活變得更愜意。

如果妳**有辦派對的打算**，請隨時告訴我。

期待妳的回覆。

保重，並好好過生日。

真誠地，
珊卓

Email 這樣寫也行！

① 寫這封信是為了祝賀您 25 歲的生日。

I'm writing this letter to you for congratulating you on your 25 birthday.

② 謝謝邀請我參加派對。

Thank you for the invitation to your party.

③ 提前祝您生日快樂。

I wish you happy birthday in quite advance.

④ 我將無法參加您的生日派對。

I will not be able to attend your birthday party.

⑤ 我下星期要出差。

I will go on a business trip next week.

⑥ 非常感謝您邀請我參加派對！

Thank you so much for inviting me to your party!

⑦ 我下週二恐怕沒空。

I'm afraid I'm not available on next Tuesday.

⑧ 遺憾地通知您，我因出差而無法參加派對。

I regret to inform you that I won't be able to attend the party due to my business trip.

06【回應】祝賀生日快樂

範例 1

Re : Birthday congratulations

Dear Mrs. Pitt ,
I am writing this letter to thank you for your congratulatory letter on my birthday.
I 'm sorry that you aren't able to make it to my party. I wish to *invite you to dinner next week*. The dinner is scheduled to take place at Happy Hours on December 20th.
I would be glad to see you at dinner.
Looking forward to your response.

Sincerely,
Dora Jones

SEND

中譯

回覆：生日祝福

親愛的彼特女士，
寫這封信是感謝您在我生日時寄來的祝賀信。
很遺憾您無法參加我的派對。我希望**邀請您下週進晚餐**。晚餐定於 12 月 20 日，地點在歡樂時光餐廳。我很高興在晚餐時和您碰面。
期待回覆。

真誠地，
朵拉‧瓊斯

照著抄 ～ Email 簡單搞定！

範例 2

Re : Birthday congratulations

Dear Sandra,

Thank You for sending me your congratulations. I am truly blessed.

I would like to **invite you to join me** as I celebrate my birthday. My party is scheduled to take place on 20th December 2020. I want to have the most memorable birthday this year. Moreover, I value your presence at this party.

If you have any inquiries, please reach me through my number 123-4567.

I'm looking forward to your prompt reply.

Yours truly,

Emily Smith

SEND

中譯

回覆：生日祝福

親愛的珊卓：

謝謝您的祝賀。我真的很幸運。

我**想邀請您參加**我的生日會。生日會將在 2020 年 12 月 20 日舉行。

我今年想擁有最難忘的生日。此外，我想邀您出現在這個聚會。

如果有任何疑問，請打 123-4567 與我聯繫。

靜候佳音。

謹此，

艾蜜莉・史密斯

① 生日派對將在 12 月 20 號舉辦，地點是<u>湯姆伯伯</u>。

The birthday party will be held at Uncle Tom on December 20th.

② 希望您能度過愉快的生日。

I hope you have a wonderful time celebrating your birthday.

③ 很抱歉我無法參加。

I am sorry but I am unable to attend.

④ 請盡早確認是否出席。

Kindly confirm your attendance at the earliest.

⑤ 很高興邀請您參加我的生日派對。

It is a great pleasure to invite you to my birthday party.

⑥ 如果不克前來我的生日派會，請來電告知。

In case you aren't attending my birthday party, please let me know by call.

⑦ 派對將於 2021 年 12 月 20 日在<u>快樂餐廳</u>舉辦。

The party will take place in Happy Restaurant on 20th December 2021.

⑧ 我真心期盼您來派對。

I am truly awaiting your presence at the party.

07 祝賀升職

照著抄 ～ Email 簡單搞定！

範例 1

Title : Congratulations on the promotion.

Dear Steven,

Congratulations on your **new position** in our company. Myself and all the others who know you in this office are not surprised to learn the news because you always showed your dedication when you were sent to work with our team. People say, **"Hard work pays off."**

We are sure that this is just the beginning in a long series of steps up the professional ladder and you will make greater success in the near future.

Good luck to you!

Yours sincerely,
Wilson

SEND

主旨：恭喜升職

親愛的史蒂芬：

恭喜您在公司的**新職務**。我和公司裡其他認識您的人對這個消息都不覺得意外。當您被指派與我們團隊合作時您是那麼地盡職。俗話說得好：「**努力終會獲得回報。**」

我們相信您會在往後的職業生涯裡更上一層樓，並且在不久的將來獲得更大的成功。

祝您好運！

您真誠地，
威爾遜

Title : Congratulations on the promotion.

Dear Mr. Miller,

I just learned of your promotion to the **Area Director** of your company. Congratulations on your new position.

You are one of the ablest men I have ever met, and I am sure you will meet the same success in your new appointment as you did in Hong Kong.

Besides, I hope that you take with you pleasant memories of your three years here in Hong Kong. Please remember that **I and other colleagues are always your friends**.

Yours sincerely,

John Williams

SEND

主旨：恭喜升職

親愛的米勒先生：

剛剛聽說您升為**地區總監**。恭喜您升遷。

您是我所認識的最有能力的人之一，因此，我相信您一定會做得和在香港時一樣好。

另外，希望您永遠記得在香港這三年的美好回憶。請記住：**我和其他同事永遠都是您的朋友。**

您真誠地，

約翰‧威廉

Email 這樣寫也行！

① 祝賀您升職！

Congratulations on your promotion!

② 聽說您升遷了，我非常高興。

I was so happy to learn of your promotion.

③ 這真的是您應該得到的。

I must say you really deserve it.

④ 請接受我們最好的祝福，希望您在新的工作崗位上獲得成功。

Please accept our best wishes for every success in your new position.

⑤ 相信您會在新的職位上獲得很大的成功。

I am sure that you will make great success in your new position.

⑥ 過去這些年您工作得太辛苦了，這是您應得的。

You have worked so hard these years and you deserve it.

⑦ 請接受我最熱烈的祝賀。

Please accept my warmest congratulations.

⑧ 請記得我們永遠挺您。

Please remember that we always support you.

08【回應】祝賀升職

Re : Congratulations on the promotion.

Dear Wilson,
I received your congratulatory letter that you sent yesterday.
It is nice of you to congratulate me on my promotion. It's
been a long search to get the right and new position. I believe
this is going to be a good match for my skills.
I'll do all that is possible to take the company forward.
Hope I will make greater success in the near future.
Thank you for your support.

Yours sincerely,
Steven

SEND   A ◊ ⊖ ☺

回覆：恭喜升職

親愛的威爾遜：
我昨天收到您寄來的祝賀信。能祝賀我升遷真好。得到正確和新的職位需要長時間經營。我相信這將和我技術完美結合。我將盡我所能讓使公司持續發展。
希望在不久的將來獲得更大成功。
謝謝您的支持。

真誠地，
史蒂芬

照著抄 ～ Email 簡單搞定！

範例 2

Re : Congratulations on the promotion.

Dear Mr. Williams,

I am in receipt of your congratulation letter. I appreciate your kind words.

The company has found out that I am a suitable person to occupy the post of Area Director. I will do my best to meet the same success in my new appointment as I did in Hong Kong.

In fact, I believe you and other colleagues are always my good partners.

Please give me a call when you have the time tosit down for a long visit.

I look forward to hearing from you.

Yours sincerely,
Alan Miller

SEND

中譯

回覆：恭喜升職

親愛的威廉先生：

我剛收到您的祝賀信。謝謝您的美好的祝福。

公司發現我適合擔任地區總監一職。我將盡我所能在新職位中，獲得和在香港任職時一樣的成功。

實際上，我相信您和其他同事將永遠是我好夥伴。

如果有空和我坐下來暢談許久，請打電話給我。

期待回音。

真誠地，

艾倫‧米勒

Email 這樣寫也行！

① 感謝對於我的升遷獻上祝福。

Thanks for your best wishes on my promotion.

② 我希望在這個新職位中獲得圓滿成功。

I wish great success in this new role.

③ 謝謝您最熱烈的祝賀。

Thank you for your warmest congratulations.

④ 努力得到回報真讓人歡欣鼓舞。

It is so encouraging that my effort has been rewarded.

⑤ 我相信在新的職位上我能游刃有餘。

I am sure that I will be great in this position.

⑥ 如果有時間來拜訪我，請與我聯繫。

Please contact me when you have the time to visit me.

⑦ 我期待您的馬上回覆。

I await your immediate response.

⑧ 收到您的來信永遠讓我開心。

Always happy to hear from you.

09 生病／事故慰問

 照著抄 ～ Email 簡單搞定！   — ↗ ✕

範例 1

Title : Comfort in sickness

Dear Lisa ,

Thank you for telling me about your ***illness***. I'm sorry to hear that.

I went to the hospital today, but hospital rules won't let me visit you.

Let me know when you feel up for visitors.

Good luck to you!

Call me if you need help with anything.

Yours sincerely,

Cindy Smith

SEND   A 🔗 ☺

主旨：生病慰問

親愛的麗莎：

謝謝您告知您的**病情**。聽到這個消息我很難過。

我今天到醫院，但是醫院的規定無法讓我探病。

當您可以開放訪客時，請告訴我。

祝您好運！

如果需要任何幫助，請來電告知。

您真誠地，

辛蒂．史密斯

Title : May you recover quickly

Dear Mr. Williams,

We have just been told that you met with *a car accident* while going to the office.

We were sorry to hear about your accident. We are thankful that you were not more gravely hurt.

Do not hesitate to call me for the same. Pray for your fast recovery.

My wishes are with you.

Yours sincerely,
Frank Foster

SEND

主旨：希望您早日康復

親愛的威廉斯先生：

我們剛剛被告知您在上班途中遇到**車禍**。

很遺憾得知車禍一事。我們感激您沒有受到更嚴重的傷害。

請不吝打電話給我。我會為您盡早復原而祈禱。

祝福與您同在。

您真誠地，

法蘭克・福斯特

Email 這樣寫也行！

① 得知車禍一事我很抱歉。

I am sorry to hear about your car accident.

② 我們將盡快拜訪您。

We will visit you shortly.

③ 希望您在康復這段時間感覺好些。

Hope you will already feel better on your way to recovery.

④ 我為您的早日康復祈禱。

I pray for your soon recovery.

⑤ 我們希望您受傷不會太嚴重。

We hope that you are not severely injured.

⑥ 若有需要，請隨時致電我。

Do not hesitate to call me whenever you need anything.

⑦ 我知道這對您而言是非常關鍵的時刻。

I understand that it is a very critical time for you.

⑧ 短時間內您的傷將會康復。

You would recover from the injuries in a short time span.

10【回應】生病／事故慰問

範例 1

Re : Comfort in sickness

Dear Cindy,

I'm happy to have received your letter. It's very nice of you to write me a letter.

I appreciate it with all my heart. Thank you for your support in the job. I am truly thankful to have a good colleague like you.

I am *out of the hospital soon*.

Please do not hesitate to call me if you *have any questions about work*.

Yours sincerely,

Lisa Jordan

SEND　　　　　　　　　　　　　　　　A ⫶ 🔗 ☺

 中譯

回覆：生病慰問

親愛的辛蒂：

我很高興收到來信。謝謝您能寫信給我。

我全心全意感激。謝謝您在工作時的支持。真的很感謝能有像您這般的好同事。

我**快出院**了。

如果**對工作有任何疑問**，請隨時來電。

真誠地，

麗莎‧喬登

照著抄 ～ Email 簡單搞定！ — ⤢ ✕

範例 2

Re : May you recover quickly

Dear Mr. Foster,

Thank you for praying for me. I really appreciate your support and good feelings.

It was so thoughtful of you to think of me. ***Your sympathy letter is great comfort to me.***

It has been such a comfort to know that you were thinking of me while I am staying at home. Your kindness and support is greatly appreciated.

Yours sincerely,
Tommy Williams

SEND   A ✐ ⌨ ☺

中譯

回覆：希望您早日康復

親愛的福斯特先生：

謝謝您為我禱告。非常感謝您的支持和好意。

您真貼心能替我著想。**您的慰問信讓我感到安慰。**

在家中休息時，得知您能想到我，真是令人開心。非常感謝您的善良和支持。

您真誠地，

湯米・威廉斯

① 感謝您的來信。

I would like to give my thanks for the letter.

② 您的話讓我備感安慰。

Your words are of great comfort to me.

③ 感謝您的體貼。

I am grateful for your thoughtfulness.

④ 謝謝您的安慰。

Thank you for sending your words of sympathy.

⑤ 我想藉此機會表示由衷感謝。

I would like to take this opportunity to express my sincerest appreciation.

⑥ 十分感謝您的支持。

Thank you so very much for your support.

⑦ 謝謝您的迅速回應。

I appreciate your quick response.

⑧ 請允許我對您的來信表示謝意。

Allow me to express my appreciation for the letter you've written for me.

PART9

商務致謝

因各家手機系統不同，若無法直接掃描，仍可以（https://tinyurl.com/wtph4hav）電腦連結雲端下載，一貼搞定！

Part 9.
商務致謝

01 感謝訂購

範例1

Title : We have received your order of...

Dear Sirs,

We are pleased to receive your order **No. CH-0012 dated May 16th**.

It is our pleasure to have the opportunity to serve you and we assure that you will be satisfied with the quality of our goods and the service of our company.

Thank you very much for your order. If you want more products of our company, please keep in touch with us.

Yours faithfully,
Huawei Company

SEND

A   ⊕ ☺

主旨：我們已收到您的訂單

敬啟者：

我們非常高興收到貴公司 5 月 16 日編號 CH－0012 的訂單。

能有機會為貴公司提供所需產品，備感榮幸。相信本公司的產品品質及服務品質定能使您滿意。

非常感謝您的訂購。如果還需要本公司其他產品，請與我們聯絡。

您忠誠地，

華威公司

Title : We have received your order of...

Dear Mr. Carter,

Thank you very much for ordering our *Photoshop software*.

Your purchase information is attached. We will send the goods to you on receipt of your payment.

If there are any other commodities you are interested in, please feel free to contact us for further information.

Thanks again for your order.

Yours sincerely,
Applied Electronics Corp.

SEND

主旨：我們已收到您的訂單

親愛的卡特先生：

感謝您訂購敝公司的 Photoshop 圖片處理軟體。

訂購確認書隨信附上，在您確認付款後，商品即會寄出。

如果您對敝公司的其他產品也有興趣，需要進一步的資訊，請隨時與我們聯絡。

再次感謝您的訂購。

您真誠地，
應用電子公司

Email 這樣寫也行！

① 感謝您訂購我們的服裝。

Thank you very much for ordering our costume.

② 感謝您對我們的產品感興趣。

Thank you for your interest in our product.

③ 您還有其他感興趣的商品嗎？

Are there any other products you are interested?

④ 收到付款我們會將貨品寄出。

We will send the merchandise to you on receipt of your payment.

⑤ 如果您對其他商品感興趣，請直接與我們聯繫。

If there is any interest in other products, please contact us directly.

⑥ 訂購確認書隨信附上。

The purchase confirmation has been attached.

⑦ 如果您想瞭解更多資訊，請不吝諮詢。

Please feel free to let me know if you want more information.

⑧ 如果有任何問題，請不吝諮詢。

Don't hesitate to ask if you have any questions.

02【回應】感謝訂購

Re : We have received your order of...

Dear Sirs,

I am pleased to receive your email.

This is the second time I order your product. Your product's quality is your most distinguishing brand factor.

Thank you for the one-time **discount for 20%** off my next order.

I might be interested in other products. I will place another order in these days.

Yours faithfully,
Larry Jordan

SEND   A 𝐈 🔗 ☺

回覆：我們已收到您的訂單

敬啟者：

我很高興收到您的電子郵件。

這是我第二次訂購貴公司產品。產品高品質是品牌與眾不同的因素。

感謝貴司對下次訂單提供一次**八折優待**。

我可能會對其他商品感興趣。最近，我將會再次訂購商品。

您真誠地

賴瑞‧喬登

照著抄 ～ Email 簡單搞定！ ── ⤢ ✕

範例 2

Re : We have received your order of...

Dear Sirs,

Thank you for your prompt reply.

I ordered your Photoshop software three days ago, but I *placed the wrong product*.

I am really sorry that I would like to cancel my order with my invoice no. 12345.

Please feel free to contact me at any time.

I'm looking forward to receiving your reply.

Yours sincerely,

Frank Carter

SEND   A ⏃ ⟨⟩ ☺

中譯

回覆：我們已收到您的訂單

敬啟者：

感謝您迅速答覆我的郵件。

我三天前訂購了 PhotoShop 圖片處理軟體，但是**訂錯商品**。

很抱歉我想取消發票號碼 12345 的訂單。

請隨時與我聯絡。

期待收到您的回應。

您真誠地，

法蘭克·卡特

① 我已經訂購貴司的商品三次了。

I've ordered your products for three times.

② 華為商品訂購可以享有八折優惠。

I can enjoy 20% off Huawei purchases.

③ 請問您對其他商品感興趣嗎？

Are you interested in in other products?

④ 我最近將會購買貴司的商品。

I will buy your products recently.

⑤ 感謝您友善的協助。

Thank you for your kind cooperation.

⑥ 請取消我的訂單因為我訂錯品項了。

Please cancel my order because I ordered the wrong item.

⑦ 請問您能告知我如何立即取消訂單嗎？

Can you please tell me how to cancel an order immediately?

⑧ 我們期待收到您的反饋。

We're looking forward to receiving your feedback.

03 感謝合作

照著抄 ～ Email 簡單搞定！ — ⤢ ✕

範例1

Title : Thank you for the cooperation.

Dear Mr. Black,

I do thank you with all my heart for your kind and close cooperation. What you have done really helped get my business back on track. Without you, I could never get back on my feet so soon.

No one believes in me like you. You will be my ***permanent VIP client***.

I believe there will be more opportunities for us to cooperate in the future, which will benefit both of us.

Thanks again!

Yours sincerely,
Daniel Robertson

SEND   A ⬝ ⊖ ☺

 中譯

主旨：感謝合作

親愛的布萊克先生：

真的非常感謝您友善且密切的合作。您所做的一切使我的事業回到原本的軌道上。沒有您，我的事業不會這麼快地恢復元氣。

沒有人像您那樣信任我。您將會成為我的**永久 VIP 客戶**。

我相信將來我們會有更多合作的機會，這將會使我們雙方都受益良多。

再次感謝！

您真誠地
丹尼爾・羅伯森

Title : Thank you for the cooperation.

Dear Mr. Schofield,

I would like to thank you for your close collaboration with our business.

We have **_gained a profitable_** year; therefore, we are keenly desirous to **_enlarge our trade in various kinds of electric appliance_**.

We do hope that we could have further cooperation with each other and achieve shared prosperity in the future. Thank you so much again.

With thanks and regards.

Yours truly,
Meg Thomas

SEND   A ⎁ ⊖ ☺

主旨：感謝合作

親愛的斯科菲爾德先生：

衷心地感謝您與我們在貿易上如此密切的合作。

我們在這一年中**獲得了許多利潤**，因此，我們強烈希望**擴大我們在電器產品方面的貿易合作**。

我們真心希望能繼續與您深入合作，共同成長。再次表示感謝。

致以真誠地感謝和祝福。

您忠誠地，

梅格．湯瑪士

Email 這樣寫也行！

① 感謝您一直以來的友好合作。

Thank you for your kind cooperation all the time.

② 我們追求共同繁榮。

We pursue co-prosperity for both of us.

③ 希望我們有機會深入合作。

I hope that we will have a chance for further cooperation.

④ 跟您合作以後我們公司盈利頗豐。

We have made a lot of money after cooperating with you.

⑤ 請代我向貴公司所有員工表達謝意。

Please send my thanks to all the staff of your company.

⑥ 感謝您給我們機會與您合作。

Thank you for giving us the opportunity to work together with you.

⑦ 能夠跟您合作是我的榮幸。

It was a pleasure to collaborate with you.

⑧ 我要感謝您與我們有生意上的合作。

I would like to thank you for your cooperation with our business.

04【回應】感謝合作

範例 1

Re : Thank you for the cooperation.

Dear Mr. Robertson,

I am pleased to have received you email.

I am glad that your business could ***get back on your feet***.

I believe we are going to achieve a lot of success in our activities.

Finally, it's my honor to be your permanent VIP client.

I am ***looking forward to*** starting our cooperation.

Sincerely,

Vic Black

SEND　　　　　　　　　　　　　　　A ◌ ⊖ ☺

 中譯

回覆：感謝合作

羅伯森先生您好：

很高興收到您的電子郵件。

很高興貴公司狀況能**日漸好轉**。我相信我們將在活動中獲得巨大成功。

最後，很榮幸成為您永久 VIP 客戶。

對於開始合作**非常期待**。

您真誠地

維克‧布萊克

410

照著抄 ～ Email 簡單搞定！

範例 2

Re : Thank you for the cooperation.

Dear Mrs. Thomas,

I am writing to let you know how delighted I was to receive your thank-you email.

It's our pleasure to collaborate with your business. We enjoy doing business with you.

We will always be here to support you.

We are looking forward to further cooperation ***in the near future***.

If you have any further concerns, please don't hesitate to contact me.

Cordially,

Ken Schofield

SEND

中譯

回覆：感謝合作

湯瑪士女士您好：

寫此封信的目的是讓您知道，非常高興能收到您的感謝郵件。

我們很高興與貴企業合作。很高興與貴公司拓展業務。

我們永遠在此表示支持。

期待**近期**能進一步合作。

如果您還有其他疑問，請隨時與我聯繫。

親切地

肯・科菲爾德

Email 這樣寫也行！

① 我們將在活動中獲得成功和達成目標。

We are going to achieve success and goals in our activities.

② 成為您的 VIP 客戶是我的榮幸。

It's my pleasure to be your VIP client.

③ 很高興收到您的電子郵件。

I am glad to have received you email.

④ 感謝您訂購我們的商品。

Thank you very much for ordering our products.

⑤ 我們期待能夠跟您合作。

We are looking forward to cooperating with you.

⑥ 我們會支持您。

We are right behind you.

⑦ 如果有任何問題，歡迎與我聯繫。

You are welcome to contact me if you have any questions.

⑧ 和貴公司合作是我們的榮幸。

It's a pleasure to cooperate with your business.

05 感謝諮詢

照著抄 ～ Email 簡單搞定！

範例1

Title : Thank you for the inquiry of...

Dear Mr. Hunter,

Thank you for inquiring relevant information about our **new version of the software**.

The detailed information has been enclosed with the letter, which we would like you to examine.

If you want further information about our company, please visit our website; www.bjks168.com.

Thanks again for your interest in our new version of the software.

Yours sincerely,
K. S. B. Co.

SEND

主旨：感謝您對於……的詢問

親愛的亨特先生：

感謝您對於敝公司**新版軟體**的相關資訊的諮詢。

詳細資料已經隨信附寄，請查收。

如果您想瞭解更多關於我們公司的資訊，請登錄我們公司的網站，網址為：www.bjks168.com。

再次感謝您喜歡我們的新版軟體。

您真誠地，
K. S. B. 公司

範例 2

Title : Thank you for the inquiry of...

Dear Mr. Miller,

Thank you for your inquiry regarding ***the fax machine KS 5008***.

The information you requested was sent to you this morning. Please kindly check your email.

If you have further questions about this product, please contact our ***Service Department***. Or directly dial the number 888-12345.

Thanks again for your attention and support.

Yours sincerely,
Neil Hanks
F. M. Corporation

SEND   A 🖉 ⌲ ☺

主旨：感謝您對於⋯⋯的詢問

親愛的米勒先生：

非常感謝您對敝公司生產的 **KS5008 型號傳真機**的諮詢。

您所需要的資料今天上午已經寄出了，請查收。

如果您對敝公司產品還有任何問題，請聯繫敝公司**客服部**，或者直接撥打電話：888-12345 詢問。

再次感謝您的關注和支持。

您真誠地，
尼爾・漢克斯
F. M. 公司

Email 這樣寫也行！

① 感謝您對敝公司產品資料的諮詢。

Thank you for asking the detail of our product.

② 隨函寄上樣品，請查收。

Enclosed find sample, which we shall like you to examine.

③ 我們已經把您需要的資料寄給您了。

We have sent to you the information you need.

④ 如果您有任何問題，請一定要跟我們聯繫。

If you have any questions, please don't hesitate to contact us.

⑤ 感謝您對敝公司的產品有興趣。

Thanks for your interest in our product.

⑥ 感謝您對敝公司紡織產品的諮詢。

Thank you for your inquiry regarding the textile product.

⑦ 非常感謝您對我們產品的諮詢。

Thank you very much for your inquiry regarding our product.

⑧ 請直接撥打號碼：400-880-8848。

Please dial direct number 400-880-8848.

06【回應】感謝諮詢

Re : Thank you for the inquiry of...

Dear Sir/Madam,
Thank you for your information of your new version of the software.
This information addresses my needs. Moreover, I am satisfied with the catalogue that contains more detailed information about your products and services.
Thank you for your kindness. The information you have provided is **very useful**.
I will visit your website : www.bjks168.com as soon as possible.

Best wishes,
Willy Hunter

SEND　　　　　　　　　　　　　　　　A 🔗 ☺

中譯

回覆：感謝您對於……的詢問

尊敬的先生／女士，
感謝您提供新版的軟體相關資訊。
您提供的資訊符合我的需求。此外，我非常滿意提供貴公司更詳細的產品和服務的目錄。
謝謝好意。您提供的資訊**非常有用**。
我會瀏覽貴司網站：www.bjks168.com。

祝願，
威力‧亨特

照著抄 ～ Email 簡單搞定！　　　— ↗ ✕

Re : Thank you for the inquiry of...

Dear Mr. Hanks,

Thank you for your immediate response.

I have checked my email; however, I didn't find any information provided in the attachment.

Please **send** the information of the fax machine KS 5008 ***again promptly***.

After you send an email, ***please feel free to contact me directly*** at 0900-383838 so we can discuss this product in detail.

Thank you for your kindly help.

Yours sincerely,

Alan Miller

SEND　　　　　　　　　　　　　　　　A ◌ ⊝ ☺

回覆：感謝您對於……的詢問

漢克斯先生您好：

感謝您即時回覆。

我已經檢查我的電子郵件；但是，在附件中並未找到任何資訊。

請盡速**再次傳送** KS5008 型號傳真機的資訊。

寄完郵件後，**請直接撥打** 0900-383838 與我聯繫，以便我們能詳細討論此商品。

感謝您殷勤協助。

您真誠地，

艾倫‧米勒

① 感謝您提供商品資訊。

Thank you for your information of your products.

② 我發現附錄內有更多有用的詳細資訊。

I found more detailed information is available on the catalogue.

③ 您寄的資料非常實用。

The information you sent is very useful.

④ 我對貴公司的商品感到滿意。

I am pleased with the quality of your product.

⑤ 感謝您迅速回覆關於產品諮詢一事。

I appreciate your quick response to my inquiry for information.

⑥ 您寄給我的電子郵件中找不到附件。

I can't find attachments on the email you sent to me.

⑦ 寄完郵件後，請直接撥電話與我聯繫。

Please feel free to call me directly after sending the email.

⑧ 謝謝您鼎力相助。

Thank you for all your assistance.

07 感謝介紹客戶

範例 1

Title : We're grateful for your introduction.

Dear Mr. Smith,

Thank you for your introduction, which helped us to ***establish a new business relationship*** with NEC corporation.

You said that you were so satisfied with our service that you would like to introduce more clients to us.

We are very happy to learn that you have a high opinion of our company. We will endeavor to meet your expectations in the future.

We owe you the greatest debt of gratitude.

Yours sincerely,
Ada Jones
Vida Co.

SEND　　　　　　　　　　　　　　　A 🔗 😊

 中譯

主旨：我們非常感謝您的介紹

親愛的史密斯先生：

非常感謝您把 NEC 公司介紹給我們，使我們建立了**新的業務聯繫**。

您說您非常滿意我們的服務，所以才願意為我們介紹更多的客戶。

得知您給予我們如此高的評價我們非常高興。我們將來一定會做得更好，不辜負您的期望。

我們在此向您表示由衷的感謝。

您忠誠地，
艾達・瓊斯
維達公司

Title : We're grateful for your introduction.

Dear Sirs,

We are in receipt of your letter dated March 24th and wish to express our deepest thanks for your kindness in recommending us and publishing our advertisement in your "Business News."

We believe the arrangement you have made will enable us to connect with reliable sources in your area and ***bring a satisfactory result soon***.

Thank you again for your assistance on this matter.

Yours faithfully,

Kaihsin

SEND   A ⬓ ⌗ ☺

主旨：我們非常感謝您的介紹

敬啟者：

我方已收到貴方 3 月 24 日來函，並為貴方之友好表達最深的謝意。

承蒙推薦，登載本公司之需求於貴雜誌「商業消息」上。

相信此安排足以讓本公司與貴地區之可靠商家聯繫，並**快速帶來滿意效果**。

再次感謝貴方在此事上之協助。

您忠誠地，

凱信

Email 這樣寫也行！

① 多謝您把我們介紹給 ACB 公司。

Thank you so much for introducing us to ACB Company.

② 我很高興地說我們應該會和對方建立新的貿易關係。

I am pleased to say it looks like we will build a new relationship with them.

③ 感謝您把 MC 公司介紹給我們。

Thank you for referring MC Corporation to us.

④ 對於您為我們做的一切我會永遠銘記在心。

I will always remember you for all you have done for us.

⑤ 我希望能儘快有機會報答您的好意。

I look forward to returning the favor at the earliest opportunity.

⑥ 我們向您表示衷心的感謝。

We owe you the greatest debt of thankfulness.

⑦ 感謝您對我們充滿信心。

Thank you for your confidence you have shown in us.

⑧ 再次感謝您一直以來的支持。

Again, we appreciate your continued support.

08【回應】感謝介紹客戶

範例 1

Re : We're grateful for your introduction.

Dear Mrs. Jones,

Many thanks for your last kind letter.

NEC corporation is a well-known company. We have cooperated with NEC corporation for many years.

I **would like to introduce more clients** to you in the future.

I look forward to meeting you soon.

Please **contact my assistant to schedule an appointment**.

Yours faithfully

Adam Smith

SEND A⬚🔗☺

回覆：我們非常感謝您的介紹

敬愛的瓊斯太太，

非常感謝您的來信。

NEC 公司是聞名的公司。我們和 NEC 公司合作已經很多年。

未來我**想向貴公司介紹更多的客戶**。

希望能早日與您見面。

請**聯繫助理安排會議事宜**。

您忠誠地，

亞當‧史密斯

照著抄 ～ Email 簡單搞定！ — ↗ ✕

範例 2

Re : We're grateful for your introduction.

Dear Sirs,

Thank you so much for meeting with us last week regarding the advertisement.

It's our pleasure that you've published your advertisement in our "Business News."

We believe the decision you have made will ***bring a satisfactory result*** soon.

Please let me know if there is ***anything else*** I can do to aid your decision.

We look forward to welcoming you as our customer.

Best regards,
Vicky Williams

SEND   A 🔗 😊

中譯

回覆：我們非常感謝您的介紹

敬啟者，
非常感謝您上週因廣告事宜與我們會面。
很高興您在本雜誌「商業消息」上中刊登廣告。
相信您的決定將盡速**帶來令人滿意的結果**。
如果還有**其他方式**能協助您做出決定，請不吝告知。
我們期待並歡迎您成為本司客戶。

最好祝願，
薇琪‧威廉斯

① ABC 公司非常有名。

ABC corporation is a famous company.

② 我很感激您親切的回覆。

I appreciate your kind response.

③ 和您有義務往來是我們的榮幸。

It was our privilege to do business with you.

④ 我們理解您做了正確的決定。

We've learned that you have made the right decision.

⑤ 我們的客戶是本司生意中最重要的一部分。

Our clients are the most important part of our business.

⑥ 我期待和您討論更多細節。

I look forward to discussing with you in greater detail.

⑦ 行程表中有空檔時請和我聯繫。

Please contact me with an opening in your schedule.

⑧ 如果您感興趣，請隨時與我聯繫。

If you are interested, feel free to contact me.

09 感謝提供樣品

範例 1

Title : Thank you for the generous offer of samples.

Dear Sirs,

Thank you for your offer of ***"Panda" pens*** samples as stated in your letter dated on July 28th.

We will check them later on and make a decision on whether to order or not.

We shall be grateful if you could quote us your ***best price*** for them.

Yours sincerely,
CPA Co.

SEND

主旨：感謝您慷慨地提供樣品給我們

敬啟者：

感謝您在 7 月 28 日的來信中表示願意提供我們「**熊貓**」**牌鋼筆**，以及附寄的樣品。

我們稍後會驗貨並決定是否下訂單購買。

如能提供該貨物的**最優惠價格**則不勝感激。

您真誠地，

CPA 公司

Title : Thank you for the generous offer of samples.

Dear Mr. Cook,

Thank you for your kindness and assistance in sending the samples that we needed so soon.

We are ***in the process of trying*** them out at present. We shall contact you should there be any issues.

Thanks for your cooperation. We do appreciate and admire a business partner like you.

Yours sincerely,

Mr. Roger White

MG Co.

SEND　　　　　　　　　　　　　　　　　A ⬮ ⊝ ☺

主旨：感謝您慷慨地提供樣品給我們

親愛的庫克先生：

非常感謝貴公司的友善和協助，如此迅速地把我們需要的樣品寄送過來。

現在我方**正在試用中**。如果我們有任何發現或任何問題，我方會隨時與您聯絡。

感謝您的合作。我們真的非常感謝和喜愛像您這樣的商業夥伴。

您真誠地，

羅傑‧懷特

MG 公司

Email 這樣寫也行！

① 非常感謝您寄送我們要的樣品。

Thank you very much for sending us the sample we want.

② 昨天您寄送的樣品我們已經收到了。

We have received the samples that you sent yesterday.

③ 您寄來的樣品得到了經銷商們的認可。

The distributors looked with favor on your sample shipment.

④ 送交的貨品與樣品不大相同。

The delivered goods were very different from the sample.

⑤ 感謝您免費寄送樣品給我們。

Thank you for sending the sample to us for free.

⑥ 我們今天收到來自貴公司的四種樣品。

We have received four samples from your company today.

⑦ 試用樣品後我們會做出決定。

We will make a decision after trying out the samples.

⑧ 謝謝您即時地寄送樣品。

Thank you very much for your prompt samples.

10【回應】感謝提供樣品

範例1

Re : Thank you for the generous offer of samples.

Dear Sirs,

I want to convey my gratitude for your interest in"Panda"pens .
I am confident that my company can provide the products you require.

Enclosed our **quotation and the price list** for your reference. If you have any problems opening the file, please let me know.

Regards,
Paul Smith

SEND   A ⌀ ⌔ ☺

 中譯

回覆：感謝您慷慨地提供樣品給我們

敬啟者：

感謝您對「熊貓」牌鋼筆的興趣。

相信本公司可以提供您所需產品。

附上本公司的**報價和價格表**，以供您參考。如果在打開文件時遇到任何問題，請與我聯絡。

您真誠地，

保羅・史密斯

照著抄 ～ Email 簡單搞定！

 範例 2

Re : Thank you for the generous offer of samples.

Dear Mr. White,

I would like to thank you for requesting a sample of our products.

It was an honor to have a business partner like you.

Our latest price list is attached. Let me know if you have questions about the attachment.

For additional information, please contact with our **_sales department_**:

Linda Pitt/Sales Manager.

lindapitt5438@mg520.com

I look forward to hearing from you soon.

Yours sincerely,

Gary Cook

SEND

 中譯

回覆：感謝您慷慨地提供樣品給我們

懷特先生您好：

感謝您索取本公司樣品。

能有您這樣的商業夥伴是我的榮幸。

隨信附上最新價格表。如果您對附件有疑問，請告訴我。

有關其他相關資訊，請與本公司**銷售部門**聯繫：

琳達‧彼特／銷售經理。

lindapitt5438@mg520.com

期待早日收到您的回應。

真誠地，

蓋瑞‧庫克

① 我們的目標是提供您品質最好的商品。

Our goal is to provide you the best quality products.

② 我們確認馬上寄出您要的樣品。

We make sure we send our samples immediately.

③ 提供幫助給您是我們的榮幸。

It was a real pleasure helping you.

④ 我們已經寄出幾種樣品給您。

We have sent several samples for you today.

⑤ 提供樣品讓公司吸引更多的目標對象。

Providing samples allows the company to reach more of its target audience.

⑥ 感謝您索取商品樣品。

Thank you for requesting a product sample.

⑦ 如果需要更多資訊，請用電話與我助理聯繫。

If you need additional assistance, please call my assistant.

⑧ 如果對樣品有疑問，請隨時用電子郵件與我聯繫。

If you have any questions about the samples, Please feel free to contact me by email.

語研力 *E055*

英語自學策略：英文 E-mail 懶人包，複製、貼上、替換，瞬間搞定！

往來應對游刃有餘，工具＋學習雙效合一。

作　　者	Sheila◎著
顧　　問	曾文旭
出版總監	陳逸祺、耿文國
主　　編	陳蕙芳
封面設計	李依靜
內文排版	李依靜
法律顧問	北辰著作權事務所

印　　製	世和印製企業有限公司
初　　版	2021年08月
出　　版	凱信企業集團─凱信企業管理顧問有限公司
電　　話	（02）2773-6566
傳　　真	（02）2778-1033
地　　址	106 台北市大安區忠孝東路四段218之4號12樓
信　　箱	kaihsinbooks@gmail.com

定　　價	新台幣499元／港幣166元
產品內容	1書

總 經 銷	采舍國際有限公司
地　　址	235 新北市中和區中山路二段366巷10號3樓
電　　話	（02）8245-8786
傳　　真	（02）8245-8718

國家圖書館出版品預行編目資料

英語自學策略：英文Email懶人包，複製、貼
上、替換，瞬間搞定！／Sheila著. -- 初版. --
臺北市：凱信企業管理顧問有限公司,2021.08
　面；　公分
ISBN 978-986-06836-3-9(平裝)

1.商業英文 2.商業書信 3.商業應用文 4.電子郵
件
805.179　　　　　　　　　　　　110011483